RIVER TRASH

L A Fields

LETHE PRESS

PART I:
RIPARIAN

AUGUST 18, 2020 — COVID-19 DEATHS
WORLD DAILY: 6,859 / TOTAL: 873,988
US DAILY: 1,262 / TOTAL: 180,264
LOUISIANA DAILY: 28 / TOTAL: 4,554

River Trash is as funny as it is poignant — and I'm a tough judge. It's not often any medium captures the disposition of a comedian quite like L.A. Fields has here. Graham Morrow is written perfectly. Somehow, Whitney Thorn may be even better. Their story is as honest as you'll find in print. Sweet but not saccharine. Hard but not drama-porn. Two men unsure of each other, falling in love. I laughed. I cried. I remembered relatives now passed who would have proudly worn the moniker "river trash" and felt grateful that an author as talented as L.A. was telling their — my — story.

Drew Morgan,
comedian and author of *The Liberal Redneck Manifesto*

River Trash is a lived-in and lovely paean to an unlovely pandemic, and an unlikely but beautifully conveyed partnership that takes place in an intimate microcosm but also an absurd universe. Whitney and Graham are a duet and a dichotomy and all kinds of other things that really make you happy and hurt and feel totally alive as you read about them. L.A. Fields writes like a dream, but also gets the joke.

Keith Banner,
Next to Nothing

River Trash is a story that blends tenderness with turmoil, humor with heartbreak. Fields' unapologetically political voice and masterful pacing make this an unforgettable, emotionally charged read. With sharp insight and raw emotion, this is a book that leaves you questioning what it truly means to survive — and to love — in the face of everything falling apart.

Jill Mceldowney,
Otherlight

Published by Lethe Press
lethepressbooks.com

Design & Typesetting: Ryan Vance

1.

GRAHAM

It was August 2020, and people gathered in an open field on the Louisiana side of the Mississippi near Vicksburg.

Were they supposed to be there? Absolutely not; there was a state of emergency declared. Were they masked against COVID-19 spread? Hardly and barely; half of those up for a good time that summer chose to disbelieve the reports that people were dying somewhere behind hospital doors and under ventilators. Were they about to have a responsible night of neighborliness? Hell no; they were predominantly open-carrying with open containers. But there was a stage set up, and speakers wired, and the show would go on.

First on the night's line-up: Graham Morrow, a de-certified nurse turned comedian at perhaps the worst time to strike out on a new career in entertainment. He knew better than to be congregating unmasked, but he was also feeling particularly fatalistic about the world and his own chances of surviving it. He missed being on a stage, where the attention and the roles he played blotted out his real self, and he'd take what he could get.

"Well, hey, y'all, you law-breakers, you," he said, greeting the crowd once he was handed the mic.

Graham started with easy jokes about Southern accents and what happens when you take them to other places. He told one anecdote to test it out on the laugh meter about mothers-in-law, though he did not have one, just using what he knew about his friends' mediocre marriages. Graham let the crowd fill in the blanks and assume it was his mother-in-law at first, but then undercut it by announcing he was 35 and gay and single, and that such a marital mess was someone else's problem. That sort of switcheroo didn't always endear crowds. Even though they knew they were at a performance, they could still feel cheated by inartistic dishonesty. Graham learned on the road to sell it as a package joke: like the idea of mothers-in-law was so unpleasant it was better to alter his sexuality entirely to avoid traditional marriage. It wasn't the nicest joke for any mothers in the crowd, but Graham was still refining it. Tonight, all that mattered was that it gained him laughs. The crowd was out, and so was he, and everyone was happy about it. Graham ended with one tried-and-true zinger, an impression of his ornery grandfather sarcastically wishing them well with an exaggerated squat-and-pop motion to go with it. Then he was off into the darkness again.

The comedown was always worse than the nervousness before a show. The bright light faded from Graham's eyes, the noise dampened, and the adrenaline left him shaky and, frankly, sad. He was sad when he had to go home again, alone in the dark, to a silent hotel room half the time, and his own screaming thoughts.

"Hey, man, that was great stuff you had out there," said a voice from the flap of the talent tent they'd erected for this makeshift show. Graham knew it wasn't one of the voices in his own head because those twerps never had anything nice to say, but he recognized this stranger nonetheless.

"Thank you, sir — always nice to hear," Graham said, approaching for a handshake while totting up: silver hair, slim face, ropey forearms, guitar in hand. Had they ever met, or ...?

"Whitney Thorn," the man said, putting a guitar pick in his teeth to shake with Graham before continuing. Graham loved that move — loved a guitar pick in a man's mouth, or a toothpick, a stalk of wheat, or some other such cowboy oral fixation thing. He'd trained himself to not find cigarettes sexy anymore by studying what they did to human lungs, but it was a struggle.

"Oh, wow, yeah, I'll have to stay for your show," he said, because it had clicked: he'd had this man's albums once, or not the physical copies, but parts of them on his digital playlists. Whitney Thorn was born in 1970 to country music royalty: his father, Avery Thorn was a guitarist and a scoundrel, and his mother, Willa Grace Sawyer, a poet and a whirlwind, or so the legends said. He was the youngest of two boys and the only one who also went into the music business. He'd had some trouble with drugs, he'd come out as queer, and yet somehow he was still gigging, still kicking, still willing to show up and sing for people. Graham loved that, too. "I'm Graham, by the way, Graham Morrow."

"I heard," Whitney said, tipping his head towards the stage, the mic, the perfectly loud sound of the second act that was up there as they spoke.

"Right, of course." Graham tried to laugh, to aw-shucks it off, failed at that attempt, but it was okay, because Whitney wasn't done with him.

"If you do stay, I was hoping someone would want to hang out for a while," Whitney said. "I don't drink anymore, but I'll buy you a Coke and a corn dog or whatever." There were people selling hard drinks, soft drinks, and snacks to the crowd from food trucks. The bars themselves were closed, but to-go sales restrictions had been lifted, and that was the loophole people were trying to exploit that night.

"Yeah, alright, that's a ... that sounds great," Graham said. "An old-fashioned carnival date, why not?"

Whitney's name was called from the stage, and he gave Graham a charming little smirk and a nod before walking away, leaving Graham reeling. The good thing was that Graham wasn't sad anymore, and his evening was no longer dark. He had an invitation to hang from a guy he'd have been honored to serve as a boot polisher. Instead of barely noticing him, Whitney Thorn had stood right there like a religious icon with the golden glow of the tent's opening around him, and offered his hand.

Graham looked at his hand and remembered the feel of Whitney's palm in it. He looked at the stage and remembered the crinkle around Whitney's eyes when he smiled. Those were the kind of wrinkles people only got when they smiled too much, according to his mother. They were the best kind of wrinkles if you asked Graham, who already had old-man folds in his forehead, the thinker's wrinkles. Those, too, were better than the ones from frowning or sadness, but the laugher's wrinkles were the sweetest.

Whitney arrived at the mic and strummed his guitar before saying hello. Graham drifted slowly towards his voice like a bug to a zapper, happy to join the crowd with the knowledge that he'd already been selected from it for a special audience with the Music Man.

2.

WHITNEY

Whitney came off the stage after singing five songs: three newer ones, and two people remembered and could sing along with, one of them being the ditty his mother was best known for writing, "We Can Make It to the Dawn," as his hopeful closing number. He went straight back to the tent to change his shirt because the one he had on was drenched in sweat. A gift from the sweltering night, the lights, the humidity, and, of course, that little twinge of dread he still felt on stage, wondering if this crowd would be one of the ones to turn on him because plenty had before.

But this set was a success, and, right on his heels, his new friend was through the tent flap to see him peel one shirt off and replace it with another. Whitney could feel the guy appraising his body. It wasn't a bad body even after putting fifty years on it and abusing it for a solid fifteen. Even in his worst state, days into a meth bender, Whitney was still a relatively good-looking disgusting mess, by comparison.

"The nerves never leave," Whitney said, slicking the sweat from his face into his hair because it was pretty on him, he'd been told more than once.

"Ah, shit, really?" Graham said, getting closer. He put his hands in his pockets, took them out, fingers in his belt loops, took them out, crossed his arms, then uncrossed them, until Whitney set a hand on his shoulder, causing Graham to still. Graham had reddishness in his skin and hair, and freckles across the bridge of his nose and under his eyes where they'd rained down on him from the sun.

Whitney smiled at Graham again, not with teeth because his teeth weren't his best feature, his eyes and his eyes while smiling were. Graham smiled back, with charmingly crooked teeth.

"See, I was hoping someone like you would have tips for stage nerves," Graham said. "Or could at least tell me it gets better the longer you keep at it."

The others in the tent noticed the touch but kept to themselves about it. Whitney turned to pack up his guitar and knapsack as he said, "It gets muted over time, but never really goes away, like grief."

"Oh, wow," Graham said.

Whitney reviewed what he'd just said and thought, *Whoops, I'm talking in lyrics.* He turned back with a bigger smile, as he hadn't meant to get so serious so early in the evening.

"Ninety-nine times out of a hundred these days it's more of a trance when I go on stage," he told Graham. "I've been in a place like this before, I'll do it again, and good or bad so long as I remember some tunes, I'm doing my job."

"Right," Graham said, nodding. "So, the puke butterflies and post-show despair, they at least calm down after a while?"

Whitney hadn't said anything about despair yet, though he knew it well — literally knew it as a well within him, a dank and echoing one with almost no barrier to keep a body from falling in.

Whitney nodded and said, "Mostly the feelings calm down, but sometimes it comes back strong, so I can't promise anything from my own experience. Last year it caught me out of nowhere and I had to dunk my head in ice water to scare it away."

It had been ice water in a tub around a keg, in a room full of some of the most shallow bro-country assholes Whitney never wanted to meet. They were young men who only got into singing because they had too much twang in them to act. They made some homophobic noise, tried to crack jokes about the water not being vodka, implying that someone like Whitney should know better how to fall off the sobriety wagon. Whitney dried his face on a Confederate flag conveniently hung in the green room right next to the American and state flag, tipped his head at the peanut gallery, and left to wait in the wings instead. They'd all be addicted to something or someone nasty within two years, and Whitney decided then that he would love to see it unfold. It isn't good for the soul to take delight in the humiliation and failures of others but ... Whitney had so few addictions left he could indulge in, and they started it first. One reaps what he sows, after all.

"It's too hot out here for ice dunks tonight," Graham said. "Ice be melting like snow cones in hell," Graham said, which made Whitney laugh a little. It felt good, and he wanted that goodness to last longer.

"Do you want to get out of here and talk shop?" Whitney asked. "I mean we can't go anywhere because everything is closed, but my place is open for some porch-sitting. There's a new moon tonight."

Graham was nodding even before he said yes.

3.

GRAHAM

Whitney Thorn's house was nice.

Graham had been living with dorm mates, roommates, and crashing with family for almost the entirety of his life. There was only one year where he lived alone the whole time, and it was his first year as a nurse when he'd been hired on in Missouri to fill an aching need for medical staff. He got a one-room utility apartment he barely saw, spent all his money trying to pay down student loan debt, and longed endlessly for a dog or even a cat he knew he couldn't have because his life and budget was too tenuous to plan further than month-to-month. He was tossed out of nursing just before that lease ended, which solved all of those problems, in a sense. After that it was back living with Momma, living with cousins, working part-time in a dentist's office at the desk only, and hating his life until he started making comedy his thing.

Graham followed Whitney's car in his own truck for about thirty minutes until he saw where he would spend the night. The house was out in the woods a bit, not so far from neighbors that you couldn't see their lights through the trees, but quiet enough, and semi-private. There was a wrap-around porch that Graham just adored which had a bench swing, some potted plants, a rocking chair and other small tables, seats, and footrests.

"Oh boy, when you said porch-sitting, I didn't realize there would be so many seating options," Graham said as he locked his vehicle and joined back up with his new friend.

"There's a hammock around the corner too," Whitney said. "Plus, a grill I never use, but there it is."

"Well, it's a law around these parts, isn't it?" Graham asked. "You got outdoor space, you must also have a grill, just like you gotta mow your lawn and maintain your mailbox, right?"

"Sounds right," Whitney said, touching Graham's shoulder again before heading up to the front door. For a few seconds Graham didn't know if he should follow or not. He was asked to the porch, not the inside of the house explicitly, so he stood in patchy moonlight just taking in a big whiff of the woods, enjoying the smell of dirt and the sound of leaves and pine needles. He snapped out of the reverie when Whitney called back, "Need an engraved invitation?"

Graham bumbled up the three short steps, over the welcome mat, and into the house as Whitney turned on a series of lamps on his way in. "I was just enjoying the breeze out there," he said, and then before he could think to stop himself, "It smells like women in here."

Whitney smirked and explained as he made his way to the kitchen why that was so. Graham wiped his feet, shut the door, and goggled around at a lot of floral print and wood furniture before following him.

"This was my grandmother's place, on my mother's side. She left it to me in her will saying something like 'because Whitney needs a place to land.' I was all over the map then, I guess she wanted to make sure I didn't become unmoored. My brother got her actual money, which was wise because I would have injected it, and he lived here for the first few years maintaining the place, going to school, setting himself up for better things. He's a lawyer in Baton Rouge now, married. About when it was time for him to take that job, I was ready to come home."

"Oh, nice," Graham said. "I've been through Baton Rouge."

The counters in the kitchen were granite, speckled like beach sand. The cabinets were all wood with golden handles and knobs. The stove, fridge, dishwasher, microwave, and toaster were all black, as were the bar stools at the island, one of which Graham sat on. He kicked his feet in the air and felt like a little kid waiting for someone to fix his cereal.

"Diet Coke, grape seltzer, tea, coffee, or orange juice?" Whitney asked. Graham was too stunned by the variety to make a fast choice, so Whitney followed up with, "There's also water. I'm having tea myself."

"Um, how about coffee for me, if it's not too much trouble?"

"No trouble at all," Whitney told him, and for the next five minutes got out a half-dozen tiny silver things to conduct an intricate beverage ritual.

Whitney put a steampunk-looking teapot on an open fire burner, pulverized coffee beans in a little grinder, slow-poured the boiled water over a fine mesh strainer with filigree handles, and that was just the coffee. For tea, Whitney mixed leaves and buds and petals from three canisters like he was making a spell, then poured hot water over those too. He brought a tray of additives out from under the counter stocked with sugar, stevia, honey packets, creamer cups, and cinnamon and peppermint sticks. Graham shook his head to all of them. Whitney had fancy coffee, Graham could tell by the smell, and he wanted to enjoy it without the interference of other flavors.

After Graham's first sip, Whitney asked, "Good?"

"Very good, yeah," Graham said, and then the deafening silence made him blurt out what he was really feeling, at long last. "I want to ask you, like, so many invasive questions, but I know that's not cool."

Whitney leaned his forearms down on the counter so he and Graham were staring directly across from each other. "I'm an open book. I kind of have to be, my parents were famous before I was born. Hard to keep secrets when you're that close to the spotlight."

"Were you on good terms with your parents when they passed?" Graham asked. He knew that the Thorn family had its ups and downs and scandals, but if they found peace with each other, that never made it into any tell-alls or headlines.

Whitney raised his eyebrows. "That's a new one," he said. "The last time I saw my father we were fine, civil, but it was four years before he died, and I don't know how he felt about me by then. Mom I got to visit towards the end, she told me and my brother to take care of each other, that it was all she wanted from us, so that was fine. I'm sure I have a lot of unresolved stuff for both of them but ... it seems like a waste of breath to try and make peace with the dead from this side of the divide."

Graham nodded a few times, before saying, "Thanks for that, man. You know you talk in rhymes?"

"I do," Whitney said, standing back up and sipping more tea. "I do it, and I know I do it, hope you don't mind."

"Who the hell would mind? It's lovely." Most of Graham's friends weren't folks of arts or letters. His grandfather was a preacher who spoke in poetic ways, though hardly ever about beautiful things.

"Any more questions?" Whitney asked.

"Yeah, one," Graham said. "Are you flirting with me or is that just my wishful thinking?"

4.

WHITNEY

Whitney grinned. He didn't know what to say exactly, but he knew what Graham was hoping to hear, and it wasn't off the table. So Whitney reached across the table and held Graham's fingers. Graham squeezed back. They were friendly, and things could get friendlier, but they had to talk about a few things first.

"I already mentioned I was in recovery," Whitney said. "Do you know from what?" Whitney didn't want to tell the whole story if Graham already knew all the salacious bits.

"It was meth, right? That's just what the gossip said though," Graham told him. He was examining Whitney's fingernails rather than looking him in the eye.

"That gossip is true," Whitney said. "It was harder to quit than anything else I've ever done, mostly because it was all bound up in sex. To quit smoking you get rid of all your lighters, right? Replace it with chewing gum or a mild vape to start. To quit booze, you get it out of your house and replace it with other drinks." Whitney took back his hand and gestured at the cups before them.

"Right, tea and coffee," Graham said.

"One of the triggers for meth is sex, and sexual desire is a natural impulse you can't quit," Whitney said. "Or at least I can't."

The self-righteous sober like to say there's no high as good as the first, but they were wrong in a thousand ways. The first time Whitney tried meth was terrible, overpowering. He was 19, he was given a regular user's dose by one of his father's dirtbag roadie friends, and he didn't touch the stuff again until he was 23. He was finally out as gay, was in a club with his own kind, feeling independent and free, feeling like himself. He was ready to make his own mistakes then, his own way, and when his dance partner told him that sex was cosmic on the stuff, Whitney believed him. The wonder and sparkle in his eyes … that man was seeing stars, and Whitney wanted to see them too.

"That's sorta like what people say about food," Graham said. "My mom and my aunt were in those weight loss groups once, and they were talking about food addiction. It's harder to quit something you can't actually quit, right? They still have to eat every day, the potential to slip is … well, it's not good."

Whitney nodded. "My granny was in those groups too, it's something like that. I quit years ago, so I've got this now, but I've also got rules I still follow. One of them is no more casual hook-ups. I've got to know people first, build some trust."

"Gotcha," Graham said. "So, no sleeping together until there's some trust."

"Oh, we can sleep together if you like," Whitney said. "Just no sex, we keep it above the waist or below the knees all night."

"That …" Graham said, and then paused to look towards the ceiling, imagine something. He scratched his reddish beard as he thought and then nodded. Whatever math he was doing had added up. "That sounds really nice, just sleeping together. You wanna?"

Whitney did want that. When he went out to break the lockdown laws earlier that evening, he never predicted his night could end so well, in a sleepover with a hot guy fifteen years his junior. Sometimes Whitney still got lucky.

They finished their beverages, talked about nonsense like hecklers, road gripes, and the foods that tasted the best at the time but did the most damage on their digestive tracts later. They took separate showers (Whitney's granny's house had two, ooh la la). Graham had some emergency spare clothes and a toiletry bag in his truck, so that worked out fine. He sent a series of texts out to people who would miss him if he logged off for the night, and then they were free to get friendly.

"I'm sorry to report that I'm living with my momma this summer, and I guess that'll be true until the world gets normal again," Graham said.

"If the world gets normal again," Whitney said, as they put their feet up in the living room and played a gentle game of footsie over the coffee table. "We're coming up on forty years with HIV and AIDS, some pandemics never go away."

Graham acknowledged that grim observation with a nod, but didn't engage with it. "She knows I'm not coming home tonight, so that's settled, but she's also disappointed that I'm risking COVID infection like this. She says I'll have to stay isolated in the garage for the next two weeks so I don't expose her, but ... you know how mommas are, she wouldn't let me sleep out there one night in the sweltering heat. Even if I had all the COVID strains and was coughing in her face she'd put up with me."

"Sounds like a good momma," Whitney said.

"That she is," Graham agreed. "Even after all I've done to quit a real job and become a clown, I'm still not the biggest fuck-up in the family, so she indulges me."

"What was the real job?" Whitney asked.

"I was a nurse for a minute," Graham said. "Got in trouble for some dumb thing and then just couldn't stand it anymore. I feel a little bit bad about not helping everyone who's still out there on the frontlines, but my license is long gone, so it is what it is."

"I like nurses," Whitney said, running his toe along the sole of Graham's foot, finding out how ticklish he was (somewhat, but not dangerously so).

"You do?" Graham asked.

Whitney nodded. "Way better than doctors. Most nurses are real working-class heroes in my book, especially the ones who can find a vein in the dark. You know the ones who've got the touch?"

"Yes, sir, I'm one of 'em," Graham said with pride.

Whitney would see about that.

5.

GRAHAM

The night was getting awfully erotic for a celibate sleepover, but Graham wasn't complaining. He was feeling pretty touch-starved after weeks in his old bedroom, which was mostly a computer room/unused gym/ junk emporium now. He had been doing grocery runs for his mom, Cynthany, and her sister, Aunt Tamella. He had been arguing with strangers on internet forums. He'd been recording what was supposed to be funny content with his comedian pals, videos for the fans they'd only just started earning, just trying to stay in touch, stay connected. His pals were all married or married with kids, however. They had what folks were calling "pods" to stay isolated with, and all Graham had was his own two hands and online porn. He felt like he was in high school again, locking doors and stuffing a sock in his mouth so he didn't make too much noise when he came. Graham had hated high school.

So, this strange ritual of searching Whitney Thorn, of all people, for his best and fattest veins was very nice. Graham marked each one with a pen, a tiny X for every injection site.

"I used to shoot up, so I know where all my best veins are," Whitney assured him. "I'll grade you when you're done."

It was a morbid yet fun little game, and it was turning Graham on a little. Being on his knees, rubbing his hands all over this lean, cool man with his guitar-calloused fingers and his stringy muscles and his surprisingly soft skin.

"Brother, do you moisturize or what? You feel good," Graham told him.

"I exfoliate," Whitney said, touching Graham's arm to feel the difference. "You should, too."

"Yeah, I'll work on that," Graham said before feeling another prime candidate for sticking a needle and marking it. "You've got a strong pulse."

"I'm glad to hear it," Whitney said.

"Did you ever shoot up anywhere but your arms?" Graham asked. "Between the fingers? Toes? You don't have to answer, I'm just out of spots to X on these arms." He clicked the pen shut.

Whitney shook his head. "I never got that far gone."

Graham nodded, not necessarily in approval, but close to it. "Well, how did I do?"

There were eight marks on Whitney, and he considered them as Graham sat back on his heels. "You get a pass," he said. "All these ones in the elbows, you nailed it, the stuff on the hands, also good. Those wrist ones ... I'm sure you're right and all, but I never found those myself."

"Those are the veins we'd use if we blew out all the other ones," Graham told him. "A little inside baseball from your resident former nurse."

Graham returned to his seat on the couch, and Whitney stretched in his chair again, hands behind his head and feet crossed over the coffee table. He narrowed his eyes and finally had an uncomfortable question for Graham.

"What happened that made you quit nursing?" Whitney asked. "You don't have to answer."

"My own words right back at me there, well played," Graham said. He was unhappy that he had to talk about this, but since Whitney had been so honest with him, and since apparently honesty was the way to this man's dick, Graham had to pony up. "I didn't kill anyone or anything. I accepted a gift from a patient and got accused of stealing it."

"He accused you?" Whitney said. "Or she, the patient?"

"He was a 'he,' an old timer, had dementia or something, but he wasn't in for that, he was in for dehydration," Graham said. "I complimented the man's bolo tie, and he said, 'Well, son, have it then,

I've got a million of them,' and I wore it around the rest of the day right next to my stethoscope. I told the other nurses about it, and no one had a problem until the guy's daughter showed up. She accused me of stealing it when she saw it on me because she gave it to him for Christmas and just 'could. not. believe.' that he would ever give away something she gave him."

"Oh, I know her type," Whitney said.

"Don't we all," Graham said. "I gave the thing back. Everyone knew what happened since I'd told them he gave it to me; they understood and all, but since she was making such a fuss about it, and I was new, and technically, we can't accept anything from patients, *et cetera*. He might have stood up for me, but he already couldn't remember that he owned the damn bolo tie in the first place, let alone that he gave it to me. To make it all go away, they suspended me for three months. Said I should have known better, that it could be misconstrued as tricking someone who was *non compos mentis* out of their possessions, the family could sue if they wanted to, blah blah blah."

"Shit," said Whitney.

"Exactly. I was out three months of pay, which I could not afford, and it was going to be a mark on my file when I wasn't even on the job a year yet, and I just thought … all them loans, all that hard work, and being there for the right reasons, none of it mattered. So, I thought, you know, screw that job. How am I supposed to do all that nasty work, literally shit work, with people fighting and yelling and puking and bleeding, and not even get the benefit of the doubt? You know they told us at orientation that nurses are the lifeblood of the hospital, that they really need us, and that's true, but those motherfuckers poison their bloodstream. Overworked, bitched at, left hung out to dry, and I couldn't even afford a car. So, I never went back."

"I understand," Whitney said. After a beat, he added, "I like you."

"Thank you," Graham told him, because he meant it, very much. "Hey, are we allowed to make out maybe?"

Whitney grinned at him. Graham was already loving that devilish grin of his. "I don't know, is your mouth above your waist?"

"Hmm," Graham said, putting a finger to his forehead to pretend to think. "Leg bone's connected to the knee bone, the thigh bone's connected to the hip, and the back bone's connected to the neck. If I remember my human anatomy correctly, I think we can kiss if we want to."

Luckily for Graham, Whitney wanted to.

6.

WHITNEY

When Whitney got clean, he had to rebuild his sexuality. His therapist called it "remapping" his sexual road atlas, a necessary task so that he had somewhere to go with his lust that wouldn't lead him down the back alleys and into the hidey holes where the meth cravings were vicious.

Whitney had to remember when just seeing another boy's knee would drive him wild. The inner thigh right above, the damp cave up the pant leg of a pair of basketball shorts ... agonizingly hot. As a teenager, just imagining reaching up those shorts could make him stain his sheets, and his sexual hunger stayed pure like that for a long time. When he finally left home and started going to bars and clubs, meeting guys he could touch and who would touch him back, he was delighted by every caress. Long, firm, shirtless hugs? Fire. Squeezing a guy's ass and having him thrust forward in a welcoming response? Intoxicating. The first time a guy blew Whitney, it was over so fast it made the man roll his eyes and mumble something about "these newbies." It hadn't even been his mouth, but his hands, one on each hip, searing into him like hot starfish. Overwhelming.

But then meth got involved, and meth made everything feel good times infinity. Where sober people saw stars, those who were high saw supernovas — stars exploding, melting, flaring. Active penetration went from thrusting to feeling sucked in, and passive penetration (which became more frequent once the drug compromised his erection ability) went from thrillingly naughty to decadently sacrilegious. He went from fresh country boy to jaded crystal slut in less than three years, and he stayed that way for a while. He'd had embarrassing injuries to explain to nurses (anal fissures), a handful of STDs (gonorrhea twice and crabs a couple times), and a few terrifying flirtations with madness when the paranoia and hallucinations came in at the end of a bender. For all that, however, it was still a drug that he missed, especially in relation to sex.

No longer doing meth was easier than learning how to stop missing it. Physical symptoms only last so long, but the mental hangover of desire was a long separation. The rewiring started with a year of abstinence, even from masturbation. Whitney didn't want to do it at all, thought surely that was only needed in extreme cases, not his own, but his therapist shut that delusion down.

Dr. Bibbins was a real professional. A cheery man with a short gray beard and dark hair, he was friendly until the doctor side of him came to talk, after which his eyes would sharpen. His will to endure uncomfortable silences was always stronger than the patient's. He explained it to Whitney the one way he could understand it best: by using guitar psychology.

"What fires together wires together, Mr. Thorn. You have to uncouple the association between sex and meth if you ever want to enjoy the one without the other ever again. The challenge you're conquering right now is that the more you try to separate out these two urges, to redifferentiate them, the more you think about them together."

"Oh good, the old *1984* problem of how to unthink the thing without thinking of it in the first place, gotcha," Whitney said.

Dr. Bibbins nodded. "About like that, yes. The treatment I'm recommending, because I've seen it work where nothing else does long-term, comes from treating 'the yips.' If you don't know what that is, it's a more common name for focal dystonia. That's a neurological disorder that causes involuntary muscle contractions. It can mess up writers, dentists, and golf players by causing wrist spasms, professional drivers and dancers if it affects their feet, and musicians who play with their lips if it shows up in the face, jaw, or neck."

"Okay," Whitney said. Dr. Bibbins didn't talk just to hear himself; he'd eventually get to a point.

"It presents in body parts engaged in overlearned tasks. Like carpal tunnel when people become highly skilled at something involving repetitive actions. You play guitar," Dr. Bibbins said, a statement that was not a question. "Musician's dystonia in guitar players could mean they can no longer move their fingers individually anymore; the fingers get neurologically stuck together."

"Hmm." Whitney winced at imagining it. He had already dreaded the possibility that his hands and voice would eventually fail him. Who would he be if the one true talent that made him special went away and left him unremarkable?

Dr. Bibbins continued. "To treat the condition, the players have to first quit playing. Starve the merged connections by letting them atrophy a little, and then when the connections are weak enough, they relearn how to hold a guitar again, like teaching a baby. First, by holding an unstrung guitar, then by using a single finger on a single string, then a second, and then a third, one by one. Essentially, the fingers are remapped in the brain as separate digits and not just one claw hand."

Whitney sighed a fierce sigh as he realized what the doc was saying. "So, I have a neuro disorder ..."

"No such diagnosis, I'm saying what you have is similar to —"

"Yeah, yeah, yeah, whatever the proper terms," Whitney interrupted with an apologetic shrug, but he wanted to get this straight before he lost the thread. "You're saying in my brain, the meth parts and the sex parts are all claw-handed together? And I have to stop both for a while to separate them."

Dr. Bibbins smiled. "Yes, sir, that's it. Stop both to weaken the connection and then remap the sex parts only, without touching any pathways tainted with meth memories."

"But I did damn near everything on meth," Whitney told him. "It's all tainted; all of it is a ghost of a feeling without the drug."

"You enjoyed sex and masturbation before you tried meth," he said, "and you can learn to do it again from the beginning."

"Puberty the redo?" Whitney asked, predicting it would never work, but willing to do as the doctor told him.

"If you want to stay clean for the rest of your life, this is the only way I've seen it work in over twenty-five years of observation," Bibbins said. "You may not get back all that you've lost, but if you allow the drug to live in your fantasies, I can almost guarantee that you will start using again."

7.

GRAHAM

"Let me kiss you first," Whitney told Graham. "If you're okay with that, I've got a little ritual."

"Ritual kisses," Graham said, nodding. "Finally, I'm at the right kind of party; let's do this."

Whitney got up and circled around to the back of Graham's chair. He leaned over Graham, and Graham closed his eyes, waiting for Prince Charming's lips to touch his, but they didn't. Whitney kissed his forehead first, right over the third eye in the center.

Next, Whitney kissed each temple, then each cheek, and only then did he come around to the front of Graham. Then it was a kiss for each ear lobe, neck kisses on either side of his throat, and at long last, a kiss on the lips. It was sweet.

"This is lovely," Graham said.

"I'm glad you think so," Whitney said. "You're welcome to participate now."

"Okay," Graham said, and he leaned forward to get some. He put a hand on Whitney's neck — Whitney fucking Thorn, who had played at the Grand Ole Opry and had met Johnny Cash, Conway Twitty, and Merle Haggard — and kissed his smirking lips with gusto. For all the struggles Graham had in realizing he was gay, coming out to everyone, and still figuring out how to deal with it in his act, tonight his sexuality was his VIP pass to know someone very special, and have the man all to himself.

Whitney said his knees were too old to keep kneeling on the wood floor, "Let's resume in the bedroom."

"That rhymed again," Graham said, following Whitney to the master bedroom at the back of the house, which had a big bed as soft as a marshmallow. "It's amazing that you can do that."

"It's just a symptom of a one-track mind, but thank you," Whitney said, frothing the sheets and comforter back. His air conditioning was good enough that it would still feel comfortable sleeping under all of those blankets. "I don't mean to poo-poo the compliment, it's just that I've met so many people with blistering amounts of talent and genius, and I'm mostly just long-practiced."

"I sort of get that," Graham said, hopping into bed and sliding his legs between deliciously soft sheets, trying not to moan at the pleasure of it. "I'll never be no Bill Hicks no matter how good I get, but I still think I can get a real career if I keep at it."

"So, you get it exactly," Graham said, before clicking off his bedside lamp and joining Graham between the sheets.

In the dark, it was easier to get past the courtliness of watching each other for permission and just feel their way into each other's arms. Graham ended up cuddling against Whitney's chest, his head just under the man's chin, and happy to be there.

"I'm afraid to say I'm just about old enough to find a good night's sleep preferable to a night of hot sex," Graham whispered to Whitney before sleep kicked in. Whitney's laughter bucked beneath Graham like a waterbed, and made him start laughing, too. "It's sad, but it's true."

"It's not sad," Whitney said, wiping a laugh-tear from his eye and kissing Graham's forehead again. "It's funny because it's very true though."

"Hey, what's with the forehead kiss, if you don't mind me asking?" Graham said, which sobered Whitney's laughter. Maybe he shouldn't have asked, but it was already out there. "Is it a chakra thing?"

"No, but I see how you got there," Whitney said. "It's something I worked out in therapy when I was first recovering. In all the regrettable places I've been and all the dirty acts I've participated in, the one thing no one ever did was kiss me right there." Whitney touched Graham's forehead with his index finger.

"Probably because it's too wholesome a place to kiss," Graham said. It was the one spot his grandparents would kiss on him as a child; even old Grandpa Hellfire-for-Queers could kiss his grandson on the forehead, at least when he was under 12.

"Maybe so," Whitney said. "I've found that if I start there, I can get turned on without getting turned down some dark memory paths."

"'Dark Memory Paths' would make a great song title, if you could go there, so to speak," Graham said.

Whitney started laughing again.

PART II:
INLET

AUGUST 19, 2020 — COVID-19 DEATHS
WORLD DAILY: 6,890 / TOTAL: 880,878
US DAILY: 1,230 / TOTAL: 181,494
LOUISIANA DAILY: 55 / TOTAL: 4,609

8.

WHITNEY

Whitney woke up to a happy morning, but Graham did not. This was because Whitney was old enough that he didn't participate in the online realms much, but Graham did. He said he had to for his career, that he needed to stay engaged and entertaining in order to reach his kind of audience so they'd come to his shows. As a result, Graham woke up to a direct onslaught of hatred and controversy over his decision to go to a public event during the pandemic, and Whitney had to hear all about it.

"These fools are trying to cancel me," Graham said as he sat up in bed and immediately disappeared into his phone. "Trying to out-medicine me when I've been a nurse, dammit." He started typing back to strangers as if their opinions mattered. "We were in ... an open field ... people stayed ... in their own cars ..."

Whitney got up and went about his morning routine: took a piss, brushed his teeth, did some stretching, and sought breakfast. Graham would shuffle back to his own affairs soon, and Whitney would have to fill his day with distractions. He preferred to stay busy creating or performing on the road, but with lockdowns in place, he felt bored and empty of artistic material. He was thinking of doing something simple and exhausting, like re-digging the drainage ditches that led from the house's gutters into the stream that flowed behind the property. Something zen but not useless. Maybe Graham would have some ideas.

"I guess I should go?" Graham asked when he emerged fully dressed from the bathroom. "I don't want to, mind you, but I don't want to overstay my welcome."

"You're welcome to have breakfast with me," Whitney said. "We can let the day unfold after that."

"The day unfolds," Graham said, looking up contemplatively before putting his hands together and opening them like a book. Whitney pointed at the breakfast table, and Graham took a seat. "You sure do talk pretty."

Whitney started singing a song about a cowboy, a horse, and a rifle as he prepped breakfast. He got out oatmeal for himself, nuked some plant-based sausages in the microwave, and made a pan of scrambled eggs from a carton of liquid egg substitute.

When he brought the feast to the table, Graham paid back all of Whitney's secrets from the night before with his own damage report.

"So, I'm living with my mom right now, and it sucks," Graham said. "Not because I don't love her and all, but she's a lot of old-woman attitude every day, and I really wanted to live on my own by thirty-damn-five. It's on me that I quit a real job to be a clown, but it's also on her that she tells me the same complaints every single day, and even when I do what she asks me to do, she has to comment about every time I didn't do as she said before."

"Classic mom behavior," Whitney said. Of course, his mother didn't quite fit the stereotype, being a wild child herself, but she still had some of the same key features as all the other moms. For example, she loved her kids for all she thought they would be and had a real penchant for criticizing them over the reality of what they became.

Graham's phone lit up and drew his attention while Whitney stirred his oatmeal. Steel-cut oats with a mixture of flax, chia seeds, and antioxidant holders like green tea powder and dried fruits. Thickened with almond milk over cow's milk because it kept longer in the fridge and because, at some point between 35 and 50, Whitney's guts had turned inhospitable to lactose.

"These people," Graham said, setting down his forkful of sausage and egg to respond to more strangers. "China's having … a pool party … in Wuhan … why are you … on *my* nuts?" He tossed his phone face-down with a scowl and returned to his food, getting a fleck of scrambled egg in his beard due to haste.

"You don't have to respond if that stuff's bothering you," Whitney said.

"Okay, Boomer," Graham said. "Wait, sorry, that was just a reflex from sassing at the jerks online. You're cool. You're probably not old enough to be a Boomer."

"Born 1970, solid Generation X. Is being a Boomer bad?" Whitney asked.

"It ain't the best, but how would I know, really," Graham said, sitting back and finding that his and Whitney's feet were bare under the table. His feet started playfully patting Whitney's. "I'm what they call an Elder Millennial, and we're not 'the best' either."

"What's wrong with you?" Whitney asked. "I know what's wrong with my ilk. We're a disaffected bunch because we had no parental oversight. Just punks, greed, and speed."

Graham snorted. "Sounds like you've got another banger of a song there. Millennials are the trophy generation, the first to grow up on the internet, so our brains are broken by it, and we've killed home buying, department stores, and chain restaurants. You know, those core pillars of the American Dream."

Whitney laughed. "Which generation is the young one now? Are they still Z?"

"Yeah, until the next batch of Alpha brats comes up," Graham said. "The Zoomers are mad at all of us because we've poisoned the whole planet. I think the Boomers gave us gasoline, you all kept the party going with hairspray, and we're about to finish the job with plastic straws."

In the following moment of silence for a destroyed world, Graham started smiling as Whitney's foot gently tickled his insole.

This foot business was safe along Whitney's lust lines, especially since he couldn't see the interaction, only feel it. There were most assuredly some unsavory memories of guys ejaculating over his feet, but it was never this soft stroking; it was hard, jamming, smacking. It also always involved staring at the feet or smelling and licking them. Feet unseen were relatively clean elements of eroticism.

"Hey," Whitney said, suddenly inspired by another wholesome idea. "Want to adopt a dog with me?"

9.

GRAHAM

Apparently Whitney had wanted a new puppy pal for some time after his last beloved dog, Sugar Bear, died the previous year.

"Where did Sugar Bear get her name?" Graham asked, suspicious of the answer, as they hopped into Whitney's car for a ride to the nearest animal shelter.

"His name," Whitney said, putting his arm up on the passenger seat to look behind him as he backed down his driveway, and managing to stroke Graham's neck as he did so.

Graham decided he was a pretty smooth operator with a move like that. "So, was the dog sweet and looked like a little bear or ...?"

"I got it from an Elton John song," Whitney said. "It's called 'Someone Saved My Life Tonight,' if you've heard it."

"Oh, I know what song it is, motherfucker," Graham said. "That is the gayest thing I've ever heard you say."

Whitney chuckled again, and Graham loved to hear it. No wonder he had the overwhelming urge to become a comedian. The thrill of getting a laugh out of someone was his drug of choice, a First Ballot Hall of Famer, unmatched.

"I thought I needed some time before I could fall in love with another dog again," Whitney said as they drove through the overwhelming summer greenery and tired-looking sun-bleached houses. "I figured I would spend a year or so touring and then come home and get a dog, but here's the year, and I'm forced to be at home for who knows how long, so why not now?"

"Sounds good to me," Graham said. "Dogs are the best souls on this earth, no question."

"Best souls, huh?" Whitney said.

That was the only excuse Graham needed to go off on his tight five about dogs being the best.

"You know it, sir," Graham said. "Most people know it. In fact, that's the one thing that keeps humankind from being complete trash; we care more about dogs locked in hot cars than babies because, let's be real, we know what we are, a bunch of ain't-shit creatures from womb to tomb."

Whitney turned off the radio to ensure Graham had the space to keep sounding off.

"Dogs are better than even little bitty babies, huh?" Whitney prompted.

"Of course," Graham said, only half kidding for effect. "I have literally hated babies; some of them are jerks, just smart enough to be mean and selfish as soon as they can grasp stuff, but dogs? Born just waiting to fall in love and be loyal."

"I've met jerk dogs," Whitney said.

"That's because someone wronged that dog, they ain't born that way, that's just true," Graham said.

"So, do you think dog fighting should be punished like murder?" Whitney asked.

"I'd be okay with it," Graham said. "I mean, you find someone who doesn't have kindness in their hearts for man's best friend, that's a psycho we don't need to share air with. Even Hitler liked dogs, so if they're missing something that literal Hitler still had, that's a late-term abortion that needs to happen."

Whitney whistled, long and slow and clear. Graham had tried to learn how to whistle like that and couldn't make his dumb mouth do it. This man driving him around and listening to his foolish rants was too cool to stand, yet Graham was withstanding him.

"Well, I'll sign your petition about dogs being the best," Whitney said, "but do me a favor and don't repeat any of that while we visit the kennels; they can turn people away if they don't think you're stable enough for a pet."

"Really?" Graham asked. "I remember just being handed puppies out of a cardboard box in someone's truck, but I guess the times have been a-changing."

The kennels, of course, stank. Graham's nose adjusted quickly enough while Whitney explained to the pet purveyors what he was looking for in a dog.

"I'm hoping for a small-ish dog who wouldn't mind road trips," he said. "I travel for work, but I don't like leaving my dog home alone."

The shelter worker nodded and started getting her keys out. She wanted to send this man home with a dog; the only question remaining was: which dog?

"Do you live in a house or an apartment?" asked the shelter worker, a woman whose name tag said Dawn and whose extremely tight ponytail said she meant business.

"A house with a yard," Whitney said. "It isn't fenced in, but the porch is good for a dog who can't jump too high."

"Hmm, and this is your house if you don't mind me asking? You don't rent? Because we have some breeds that landlords don't like."

"I own the house outright," Whitney said. "Are you talking about a Doberman, a pit bull?"

"A pit mix, yes," she said. "You said you want a small dog. She's a chihuahua-golden-pit mix, possibly, among others, but we think she'll stay tiny, and she's such a sweetheart."

Dawn marched to the one cage she wanted empty today and presented the little dog for viewing. Hardly a foot high, the dog had a uniformly pale gold coat, and hazel-brown eyes that looked at you like they'd been missing you for years.

"Aw, c'mon," Graham said when he spotted her. Dawn shot him a look like he was being disparaging, but he was just dropping to his knees in a sweet agony. "Man, pit bulls always look like they've had their eyebrows shaved off, don't they? Their little faces are so expressive."

Dawn was satisfied with Graham's reaction and waited to see about Whitney's.

Whitney squatted, too, and put his fingers through the fenced gate keeping the dog in her kennel cell. She got up from her towel bed, approached for a sniff, and then started licking.

"Look at that floppy tongue," Graham said. "Bet it's all velvety too, man, she's perfect."

"What do you think, sir?" Dawn asked Whitney. "We have a playroom if you'd like to interact with her for a while. She really likes the rope toy."

Graham saw that Whitney was lost in the pup's eyes. Whitney said, "Let me just try one thing here." Then he let out an "Ahrrooo!" howl.

Several dogs howled back at him and came crashing into their cage doors to see what was up. The golden puppy hesitated a moment, looked at the other two humans, and then back at Whitney before singing out one long, "Roooooo!"

Whitney had found his new dog.

10.

WHITNEY

Whitney struggled to keep his eyes on the road with the new puppy sleeping angelically in her carrier as they drove back. He hadn't realized how much he missed loving another creature all day, having them come and go from rooms and seek him out for attention. Now that he had another pet, he also realized why he was so quick to invite Graham back to his house, into his bed, into his confidence, and ask him to say for lunch when he stood around in the driveway of the house this afternoon saying, "I guess I should get back to it, then."

"How about a sandwich first?" Whitney asked. The new puppy got her lunch, too, from a bag of the preferred brand sold at the adoption center. Whitney decided to name her what he first called her when he turned to the dog and asked, "What about you, Honey Bun? Want some lunchies?"

Graham managed not to make a face at the baby talk. He came back inside to eat. Whitney wanted him to stay too. He broached the subject.

"You said your living situation isn't ideal right now?" Whitney asked.

"That is correct. I'm basically grounded until this pandemic is over, and it's barely started, looks like," Graham said.

"Well, I have enjoyed your company, and I'm not looking forward to spending this pandemic all by myself. I get squirrelly and restless with too much time on my hands."

"So ... you're making me an offer you think I won't refuse?" Graham asked.

"I'm saying if you want to keep coming around, staying over, leaving some things in a drawer, I'd like the company," Whitney said. "And so would Honey Bun, it seems," he added as the dog finished inspecting her bowl for every crumb of food and stuffed her face next to Graham's crotch.

"Well, I'm thinking I like this idea," Graham said, leaning down so Honey Bun could snuffle around in his beard. "And bonus, if we shack up tight, we become one of them pods they talk about, little isolation pods from the 'rona."

"That's the idea," Whitney said. "So, want to have an extended sleepover with me during these here end-times?"

Graham did. He first had to go home and pack some things and make nice with his momma about this and other recent rash decisions. While he was gone, Whitney took the window of free time to get his house in order.

First, the needs for Honey Bun. Whitney got out and reassembled an old puppy pen and a crate, layered it with towels, and set up the girl's water bowl. He would let her have run of the house for now to see which foibles she came with. Did she chew armrests or cords? Was she a trash digger? Would she cry when left alone or shut out of a room? Depending on what she brought, Whitney would respond with the appropriate training.

Whitney did some laundry, some grocery inventory to get a list going for two instead of one, decided to defrost some vegan beef crumbles and dig out a jar of salsa and a bag of tortilla chips for a taco skillet dinner. He got a request for a video call from an old friend while he puttered around, and picked it up with a smile.

"It's been a while, Lyle," he said. Lyle was a man in his sixties who had a modest business filming amateur porn in Akron, Ohio. He was one of the cheeriest degenerates Whitney had ever met, and he was also squeaky-clean regarding drugs — Lyle he didn't even drink coffee. He was a great friend during Whitney's sobriety and sexual reawakening, truly heaven-sent.

"How you doing, friend? You smilin' so you look like you're doing well," Lyle said. He had white hair, a toasted-coconut tan, and a gap-toothed smile.

"I'm getting a house boy for the pandemic," he said. "Met him last night, he's moving in today."

"Ooh, you ho," Lyle said. "What's his name?"

"Graham," Whitney said, "and this ..." He went to find his new puppy to lift her into the shot. "This is my new house girl, Honey Bun."

"You're on a real tear, it seems," Lyle told, a note of worry creeping in. "Hope you're not getting manic or anything. I don't mean to yuck your yum or nothing, but these are hard times for people in recovery."

"I ain't mad," Whitney said, as he gently discouraged Honey Bun from licking the inside of his mouth. "It's nice to be worried over. I think I want someone else here precisely because I don't want to get too wrapped up in myself."

"Right, but if you get wrapped up in him, and something goes wrong, it's like having a crutch kicked out from under you," Lyle said. "Or it could be, there's just a risk is all."

"If something happens with the guy, I've got the dog. If that goes wrong too, I've got you, right?"

"You know it, brother," Lyle said. "Well, I was calling to see if you wanted to come to a remote orgy. Interested?"

"I'm sorry," Whitney said, blinking rapidly as if that would fix what he'd just heard. "A what now?"

11.

GRAHAM

"Cuffing?" Graham asked his momma, as she stood in the doorway of his room, disapproving. "Is that what the kids are calling it? And how would you know?"

"I learned it from one of my late-night shows," Cynthany told him. "It's when people decide to move in together before the winter, so they won't be alone when they're snowed in." She nodded with the wisdom imparted to her by the television. "They want to be, like, handcuffed to somebody for the dark days, but they usually break up after Valentine's Day."

"But it's summer," Graham told her.

"The winter is this Corona lockdown," she said. "I'm not telling you it's a bad idea, I'm just saying it probably won't work out."

"Seasons of bondage rarely do, Momma," Graham told her, in response to which she swatted his shoulder for saying the tasteless word "bondage."

Graham had his clothes and undies packed, along with his toothbrush and the charging cords for his phone and laptop. He didn't own much, which was both sad yet convenient. He took a thorough shower and paid a great deal of attention to cleaning his ass, because he was pretty sure he was getting laid that night. He hadn't had a date since arriving back in this town during the spring, and it was the dead-end of summer already. On the road he'd been having a good time matching with strangers on apps every other week, just gorging himself. Then it all stopped: the gigs, the guys, the glory days. From April to August, he'd been lotioning his hand and keeping his voice down like he was 14 years old again. Whitney wanted some company? Well, Graham wanted somewhere else to jack off, so everybody was in perfect alignment, except for Momma.

"What am I supposed to tell people who ask where you've gone?" she asked as she stirred her TV dinner on the couch because what was the point of cooking a meal if there was no one else to eat it? She'd pulled her stringy brown-and-gray hair back into a ponytail so it wouldn't draggle in the sauce, and she was definitely pouty to see him go.

"If by people you mean Aunt Tamella and Cousin Sage, just tell them I'm staying with a friend," Graham said, putting his second pair of shoes in a grocery bag, and his main pair on his feet in one awkward dance by the door.

"They're going to know what 'friend' means," Cynthany said.

"Well, I guess they're smarter than people say then," Graham said, approaching for his goodbye kiss. "I'm still doing your grocery shopping for you though, just text me pictures of the kind you want, and I'll get them for you, okay? I don't want you in the stores with people sick."

"It's not that big a deal," she said. "I know you think you're a doctor or whatever because you got your nursing license, but it's not the plague, I think we'd notice if it was. The news just wants drama."

"Okay, but if I find out you're out shopping when you don't have to I'm gonna come over here and kick all your garden gnomes in the face," Graham told her.

"You would not, I'd beat your ass if you did, buddy," she told him.

"But that wouldn't unstomp their faces, would it?" Graham asked. "So just stay home, okay?"

"Whatever," she said, turning back to the TV.

"Promise me," Graham said, and when she didn't speak up fast enough, he quit the hokey threats and reminded her of the real reason he insisted. "You remember what it was like seeing Dad on that ventilator, you know neither of us want to do that again, Momma ..."

"I know that — I'll stay home," she said with a scowl. "Bye!"

Graham nodded and walked out. His mother didn't like to think of that time. The lung cancer that killed her husband. The struggle it took her to quit smoking in solidarity and for his health as much as hers. The hopelessness of caring for someone who was gradually dying, all while his father (Preacher PawPaw) insisted that praying mattered a damn and blamed her for taking his son into the trashy life he died living.

All that drama happened during Graham's senior year of high school. When Dad finally died, Graham was gone to college, and Grandpa gave up the illusion of caring about them anymore. Without his son there to make the connection, Cynthany and Graham weren't really family as far as he was concerned. Grandpa died just a few weeks prior to Graham's return home to Louisiana, possibly from one of the early COVID cases, though Graham neither knew for sure, nor cared. Grandpa would have called it the Kung-Flu with his dying breath, he was that kind of Christian.

Graham walked back into Whitney's house with relief. It was glowing with lamplight as the evening surrounded the property. It smelled of food, and the puppy was the first to greet him, wiggling and ecstatic and also freshly bathed, so they had that in common. Graham fell to his knees half in gratitude, and also so that the dog could inspect his new smells. This place was so much less fraught than Cynthany's house, with its memories, obligations, and emotional landmines. Graham felt grateful to be there.

Whitney's head popped around the corner so he could make sure this bold intruder was the one he was expecting for the night.

"Hi there, dinner is almost ready," Whitney said, before disappearing back into the kitchen, and speaking louder. "I prepped the guest room for you, first door after the bathroom, not because I want you to sleep in there instead of with me, but more so like you *can* sleep in there if you want to, have your own space."

"Sounds good," Graham said, following his voice as the puppy followed him. "What's cooking?"

"Taco scramble, and for dessert, boom," Whitney said, slapping down a box of Little Debbie's Honey Buns. "In honor of this Honey

Bun." He picked up the dog to show her the box of Honey Buns too and tell her, "That's you, baby, you a Honey Bun."

Graham was briefly jealous, wishing that he was the one in Whitney's arms, but a voice in his head reminded him, *Soon*. That was the plan for the evening, no need to rush.

"Funny story," Whitney went on, releasing Honey Bun back to the floor. "An old friend of mine called to invite me to — get this — a socially-distanced orgy. Apparently, that's how people are keeping it spicy right now, naked video calls."

"Oh, damn," Graham said. "Did we RSVP?"

He said it as a joke, but ultimately, he wasn't joking.

12.

WHITNEY

Whitney and Graham decided to put dinner on the back burners and attend the e-orgy.

"I am no longer a serious person," Graham told Whitney, "so I don't really have a problem showing my ass on the internet. In a lot of ways, that's exactly what my social media presence is already."

"Alright," Whitney agreed, donning a deerstalker hat and a pair of sunglasses but taking everything else off. "Let's get at it."

Whitney lent Graham a ski mask so they could show their bits and buttholes without their faces being identifiable. Whitney brought a small table out of his bathroom to set the laptop at the foot of his bed and put a towel across both their laps to start modestly before finding the link and getting the code from Lyle.

The moment before he clicked to sign in, Whitney turned to Graham to make sure this was still funny to him, not just a bluff that went too far. Graham was perfectly perked up, curious to see a window open up into a dirty world he'd never been even to the edges of, whereas Whitney had been to the deepest dungeons.

Whitney then took a moment to check on himself. Was this too close to bad old memory terrain, or would the novelty of seeing lonely sex acts in a series of Brady Bunch squares keep it new enough to stay safe?

While Whitney worried over these subtle distinctions, Graham snapped him out of it with a kiss, a sweet bird-like peck from someone who looked like he was here to rob some booty. Whitney grinned and got over his concerns. This definitely was something new, and so far, something that felt very safe.

"Ready?" Graham asked. His hand was already stroking himself beneath the towel.

"Ready, Freddie," Whitney said, and hit the log-in button.

As the camera engaged, Graham said, "I know that's from a Queen song. If you start singing Cher songs we may have to rethink this arrangement."

Whitney was heard laughing as soon as his microphone turned on, and Lyle's voice as the moderator came on to say, "Please mute."

Laughing was not appreciated at the orgy.

Within fifteen minutes, there were eleven screens going, and Lyle's voice made small talk as people got comfortable enough to start opening their pants and showing their cocks to the other folks at home.

Lyle said, "I encourage people to unmute if they're making sex noises, but try to stay muted if you've got TV on in the background or pets. Definitely let me know if you're about to cum, so I can feature your camera to make sure we can all enjoy it."

In the grid view, it was a gallery of dicks, bellies, butts, and slack jaws over tweaked nipples. When switched to the view Lyle was showcasing, he kept a steady revolution going between views that looked good. Every once in a while, someone would join the group and Lyle would welcome them with, "Hi, we're all jerking off in here, please mute," and someone else would ejaculate and then leave, departing with a thumbs-up or eggplant+squirt emoji combo in the chat on the side.

For Whitney and Graham, they first started by jerking themselves, and then crossed arms to fondle each other. Whitney bent the laptop lid and then himself down to blow Graham, give the people a show that only a couple could put on. This was much appreciated until a threesome showed up and started spit-roasting: one guy on all fours as the other two entered his mouth and ass on either end. This was obviously not the threesome's first rodeo.

Once the room's attention was elsewhere, Whitney and Graham started performing a bit more for each other than the anonymous guys online, kissing and spitting and whispering until it was agreed that Graham would crawl onto Whitney's lap, face-to-face, and grind on him that way.

Whitney had condoms in the bathroom, but didn't want to go get them, nor did he want to try and discuss sexual health data so close to coitus (it likely wouldn't be believable, actionable information, just like confessions under torture weren't worth shit). Instead of fucking Graham, he just enjoyed the hot, sweaty seam of him, and put his fingers up there to prod Graham towards orgasm.

"I'm about to shoot," he said, and that got them the top spot at the show again, with Whitney shifting so that people could see the spurt between them.

They hugged as a few men spoke favorably saying, "Hot," and, "Nice."

After some huffing and puffing and more kissing, Graham got down on his knees to blow Whitney, returning the favor. Once Whitney had cum all over his own ski mask, Graham stepped out of view to slip off the mask. Whitney showed it off to the rest of the group — white lines and dots like Morse Code over the black fabric. It helped a couple more guys unload, and then sign off. Whitney waved goodbye, and exited the orgy via click.

Graham started laughing as soon as they were alone again, which startled Honey Bun out of her nap momentarily. She took one look at them, then tucked back into a sleep ball.

"That was fun!" Graham declared. "Also hilarious, I can't wait to talk about this on stage."

Whitney took off his hat and sunglasses, smiling. It made him happy to see someone so jazzed by something as simple and silly as strangers showing their unphotogenic penises to each other online. What a sweet summer child he had to enjoy for now, for a season.

Graham grabbed Whitney's face in both hands to give him a big kiss on the mouth.

"Are you hungry? Because I'm starving," Graham said, before walking buck naked out into the kitchen.

13.

GRAHAM

Once the first sexual encounter was out of the way, their jollies had and their bellies full, Graham and Whitney found a comfortable silence. They cleaned up and got into their sleep duds. Graham set his things up in the guest room while Whitney took Honey Bun out for a romp around the yard. They sat next to each other with some music on, checking their phones for fresh bad news.

There were fires in California, flooding in China, an official Democratic nominee for president, and nothing two pieces of river trash could do about any of it. They went to bed early, but did not sleep right away. In the dark, Graham started talking.

"What's one of the best and one of the worst things about you?" Graham asked. "I'll go first. The best is my ability to make people laugh. My cousin said I talked her out of suicide once just for cracking jokes when she needed it most."

"That's a very nice review," Whitney said, his voice half-muffled by the pillow as he lay on his side, facing Graham in his big, wonderful bed. Graham lay face-up, watching the ceiling fan spin.

"Right? But I'm not all good, you know. I let my mother deal with my dad dying alone. I did not come home to say goodbye, I did not help with the funeral, and I made a choice to do that. I could have helped a lot, I should have, but I just didn't want to so I made her deal with it instead."

"You were how old?" Whitney asked.

"In the end, 18 turning 19," Graham said.

Whitney found Graham's hand in the dark and brought it to his mouth to kiss. "That's not so bad, you were still a kid. Kids don't sign up to care for their parents, spouses do sign up to care for each other."

"It was still shitty to my mom, I'm ashamed of it," Graham said. "I'm kind of leaving her to deal with this pandemic crap right now, but I did say I'd still get her groceries, she's too high-risk for that. And we were getting on each other's nerves, maybe this isn't so bad either."

"Hmm," Whitney said. "The worst things I've done were because of the drugs. Stole money, used people up, still have some apologies I owe that the folks I wronged don't want to hear. And I'm ashamed too, but I can't let myself dwell on it, that's not helpful to me or them or anybody."

"Yeah," Graham said. He also knew asking Whitney such probing questions could be triggering, but he did it anyway. Graham was selfish in a lot of ways, but Whitney probably knew how to say "no" if he didn't want to play these games. "So, what's good about you?"

"My love for music," Whitney said, answering so fast he must have thought about it before. "It's the purest thing about me, and I can't seem to tarnish it. I never get so empty that the right song can't make me feel something, and I think music is one of the best things humans have ever done, so I can't ever really give up on us as a species either. And when I perform it feels spiritual in a way that church never did for me. It feels like for better or worse, I'm connected to something real, and something that can never die, because music is movement, vibration. It exists in some form as long as there's a rhythm to the universe."

Graham felt half-hypnotized listening to all of that. When Whitney quieted, Graham turned to kiss him, and then rolled over on top of him when Whitney reciprocated. Graham still had a few more questions though, before he could rest easy.

"How long am I going to be here, do you know?" Graham asked. "It's okay if you don't know, if we're just having fun and shacking up until the fun stops and the lockdowns are over. I just want to know my expiration date if you know it, if that's okay." Whitney didn't answer right away. Instead, he looked up at Graham in that strong new-moon light from the window, and raked his finger through Graham's beard, contemplating. "I don't want to overstay my welcome," Graham explained further, desperate for validation. "Whenever we part, I just want it to be on good terms."

"Who says we have to part?" Whitney asked, and before Graham could form another downer comeback (entropy said they must part, and that all things would end, for example), Whitney went on. "I don't have any end in mind right now. I just know I don't want to be alone all year, or however long this virus lasts, so I'm glad you're available, and that you helped me get a dog. My friend Lyle, you remember him ..."

"The great and powerful Oz of the orgy, yeah," Graham recalled.

"He's already worried I'm being too impulsive, it's what addicts do sometimes when they're about to lose keel, relapse." Whitney started stroking Graham's hair then, and Graham leaned into the touch like a pet might respond to his master. "All of a sudden after a lot of slow, safe, and steady, I'm inviting a lot of new variables into my life. Is it just a coincidence, or am I becoming manic in response to what's going on in the world? I think I'm fine, but I can't always tell with me. There are a lot of people in recovery right now who will be off the wagon or in the ground by the time this is over."

"I don't think this is bad," Graham said, though he wouldn't be able to tell either. "I think this was a happy happenstance, you and me meeting the way we did. I was feeling pretty suffocated at my mom's, and you need some healthy energy around, right? I mean I'm trash, but that puppy's going to be good for both of us, don't you think?"

Whitney smiled. "Yeah, let's put all our emotional labor on that baby dog, sounds like we're both making a sensible, grounded decision there."

"Totally rational," Graham agreed.

Whitney's laughing belly tickled as it undulated beneath Graham.

14.

WHITNEY

Whitney slept peacefully for about half the night, but when he got up around 3 AM to pee, he walked into a pocket of strange and couldn't shake it.

Graham was sleeping soundly, no jitters about a new bed, perhaps because as a fellow road dog, he had learned to sleep wherever he landed. Whitney looked at him from the bathroom door, and for a moment felt a flare of paranoia. Who was this man who so easily walked in when invited? Was that not a red flag? What if he became some kind of nightmare squatter who refused to leave if Whitney wanted him gone? What if he told lies someday to tar Whitney and gain fame? What if he told only the truth, but still cashed in on whatever days they would spend together, exchanging it for cheap attention, no matter how honestly it began?

This was what those in recovery called "stinking thinking," and Whitney recognized it as such. He was only second-guessing Graham because he was asleep, unanimated. Graham's vibes had no false notes all day long, but when unconscious, it was easy to forget who was really in there, and just see a man, a stranger, with motives unknown.

Whitney shook his head physically and shook off the noir mood by seeking out Honey Bun, who also slept beautifully on a wadded-up blanket in her new crate. When Whitney got close enough, she stirred by the nose and made a tiny, inquisitive call toward him.

Whitney let her out so he could hold her. She had such silken fur that showed glossy in the moonlight. Even though it wasn't the best idea to start a midnight cuddling routine, he couldn't stop the impulse that night.

With the puppy in his arms, Whitney lay down on the couch. Honey Bun was too excited to settle at first, wriggling and scratching him lightly as she tried to climb on top of him rather than stretch by his side, but Whitney tried an ear-scratching technique that Sugar Bear had liked, and that massaging felt good enough to hold still for.

Once tranquility had returned to them both, Whitney started to whisper to his new pet, kissing her head and ears as he did so. He was trying to dispel sad memories of missing Sugar Bear, and so painted a new picture of the future.

"I love you, do you know that?" Whitney asked her. Honey Bun just looked up at him, but when the question intonation didn't come with any other excitement, she set her head back down on his arm. "We're going to have such wonderful days, you and me. We'll get to play in the crick, and lay in the hammock, and I bet Graham will play fetch with you, ooh, won't that be nice?"

Honey Bun's tail smacked up and down. She liked the sound of that.

"That's right. You'll get to lick all my bowls so long as they aren't too spicy, and you'll get to pee on all the trees in the yard, and you'll get to chase squirrels and dig holes, cuz I don't care about this yard, Honey Bunny, it can look like a dirt farm all year, nobody pays me to mow anyway."

The dog farted. Whitney almost laughed, but managed to choke it down, so they could keep still even as the smell dispersed through the room.

"We're gonna stink together, and we're gonna sing together, and if you're like this every night my darling, maybe we can even sleep together," Whitney told her. "I'm not the biggest fan of crates, we're just … starting from scratch here."

In the bedroom, there was shuffling, the sound of piss hitting the toilet, and then a flush followed by a quiet, "Oh shit."

Honey Bun popped up her head to see Graham come around the corner, looking for Whitney. When he saw the two of them snuggled on the couch, he stopped in his tracks and waved.

Honey Bun's tail started wagging again, making a loud *thwap thwap* on the couch and smacking Whitney's leg rather hard. She was ready to defend her new master but understood that Graham was not a threat.

"I didn't think before I flushed, thought it was going to wake you up, but you're already out here," Graham said.

Whitney didn't reply, just held out a hand so that Graham would come to join the sitting area. He seemed to be waiting for permission, standing awkwardly like a kid at a sleepover, lost in the dark.

Graham sat down on the coffee table, a beastly sturdy thing. He went to give Whitney a quick kiss on the mouth, but Honey Bun beat him to it, licking her tongue between them both.

"Oh gross," Graham said, wiping his mouth, while Whitney let the dog lick his face as much as she liked.

"What's this?" Whitney asked, as puppy tongue got slightly inside his mouth. He put his hand around Honey Bun's snoot so he could talk, but he wasn't gagging like Graham. "Are you too good for her kisses?"

"Buddy, I've got a dirty mouth, but not dog-dirty. They eat poop, and she's new here, so we don't know where she's been licking."

Whitney chuckled. He never understood people who would eat ass, suck dick, make out, but still think their mouth was too clean to befoul with dirt on potato skins or hair in a soup.

"Guess we won't be sharing a toothbrush, huh?" Whitney asked.

"Ah, no sir," Graham said, as Honey Bun realized the humans were talking, and hopped down to find her water bowl and then return to her crate. "I'll have you know, the human mouth has more germs than a toilet seat, more than any given anus."

"Any given anus," Whitney said, sitting up and impressed by the phrase.

"It's true. People who came into the clinic with fight bites had to be dosed up with all the antibiotics because they could get infected and poison their blood, our mouths are toxic."

"So, they'd be better off punching a wall than punching someone in the face?" Whitney asked.

"One hundred percent," Graham said, nodding and surprisingly serious, just as he was about the purity of a dog's spirit. The man had a stridency about him and would expound unexpectedly. Whitney wondered if that came from performing, or if it came before and found natural use on a stage.

"So, but then isn't a dog's mouth cleaner than yours?" Whitney asked. "Where do you get off acting like your mouth is dirtier now, when really it's Honey Bun who should be complaining?"

"I'm sorry her standards are so low, you have my condolences," Graham said. "Are you coming back to bed?"

Whitney checked with himself, and found his spell of sadness had passed. He always worried when those arrived that they would drag him down, but tonight's crisis was averted by just a little kind company.

PART III:
VORTEX

SEPTEMBER 2, 2020 — COVID-19 DEATHS
WORLD DAILY: 6,516 / TOTAL: 965,030
US DAILY: 1,056 / TOTAL: 195,258
LOUISIANA DAILY: 20 / TOTAL: 5,004

15.

GRAHAM

For the next two weeks, Graham and Whitney enjoyed a top-notch and rare honeymoon bubble.

While a Black man was shot 11 times by Lafayette Police outside of a convenience store, they were white men who had groceries delivered to the front porch. As the Category 4 storm Hurricane Laura ravaged the western parts of Louisiana, knocking out power and leaving people to die from the heat, all they felt was cooling cast-off rain. When Lake Charles and surrounding neighborhoods were being polluted extra by nearby chlorine and oil refining plants damaged by the storm, they were playing squirt games with the hose as they gave Honey Bun a bath in the yard.

"I hate to ask," Graham said one day, mid-week, not that calendar time mattered to them in lockdown. "But would you be willing to help me make content?"

Graham had been on the cusp of building an audience before this shutdown business. A new comedian couldn't survive if he couldn't make connections with other comics, with club and bar owners, with agents and bookers, and with the crowds that came out to comedy shows. He had to be seen, he needed to build interest in people who would buy tickets in advance, he needed to put on a show. If he couldn't get on to a stage during the pandemic, he would have to get online in a big way. His first idea was to film himself doing sketches, and he would need a cameraman.

"Content like what?" Whitney asked. "Also yes, I'll help."

"Yeah?" Graham asked, stepping into the dog bath water to rinse his feet before putting them back into his sandals. "Fair warning, it's going to be embarrassing fare."

"Sweetness, you're a clown," Whitney said. The dog knew her name was Honey, so Graham had to be called other affectionate names. So far, he was Sweetness, Sweetheart, and the more formal Sweetheart Darling, while the dog was Honey, Muffin, and Pumpkin. "Clowns gotta be fools, so of course it's embarrassing."

"That's a good point, can't have a dignified clown," Graham said, whipping out his phone to type *Dignified Clown* into his notes for a future sketch.

Whitney finished scrubbing Honey Bun dry with a towel, and shook his head and shoulders along with her as she wriggled free. She immediately found some sand to roll in, but they would just have to give her a good brushing before bed. They couldn't fight the puppy's messy nature, they could only accommodate it.

"You know I've got a lot of stage outfits if you want to go closet shopping," Whitney said.

"Oh, do any of them have rhinestones?" Graham asked, trying not to get clappy.

Whitney smiled, crooked a finger, and led Graham back inside to his other closet, what should have been an impressive pantry off the kitchen, but instead had a new use.

"This is my Pageant Pantry," Whitney said, rolling up the double door.

Graham stepped in feeling like he was some game-show contestant who picked Door Number One and nailed it.

There were shirts embroidered with birds and roses, and hats with feathers, buckles, and beads. There were jackets with fringe and leather vests that smelled amazing. There were cowboy boots with turquoise, hand-stitching, and one very special one with decorative spurs that yep: glinted with rhinestones.

"It's all so beautiful," Graham said in a breathy whisper.

"I think a lot of this will fit you fine, especially if you just wear your own jeans or we film from the waist up," Whitney said. "I've got a fake snake and a skeleton in some Halloween decorations too, we can go through those like a prop department and —"

Graham kissed him because he didn't need to hear anymore. This man was saying yes to the dress-up closet today.

16.

WHITNEY

While Graham was inventing new characters and finding their wardrobe choices, Whitney was remembering his music video experiences. It was the 1990s, he had blond tips in his hair, smooth skin, and he was the next hot thing. Famous parents, a pretty face, and fairly talented. The world was his for the taking and he took it with gusto. Up the nose, up the ass, and ultimately on the chin, he took it.

Every item Graham touched held both shiny and grimy memories, all of which Whitney kept to himself under a serene smile. A leather jacket that had been slid onto his shoulders like a cape over a king in a very nice store by the man that signed him to his record label. That same man ultimately spat at his feet when Whitney's attention-grabbing exploits were gay, not straight.

Speaking of feet, every pair of boots held something nice and something drab. The ones Graham ultimately selected smelled amazing, Graham said so himself, as had someone who blew Whitney at an afterparty once (the guy caught a whiff while he was down there and had rubbed his face against the leather, which was hot). By the end of that afterparty, Whitney was puking in the alley, but he managed to miss the boots. He was proud of that while he nursed a wretched hangover the following day. Alcohol was never his preferred drug after that, *too messy*, he thought.

And then the hats, one he had for a photo shoot for album art, great for tipping over a rakish brow, a move that nothing but compliments and swoons from the ladies, which Whitney still enjoyed as much as any straight man, just for different reasons. But of course, there was one who finally got close enough to tell him "what a waste" it was that he was gay, like what was the point of him if not for being with her or someone like her?

Graham's hands were full of items by then, and Whitney pulled out a retired drinks cart from beneath some hanging pants. It used to carry liquor, but was too nice of a cart to get rid of once Whitney sobered up. He put it out of sight and out of mind until he could look at it without noticing his thoughts leading him back to a meth craving, but hadn't thought of it in years once it was tucked away with all the rest of these problematic recollections. It would now serve as a little shopping cart for Graham, and maybe it could live in the kitchen after that, under all his tea fixings and whatnot.

"Man, you must have been a pretty big deal back in the day, with all this stuff," Graham said. "Not that you aren't a big deal now I mean, but ..."

Whitney kissed him to avoid the *mea culpas* about how he wasn't that defunct now, wasn't that old, *et cetera*. Instead, he offered Graham a distraction.

"They thought I was going to be bigger than I got," he said. "Want to see the director's cut of the video with that shirt?" He pointed to one with a phoenix stitched across the chest.

"Yes, I do," Graham said. "Maybe it'll give me some inspiration for filming my little two-minute goof-em-ups."

Whitney had the video in a digital storage file. It was much simpler to turn on his computer and use the search function than find a tape or sort through an album, though it did cut to the chase rather quickly. In the old days, finding that one picture or video would have been a stroll down memory lane, now it was a bullet train from point A to point B.

"Ooh, look at you dance," Graham said as he watched over Whitney's shoulder. "They keep cutting away like you're too good at it, what's that about?"

"They wanted me to be a young, cute version of the old stuff, kind of stoic, just a simple country boy," Whitney said. "My dance moves were too sexy."

"They actually said that?" Graham asked.

"Yes, they did," Whitney said. "Told me to only dance above the waist because the gyrating could get them letters of disapproval. I was supposed to be a clean young man their daughters could bring home, that was the image we were selling."

"This was the 90s? The post-AIDS, grunge band 90s?" Graham asked.

"The very same," Whitney told him, "not the top-hats-and-waltzes 90s that came before it."

"I just can't believe they were still on that Elvis-the-pelvis, only film him from the waist up 1950s bullshit," Graham said.

"Believe me, Sweetheart, they're still having that conversation right now today," Whitney said, leaning into Graham's kiss on his neck. "Some of those old fuckers and most of their old ideas refuse to die."

"Oh man," Graham said, pulling out his notebook. "That would make a great series of a 1950s dude color-commenting on popular dance moves, can do that one in black and white and an old-timey voice."

Whitney closed the video of his bright-eyed, baby-faced self and turned away. He was glad to be behind the camera today, rather than in front of it. Whitney had once gotten a taste of everything he thought he wanted, and most of it was bitter or fake. Like a beautiful cake sculpted in flavorless fondant and stacked on Styrofoam, the beauty was there to *look* good, not to *be* good.

"Are you ready for your close-up?" Whitney asked Graham. Whatever fame his new friend wanted, Whitney would let Graham discover its disappointments on his own.

17.

GRAHAM

Graham found a plain wall in Whitney's living room he could perform in front of, and lost his reluctance to use the man as a director when it was time to put on the show. Whitney said yes, so if it became tiresome as it surely would, they would just have to cross that bridge when they came to it.

Graham had a few characters he wanted to explore, some he could do in rapid-fire one-liners, others who would need a script and some film-ification tricks from his smartphone, like backgrounds and filters. One idea that would have to wait was Stetson Stat, a cowboy doctor. One of Whitney's hats plus a stethoscope and a pair of Graham's old scrubs, and boom: he's saying tarnation in the OR. That would require a trip back to his momma's for the medical props, so it was tabled. He had a vision for a Lonesome Line-Dancer, a guy in a jazzy shirt and boots who had all the right moves, but no one else would join in his dance. It would start at a jukebox joint, but become increasingly funny as the Line-Dancer did the same do-si-do nonsense with every line he was in: grocery store checkout, DMV, amusement park, police line-up, then finally a firing line where he's executed for bothering folks too much with his enthusiastic solicitations of, "Come on, y'all, who doesn't like to dance?"

First up though, was Gussied-Up Gus: the man who overdressed like he was going to a dinner theater for every semi-nice thing he did. The background: A dumpy-looking chain food restaurant. Gus: "It's actually quite classy to wear a bib." An inner-city airport with Gus saying, "People used to wear suits and Sunday dresses to travel through the air." A crowd of sloppy and shirtless football fans and Gus says, "I show team pride with a bolo tie."

"Bolo-tied and showing pride," Whitney said after hitting the stop button for the video, finding the lyric in what Graham had come up with.

"That's good," Graham said as he put back on his own schlubby clothes and returned a painting of a horse to Whitney's wall. According to the rule of thirds, Graham had enough for one reel, and they were done filming for the day. "Want to record Gus a theme song?"

Again, he thought he was joking, but Whitney went for it by finding the voice recorder on Graham's phone.

"You don't mind?" Whitney asked.

Graham threw up his hands and said, "By all means." Graham figured Whitney must record his own tune ideas on his phone whenever inspiration struck, and now Graham was getting a tasty-taste of that talent.

Whitney's voice was shockingly pretty all of a sudden, with no warm-up at all, and the man didn't even clear his throat. He just sang out sweet and clear, "Bolo-tied and showing pride, this cuss gussies up: Gus!" He hit stop and recorded it two more times with different emphases and final landings on the punctuating "Gus!" He then handed the phone over like it was nothing, just a napkin-doodle from a genius *artiste*, no big thang.

"You gifted son of a bitch," Graham said, taking back his phone and careful to make sure it was all saved properly not only to his phone, but also emailed to his inbox for later remixing.

"It's mostly practice," Whitney said. "A little bit of talent, a lot of stick-to-itiveness, and that's how it's done."

"This is your advice to young upstarts like me?" Graham asked.

"Young guns do ask me after shows, people want to know how to break in," Whitney said. "You can see how long I've been in the biz by the lines on my face, it really is good advice to just keep at it. The same applies to singing, to your little skits and routines, to all of the arts that get better with age."

"Alright," Graham said, pulling his regular t-shirt back down over his head and going to stand between Whitney's knees where he sat on one of his barstools (recently in service as a director's chair). "We need to make a few things clear. First of all, skits are what people do in high school drama class, professional comedians do sketches. That's the most important lesson they teach after how to 'yes, and' your teammates during improv so no one loses the momentum."

"Oh," Whitney said, amused to high-heaven based on his big, beaming smile. "I stand corrected."

"You sit corrected," Graham told him, earning a guffaw. "Second, I believe you with that ten thousand hours stuff, but only if you start with some aptitude first, and then have the luck and good fortune to have time to practice, right? There are a lot of virtuosos out there who are going to burn out over a vat of French fries, aren't there?"

"There are," Whitney said. "But don't let that excuse wasted luck."

Graham nodded. He had a real philosopher under his fingertips, and revolved him back and forth on his spinning seat top while he pontificated.

"Third of all," Graham continued, "you look hotter than you did back in the 90s."

"Stop," Whitney said, rolling his eyes. "I don't need to be flattered, young man, I'm perfectly proud of my age. With the way I behaved when AIDS was still felling guys, the close calls I've had with overdoses, the danger I've been in behind a wheel, it's an absolute privilege to be old enough to look it."

"I acknowledge all of that," Graham said, "but I'm still telling you I'd personally rather fuck with you as you are today than that boyband-looking kid you used to be."

"Oh, I see, this is just your own preferences we're talking about here," Whitney said as Graham ran his hands up to pull the man's face a little more taut, lifting a few of his characteristic wrinkles.

"Maybe," Graham said. "You look cooler with wrinkles, weathered, it's sexy. You look like you've seen some shit, that you'd stay calm under pressure. You like you can shoot a gun, change a tire, *and* play guitar. It's very appealing."

"More like I can shoot a tire," Whitney said.

"Shh," Graham said, putting his fingers over Whitney's lips. "You look so much prettier when you're quiet, Angel."

Whitney started laughing again. Nothing sounded better than a grown man's genuine laugh to Graham, not even silence.

18.

WHITNEY

As the day waned, talk veered at last into controversial subjects. As Graham sat with headphones half on working with video editing software on his computer, Whitney put a record on the turntable, started dinner simmering, and tried to teach Honey Bun how to sit and roll on command.

It was the music medium that started the debates.

"That's a real album," Graham said. "Does it ever bother you that people say they're 'dropping an album' when they're actually clicking publish online?"

"Not enough to do anything about it," Whitney said though he had noticed it sounded incongruent before. "The phrase is a little outdated maybe, but an album is a collection, right? They're not dropping records, they're dropping collections, and some still do issue special vinyl editions of their albums."

"Right, for the hipsters and the old timers," Graham said. "Sort of like an online photo album, people still call them albums when they aren't physical books, more like digital folders."

"They aren't folders either, or files, or pages or none of that," Whitney said. "We just call them what they used to be."

"Future historians will be so confused," Graham said, shaking his head and saving something that needed time to finalize. "Here I am saving a film without celluloid."

"Celluloid," Whitney said. "Haven't heard that word in a while."

"Well, I'm an educated fool," Graham said with a smile, leaning back as his computer buffered, zipped, or converted, whatever the spinning wheel meant. Whitney was busy scritching the dog in his lap, so he was fully occupied. "Got any pet peeves about the music business?"

"I hate the word *merch*," Whitney said, "and I deeply hate seeing my face on the merch."

"Merch is a stupid word," Graham agreed, "makes me think of merkins half the time though, so I don't mind it. Pubic wigs are just plain funny, there's no way around it."

"Hmm," Whitney said as Honey Bun suddenly twisted out of his lap and ran off. "Any complaints about comedy?" They were making small talk for the sake of the noise it seemed, but Whitney didn't mind. They would have to start really talking to each other sometime, rather than flirt their way through conversations as they'd been doing for the past couple of blissful weeks.

"Comedy about how comedy is being canceled is the most useless thing I can think of," Graham said. "I hate to be such a purist, but like where do these guys get off thinking twenty minutes of a half-hour special should be filled with them complaining that they can't be as mean and dumb as they want to be?"

"Not very canceled if they have a special, are they?" Whitney asked. He had a couple of lifetime bans to his name from places where he'd irrevocably damaged his reputation, so Whitney knew the difference between being truly silenced and being publicly criticized. The real bans happened in back rooms, whereas the outrage machine was like a summer storm: showy but short-lived.

"Exactly," Graham said. "I hope I never turn into someone like that, but I'd have to get fame and fortune before it could corrupt me, so I don't worry too much. Might as well spend time being concerned about how much rich people get taxed, it's not a problem I'm likely to have."

"You never know," Whitney said. "Fortune in entertainment strikes like lightning."

"There you go again with your poetry," Graham said. "I just hope I'm never such an entitled has-been that I turn on my own. Don't want to be the Southerner calling people pill-billies like that ain't my own cousin, or the gay guy complaining that people are too sexy at Pride like 'what about the children who want to come to the Folsom Street Fair' or whatever."

"Or the liberal voting third-party because not all Democrats pass the purity test," Whitney suggested, thinking that his point was just the same as the others, until Graham revealed it was not.

"You're actually talking to a Green Party voter, my friend," Graham said with a cautious smirk.

"Ah," Whitney said, smiling as well while wondering just how fractious this would get. "And you don't see any hypocrisy in that?"

"Their platform has my values and the Democratic one doesn't," Graham said. "And if you're worried about lesser-of-two-evils stuff, I've only ever voted in deep Red places where Democrats never had a chance anyway. Just logging my protest like a good American."

"Okay," Whitney said.

"You disagree?" Graham asked after a silence. "Or disapprove?"

"I just wouldn't do it myself," Whitney said, "but I don't feel the need to dissuade you. You do it ranked-choice style? Like Green preferred, Blue when it's not available, and never Red?"

"That's right," Graham said. "Let me guess why you don't though. Supreme Court picks? Healthcare? Gay rights?"

"More or less, yeah. I remember the AIDS response from the other side, and here we are in another public health crisis, and you know the Dems would have done better."

"I do," Graham said. "I also know they promised us point-blank that they were against public healthcare, which is the actual solution, to the point of stealing the nomination from an Independent just to be aggressively Not Enough. I don't have health insurance either way, so I vote my conscience."

"Even if it's useless?" Whitney asked.

Graham nodded. "Your vote was useless too. Even when Dems win, we lose. They pass Republican healthcare bills and leave us with a right-wing Supreme Court anyway. I can't vote pro-fascist because I don't want to be on that list in hell, but I don't want to be on the Democratic mailing list either."

"You don't want to give fifteen dollars to people who quibble about the fifteen-dollar minimum wage?" Whitney asked. "Weird, because there's poetry in that too, poetic irony."

"There is," Graham agreed, just before his video maker dinged, and the debate forum closed without fisticuffs.

19.

GRAHAM

They watched Graham's little sketch, with musical intro and everything, and Whitney asked a few polite questions about where Graham posted such content, why it made money, and how much. Graham told him: it was a pain in the ass to spam across multiple platforms, it made money with views and clicks sometimes, but not much at all, it was mostly to build name recognition.

They were sitting side by side, knee-to-knee during this viewing party, and quickly their close talk and leaning over one another got them in a kissy mood, a sexy mood. They retired wordlessly to the bedroom with nothing more than a look and a nod.

This attraction between them made so much sense to Graham, he had yet to let other questions cloud his mind. Was he in love with this man? Dunno, but certainly he did not hate him. Could they work as a couple with fifteen years of age difference, a true generational divide? Maybe, but it's not like they had to worry about social group cohesion in isolation. Would it always be this easy? Hard to tell. If yes, they could grow old together, if no, then they'd each become somebody that the other one used to know.

Whitney was good at sex, far better than Graham had the ability to be, due to an unfortunate lack of practice. Whitney had an empirical, hands-on knowledge of carnal matters, along the lines of practical hacks learned during the years when he "regularly abused himself" in his own words. Unsexy sexual information like saline douches rather than scented ones, and which ointments and salves were best for ass and cock chafe.

Whitney also held wisdom that made him seem almost magically intuitive when he was in Graham, on him. He was over there reading micro-emotions, really dialed-in and focused on the moment, eyes open and intentional. Graham was consciously trying to learn from him, mirror him. The eye contact during the act was particularly intense and Graham was slowly learning not to flinch away from it. He was no child, no blushing bride, why couldn't he be bold in his sexuality too? Better late than never.

Graham was thinking all his thoughts on this subject, gazing at the ceiling, and trying to generate something to say in the post-coital calm and quiet. He opened his mouth like a gasping fish to allow out whatever would float up — probably something about nipple sensitivity, he'd been wondering about it — when another noise came from the living room.

It was a nuzzling little noise between a purring engine and a tiny grunt. It was the sound of a puppy chewing the heck out of something real good.

"Uh oh," Whitney said, and popped up to see what was getting gnawed on. Graham got his pants back on first before following. He brought Whitney's shorts with him to find out the damage report.

"Oh no, she got one of them pretty boots," Graham said, for indeed one of the blond and buttery boots with tassels and embroidered flowers of the valley had been slobbered on and munched up like a piece of beef jerky. "I shouldn't have left them out, I'm sorry."

Whitney told Honey Bun, "No, not for doggies, no-no," in a low voice as he led her back to her crate and locked her in. She seemed very concerned that she was no longer getting happy praise, and whined as she pawed at the cage door that would not open at her nudge this time.

Whitney returned to take the jockeys from Graham and slipped them on so he wasn't free-ballin' all around the living room. "Thanks," he said, "and it's not your fault she got at the boots, we both left them out, and we didn't know she was a boot-chewer, she leaves our sneakers alone."

"Must be the leather," Graham said, picking up the savaged boot as Whitney recovered the pristine one.

"Probably the leather, I'll have to get her something similar she is allowed to chew on," Whitney said, taking both boots to the trash can in the kitchen and dropping them in.

"Those aren't worth trying to save?" Graham asked. "I'm no boot doctor, but they seem expensive enough to, I dunno, like cuff down the top and restitch?"

"I don't like them that much," Whitney said. "Matter of fact I bought those boots with one of my more embarrassing exes who treated the sales girl like shit, so I'd rather not remember that day ever again if I don't have to. Honey Bun did me a favor there, really."

Whitney went to the fridge to write down another item on the shopping list: *puppy leather chew thing*. Graham saw it when Whitney next opened the fridge door to see about dinner, and it made him smile.

"What's that look?" Whitney asked, though he was smiling too, nearly blushing, because Graham was beaming at him and, shock of all shockers, this headliner was still shy.

"I like that you didn't yell at her," Graham said. "You're not even mad."

"Well, you know, I can't get mad at her for something she didn't know she shouldn't do yet," Whitney said. "It would be like yelling at a little baby, who does that?"

"When it's a dog? Tons of people do. And plenty yell at their babies too," Graham said. "My grandfather was one of them, may God piss on his soul, and I guess I'm just really happy that you're nothing like that."

Whitney rolled his eyes, but he was still apple-cheeked over the adoration Graham was blasting on him. "Don't compare me to your grandfather, please, it makes me sound old and decrepit."

"Don't turn down the comparison until you see a picture of my grandfather," Graham said. "He was a hot piece of ass all his life, it's why he was so successful preaching. People like listening to a man who's easy on the eyes."

"Is he why you're so good-looking?" Whitney asked. "You got it in the genes?"

"Yes," Graham said, though he got most of his looks from his mother's side, they of the ginger-auburn hair and freckled skin and undiagnosed manic depression. "That and my unquenchable thirst for attention and approval."

"Hmm," Whitney said. "You're a very good boy, then."

He laughed when Graham did a double fist-pump, hissed "yesss," and then smoothed his hair back like he was too cool to care. In truth, Graham and Honey Bun were probably developing some of the same feelings for Whitney: devotion, guardianship, and a preference for being hand-fed.

20.

WHITNEY

Whitney and Graham ate dinner together, really together, with no phones or tablets or computers going. It had become their last moment of true engagement each day, to be present with one another for dinner discussions before taking up their evening interests.

To wind down each night, they had options. Sometimes they would watch a movie together. Sometimes they would watch separate things in the same room, headphones connected to their own devices, but still close enough to snuggle or appreciate the sense of company. Some evenings were a little more solo — Graham might go to his room for alone time, or Whitney to the porch hammock to read or work on something or call an old friend.

The people Whitney knew were more into phone calls and letter-writing than they'd ever been before. Friends from his twenties or thirties suddenly would reach out in the hopes that somebody they used to know would talk to them for a little while during a lonely moment. Many friends were experiencing indefinite financial woes, bills stacking up as income was reduced on unemployment. The friends who still had work were getting severe burn-out, because they were making the same crap money but now with invasive or isolating safety protocols. Everyone seemed to have their moments of a special kind of fatalistic depression the kids were calling "doom-erism." Twice a week someone wanted to talk, and Whitney was in a good enough place that he wanted to be available.

Whitney knew that listening to his friends' complaints could keep them from using again, or thinking about death as the one solution to every problem they had. Sometimes the friend didn't have the energy to talk, and so Whitney would distract them by chattering about entirely silly in-depth discussions like, *What's worse, a noisy roommate or a nosy one? Possum vs. raccoon, which is better? Are sunrises and sunsets really that different, and why?* After a while and a laugh or two, the person would feel lighter and go to bed.

Folks were reaching out from across Whitney's history. An ex from before the drugs, now with a husband and a suit-and-tie job in Savannah. An old backup dancer buddy still living in L.A., swearing he was going to move back to Arizona but he never did and probably never would (even if it meant a few stints of couch-surfing homelessness). A friend from rehab called to make sure Whitney was okay, maybe out of care, or to cover her need to talk to someone, or a little bit of both. His mom's old agent who knew Whitney as a little boy and still called him around Christmas each year, to talk about her memories of Willa Grace and catch up with the woman's wayward son.

Whitney's brother Nash also called to find out just who exactly was staying in the house with him, was this person reputable? Nash still knew neighbors around here, and someone must have noticed the second vehicle in the driveway or their romping in the yard. Whitney talked about the puppy as if that's who Nash was asking about. "Don't worry, they're really well-behaved and not too rough on the furniture …" He only let up when Nash got huffy and said, "Grow up, would ya? It's fair that I worry."

Whitney reassured his brother that Graham was just a nice local fella who needed somewhere else to stay than his momma's house, and yes they were romantically involved, but they weren't sending out wedding invites or anything. Graham had overheard his name and called out, "Tell 'em there's nothing else to do during lockdown so we're doing each other!" Whitney laughed as Nash sighed and said, "Sounds like you're well matched in maturity if not age, just be safe." Safe from what he did not specify. Robbery? Disease? Heartbreak? Maybe all of the above.

That night, after watching Graham be creative all day, the topic got around to how Whitney did it.

Graham asked, "When you write songs, is it words first or music? Is there some kind of lightning strike of inspiration or is it just work?"

Whitney moved clean dishes out of the dishwasher as Graham cleared the table and brought the dirty ones to the sink.

"It can go either way, sometimes tune first and topic later, other times I'll run across a phrase or a rhyme and let it repeat until it gains a beat or a tone," Whitney said. "It's magic when I have a tune from one place and a snatch of lyric or thought from another, and they finally pair together and just click ... those are Eureka-Jesus-Muse moments, those feel like lightning strikes."

"Yeah, but like real lightning," Graham said. "Like it takes a charge from the air and the ground building up and down in both directions, meeting in the middle, and then boom the electricity surges in one pulse."

"Is that how lightning works?" Whitney asked. It sounded about right to him as far as the creative process, but too good to be true for real life.

"Is it?" Graham asked. "I thought I knew that from somewhere, could be true, or could be fake news."

And thus their plans for the night were settled: together they would research lightning.

21.

GRAHAM

It turned out cloud-to-ground lightning strikes started when electrical energy sorted itself in a cloud: positive charges up top, and negative ones towards the bottom, closer to earth. Negative energy would start to reach towards the ground in "stepped leaders" (not step ladders) branching their way down sometimes in multiple directions. At the same time, positive energy in the form of "streamers" would start to reach up, usually through tall objects like trees and buildings. When they met, the charges rapidly switched places — the negative rushed down the streamer track, while the positive energy lit up the stepped leaders' connected branches. That was what illuminated the sky, from the bottom up. If it looked like lightning struck down, it was only because it happened so fast the human eye couldn't tell through the dazzle.

"So I was right, good for me," Graham said, relieved that he hadn't been repeating misinformation and nonsense. "The charges meet in the middle, and the light flashes through only when the two ends connect."

"Man, lightning is so beautiful," Whitney said. "Don't you just love thunderstorms?"

"So long as I don't have to go to work in one, yes," Graham said. "They were better as a kid when I could stay home, not so fun showing up to hustle through the hospital in soggy sneakers."

"True, true," Whitney said. "I was in Texas once during an apocalyptic storm, I just went spinning around in a field in the rain like Maria in *The Sound of Music*, it was transcendent. All that sky surrounding me, so full of fight and boom, almost makes you believe in God."

"You don't?" Graham asked. He decided he was an atheist at 13 to anger his grandfather, and had yet to find a reason to take back that assessment. He couldn't assume anyone else he met felt the same way though. Regardless of how selfishly and myopically they acted, they still swore they believed their eternal soul would be judged and forgiven of all the petty ugliness they spread day to day.

"I mean if a fan asks me, I say I believe there's more to us than what we can see," Whitney said. "But I can't pretend to myself what I don't feel. That big storm let me feel the edges of what I imagine true believers feel though, so I get why they insist so much."

"Still wish they wouldn't though," Graham said. "Hey, if we get a good summer storm while I'm here, let's go out and roll around in it just like Honey Bun would, yeah?"

Whitney slipped his arms around Graham, one around his neck and the other up his torso under his shirt. "Sounds good to me. Thunder might scare the dog though."

"Maybe if she sees us liking it she'll join in," Graham said.

Whitney kissed his cheek a few times in rapid succession and told him, "What sweet thoughts you have."

Speaking of Honey Bun, before they could let her roam free again, they had to go on a scavenger hunt to find and hide any low-hanging leather. Graham got on his younger knees to look around from a dog's-eye view, and Whitney packed up all the costumes Graham had selected.

"I'll keep these separated from the rest so you can keep playing dress-up for your skits," Whitney said.

"Sketches," Graham corrected, though the smirk on Whitney's face said he knew, and was teasing. "Watch your mouth, sir."

"I think I've got a clean plastic bin or something, I can just stash this stuff up in the closet for later," Whitney said, before wandering off to other corners of the house in search of storage solutions. The next sound he made was muffled but concerning, a soft, "Uh oh," from the costume closet.

Graham dropped the blind string he was worrying about as a possible puppy chew toy and went to find his fella. Whitney had his shirt tucked up under his chin, and was looking at his belly in the mirror. The clothing box was dropped on its side, and Whitney had a little bump sticking out of his otherwise flat stomach.

"Well, that's not good," Graham said, before getting right back on his knees to palpitate around the bulge, his old diagnostic training kicking in.

"What is it?" Whitney asked.

"Hernia," Graham told him. "There's no need to panic but it'll need surgery to fix."

"Surgery?" Whitney asked. "How painful is it? I've got to be careful with pain pills."

"I had my appendix out when I was 14," Graham said. "You can probably grit through it with ice and aspirin if you have to. If you've got a doctor you like, we can call him or her tomorrow for their advice, referral, whatever."

"Tomorrow? It's not an emergency?" Whitney asked, poking this soft little lump back in, where it stayed temporarily before oozing out again.

"You popped a hole in the muscle, and that's a little loop of your intestine sneaking out," Graham said, also poking it back in to watch it slide slowly out again. "It could get serious if that loop gets stuck outside with a blockage and can't get back in, but we'll just keep an eye on it, until they can schedule you for surgery to patch that muscle back shut."

Whitney sighed, and his face blanched as he let his shirt back down and rubbed his temples. Graham gathered the box of clothes back up and put it on the high shelf Whitney was probably lifting it to when this happened.

"This is a pretty minor thing," Graham said. "Some people can't see a hernia if they're too fat to feel the bulge or something. It gets impacted, hardens, bungs them up, strangles, gets necrotic, bursts, stuff like that. But those are extreme cases, most people just get their pink, slippy guts put back inside, easy peasy."

"I'm falling apart, this is how it begins," Whitney said with a sigh. "I'm not trying to be dramatic even though I am, I just … this sucks."

"It does," Graham said, "but we can make the best of it. How'd you like to explore a medical fetish with your real-life private nurse over here?"

PART IV:
EROSION

SEPTEMBER 11, 2020 — COVID-19 DEATHS
WORLD DAILY: 5,878 / TOTAL: 1,015,098
US DAILY: 924 / TOTAL: 202,826
LOUISIANA DAILY: 41 / TOTAL: 5,202

22.

WHITNEY

It took a week to get Whitney an appointment for this "non-emergency" surgery. They had to call around to hospitals and clinics until they found a private one in Vicksburg that had an opening on the inauspicious day of September 11th. The Coronavirus was taking up a lot of space, sucking up all the gloves, gowns, and surgical masks usually overflowing operating theaters and recovery wards. Beds were scarce, but Whitney finally got one.

The doctor was Indian with a British accent behind his mask. He had never heard of Whitney Thorn or his parents, which was great as far as Whitney was concerned. He asked if Whitney cared what kind of incision was made for his procedure because, "We can do the laparoscopic method with minimal scarring, but I've found a full incision leaves more room to get it right on the inside."

"Sir, whatever my surgeon likes best is my choice too," Whitney said.

"Indeed," Graham added. "We want a cool, confident, and comfortable surgeon every time for optimal results."

"Your son is funny," the doctor told Whitney, nodding at Graham. "He is also correct, that is the best-recommended policy."

Neither of them corrected them on the "son" part, instead Whitney said, "Well, the boy's a nurse, so he knows."

"Ah," the doctor agreed with his wise old healer nod. "So he knows."

They were left alone for a moment after that, Whitney in hospital whites all tucked into bed, and Graham about to be ushered into the waiting room after their goodbye.

"This is our moment of zen, Dad," Graham said with a sly smirk. "Quick question, am I in the Will?"

"I guess I am old enough to be your father, technically," Whitney said, as Graham sat at his bedside. He didn't hold his hand, which Whitney appreciated, as it would have made him feel like an invalid. Instead, Graham slid his warm hand up Whitney's chest and rested it over his heart.

"Oh, for sure," Graham said. "I've met a 30-year-old grandma or two, it's a reasonable assumption 'round these parts." A beat of peace and then, "Feeling scared at all? If it helps, the surgeons I've met consider hernias to be ho-hum. One said it was as simple as patching a tire for a mechanic, easy, uncomplicated, stellar success rate."

"I'm not worried about the surgery," Whitney said. "I mean I'm not excited about it, but it's not really a choice, you know? I need it, I need it sooner rather than later, and we're already here, so whatever happens is what happens."

"You just don't want to feel like an old blown tire?" Graham guessed.

"You got it," Whitney said.

"The doctor said you're in good shape for your age, at least, strong heart and all that, no other complicating conditions," Graham reminded him.

"No conditions that they know of at least," Whitney said. He was always surprised that his body didn't show signs of ravage, some leftover from years of meth. He suspected that somewhere within him there was a weak artery wall or some erosion of tissue that could be triggered at any time like a forgotten landmine.

"I'll just be out here sweet talking the nurses, making sure they like you," Graham said, standing up and popping down his mask so he could peck Whitney on the cheek. It was a kiss so innocent it wouldn't startle anyone who thought they were related. Some families were that affectionate, just not Whitney's. "I'll see you on the other side," Graham said at his departure, and left Whitney with a few moments of blinking silence before the nurses came in again.

Whitney was then rolled through fluorescent hallways to a staging area outside the surgery room. He was asked basic questions like his name, the date, and what procedure he was about to have. Then it was time for the inner chamber, where a needle in his arm knocked him into the black, a void without time or dreams or shades. His last thought was one of mild disapproval and discomfort at feeling himself hefted and moved from one table to another in a way that slid his ass unevenly and meant he would settle lop-sided for the duration of the procedure. It was a fleeting discontentment, because mid-thought he was rendered dead to the world with anesthesia.

When he came to again, Whitney was back in the staging area, briefly worried something had called off the operation before he felt for the bandage over his gut. Whitney had time to check his fingers, toes, and genitals were all still attached to him before a nurse popped back in with a cheerful, "There you are!" She asked a few more questions to check his alertness that Whitney answered slower this time: his name, his operation, who's the president?

When Whitney said, "I'd rather not remember him," the nurse's cheeriness notched down a bit. She must have voted differently than Whitney, because it was all business and no jolly after that. If this was one of the nurses Graham had sweetened up, Whitney had soured her in an instant, but at least he could blame it on the fog of surgery.

"Looks like you're fine then," the nurse said. "The operation was successful, no surprises. You should be able to go home soon." She left, and it was a different nurse, this one male, who delivered Whitney back to his original room and asked him to wait for the doctor's debriefing before getting up or getting dressed.

Whitney didn't listen to that advice. He stood up to explore how he felt right away, and sought his pants so he could find his phone and message Graham that he was back, awake and alive and waiting for him.

23.

GRAHAM

It wasn't even noon when Whitney was wheeled out of the hospital and released home. The day was perky and bright, and Whitney was feeling fine for the first half of the ride, but Graham noticed him start to flag and clam up about halfway through the drive.

To distract him, Graham kept up a running commentary on all his accomplishments and plans for Whitney's recovery. The big news was there would be some company later in the day.

"My momma insists that you need a woman's home cooking to recover, so today she's making her best lasagna, and my aunt's baking her award-winning pecan pie."

"You say pee-can, not pi-cahn," Whitney observed, but then closed his mouth again like he was feeling sick.

"I do, indeed," Graham said. "Pee-can pie on rat-tan furniture, sittin' on the porch and not the lanai or sun parlor or whatever fancy people call it."

"Veranda," Whitney supplied.

"That sounds like a great drag name," Graham said, "but porches are porches, decks are decks, and stoops are stoops."

Graham made a mental note to see if he could tease all of that out into a stage joke, and kept telling Whitney about his grand plans for the coming days.

"So Momma and Aunt Tamella have agreed to stay on the porch for their visit, you know, to socially distance. We'll stay inside, they'll stay outside, and that'll keep the visit short because if they need the bathroom they'll have to go home."

"Tamara?" Whitney asked.

"Tamella," Graham repeated. "Half Tamara and half Pamela. Just like my mom's name is half Cynthia and half Tiffany or Bethany or something, she's Cynthany."

"Talk about drag names," Whitney said. "But I won't make fun, I promise."

"They've heard it all before," Graham said. "Their mother, my grandma, was a piece of work I've heard, can't remember the few times I met her. Probably she was chemically nuts, but a real hoot all the same. I'll write down Cynthany and Tamella for ya, little cheat sheet on your hand or something, it can be hard to remember when you meet both of them at once."

"And they're good cooks?" Whitney asked.

"Good at cooking what they're bringing, I wouldn't let them bring any food over if I didn't want to share some myself," Graham said. "I did some grocery shopping for fresh ingredients while you were in surgery, so they're cooking this morning, blessing us with hot food this afternoon. I also went and picked up your prescription, some laxative they recommended, and a nice ice-and-heat combo pad, very versatile."

"Prescription of what?" Whitney asked, turning a pale, greenish-looking color due to some discomfort he was feeling. "I can't take pain meds, I told you." Whitney closed his eyes like watching the scenery go by was making him woozy.

"It was both pain meds and some antibiotics, but don't worry, I've already hidden the good drugs," Graham said.

"You shouldn't have brought them back with you, you've got to get those out of my house. The second we get home, promise me," Whitney said.

"But what if the pain gets really bad?" Graham asked. He'd seen brave patients lose their nerve once the reality of pain hit, and he didn't want to deal with a tantrum from Whitney of all people, begging for pain relief Graham could no longer provide. "Seems foolish to throw it out now when you don't know how much this will hurt once the stuff they already gave you wears off."

"Didn't say … get rid of it," Whitney said, his speech slow as the very pain Graham was worried about started overwhelming him. "Said out of the house."

"But doctors say it's okay for folks in recovery to take pain meds if you're in pain," Graham said. "So long as you have someone else like a trusted friend, that'd be me, doling it out."

"Graham, listen to me," Whitney said. "I don't care if I need it. I don't care if I'm allowed to have it. I don't care if I ask for it later. If I even find the bottle, I will throw you out of my house. And I will get a restraining order … if you try to come back."

"Damn, well, if you insist," Graham said. "I'll make sure my momma takes it and keeps it at her house, then. She'll like having some Vicodin around when her back aches."

"Don't know if that's a good idea for her," Whitney said, sighing and sinking back into a calm misery now that Graham had acquiesced to his demands. "A lot of addictions start as back aches. But she's an adult. Y'all make your own decisions."

Graham reached over to squeeze Whitney's shoulder. His staccato speech was sad to hear, but they were almost home. Graham was going to tuck in this man and baby him with all the best nursing he could dredge up. He was still so grateful that Whitney had taken him in, this would be his way of paying back all that kindness.

"My momma knows her moderation," Graham said, returning to the wheel and the task of driving safely. "And she knows from addiction too; my cousin Sage was a pill-billy, her sister's kid. Still is I guess, though she cleaned up a few years ago after some trouble with the law."

"Oh my," Whitney said. "Sounds like she had a rough go of it."

"Yes, she did," Graham said. "She may be stopping by tomorrow too, don't know for sure, but like I said, they won't stay long, and won't come in and cough on you. Honestly, I think they just want to lay eyes on someone a little famous, they're tired of me having all the fun."

"Right, the glitz and glamor of nursing an old man, lucky you," Whitney said. "Did you remember to pick up an adult-sized bib, too?"

Graham started laughing as they turned onto Whitney's street. He wasn't the only comedian in the car today, apparently. Even wan and worn out, Whitney still smiled to hear his joke land.

24.

WHITNEY

Whitney started to feel sick on the way home, but only found the depth and breadth of it as he walked from the car to the house. Even though the bed was fresh and clean and ready for him to rest in, Whitney sat down in the first seat that crossed his path and didn't plan on moving from it for a good long while.

Graham did right by him. He moved the chair, gently, with Whitney in it, to the most comfortable spot near a warm window. He then pulled over a footrest and turned a sideboard cabinet longways, so Whitney would have a surface that was easy to reach. He lined that surface up with water, snacks, and a plastic office trash can for piss (or puke should the pain overwhelm him and make him nauseous). He supplied a few ibuprofen to start Whitney off with, a blanket for his feet, and a bag of frozen peas for his incision site.

"If you get hungry, tell me what for," Graham said. "If you want to nap, I'll tie something over your eyes for a sleep mask or something. You've got your computer right here for entertainment cuz I guess you don't have a TV that was hidden behind one of these paintings the whole time, right?"

"Granny didn't believe in television, thought it was making people stupid," Whitney said.

"She was right about that, but it's good to have the idiot box around sometimes," Graham said. "You have TV on the internet though, so you're all set. Try not to rest the computer on your stomach."

Honey Bun had been waiting, watching all this frantic activity, and finally approached to hop up on the footrest and settle on the blanket between Whitney's feet.

"Hi there," Whitney said, patting the dog with his foot. Her tail wagged up and down on Whitney's ankle, patting him back.

"Look at that little angel," Graham said. "Don't let her jump up on your stomach either, but it looks like she gets it."

"Guess I've got two nurses, lucky me," Whitney said, as a cold ripple rolled beneath his skin, the opposite of a flush. The feeling must have shown on his face because Graham rushed to his side and lowered his voice.

"Take it easy, breathe in and out nice and deep, and just let me know if you can think of anything you'd like. Otherwise, I'll be in my room being quiet." Graham kissed Whitney's cheek and murmured, "If you want company just text me to ask my opinion on whether pancakes or waffles are better or something, and I'll come out here and give a whole presentation, alright? And it's waffles, by the way."

Whitney started laughing and pressed his hand over the veggie bag on his belly. "You can't make me laugh," he whispered. "My guts will fly out."

"If they did, I'll add '*literally* gut-busting funny' to my resume, so it won't be all bad, will it?" Graham asked.

"Get out," Whitney said, laughing through the pain.

Graham gave a couple of squeezes to Whitney's shoulders and retreated. They agreed before the surgery that Whitney would rather not be babysat if it wasn't necessary, but he might summon Graham later and ask for a back rub, or a foot rub, or a blow job if it didn't feel too gross to request. He'd have to wait to feel better first though, because in his current state, he'd refuse every bodily pleasure under the sun.

Whitney closed his eyes and imagined his guts like a turbulent ocean. Waves and humps undulated together, giving him that queasy seasick feeling, but he knew how to overcome it. He took in one slow breath all the way down and thought of other things, simple things, like the sunlight beaming from so far away just to settle at last upon his skin. Another breath in, and he thought of Honey Bun, her weight at his feet, so sweet and loyal and kind. One more deep breath, and he heard the sounds of Graham puttering around in the other room, a real comfort.

Whitney fell into a strange, silent sleep, and was surprised to learn that three hours had passed the next time he opened his eyes. Birds were tweeting outside, food was warming in the kitchen, and Whitney found that the sun had moved away from him while he slept. He missed the warmth.

Graham was alerted to Whitney's return to the waking world by the jingle on Honey Bun's collar when she looked up at him and stood as if awaiting instruction.

Graham popped his head around to ask, "Are you hungry? Got some nice chicken soup and buttered bread over here cuz I like dipping it in the broth myself."

"What kind of heathen doesn't?" Whitney asked, and felt his insides turn over in hunger as he thought about eating sopping-warm bread with cold butter spread. "That sounds good," he said.

"I'll bring you a tray then," Graham said. The tray he'd found was a serving platter with a bowl of soup in the middle, two pieces of bread around the sides, and a cluster of green grapes. It reminded him of the spread in rehab, but Whitney pushed that thought aside aggressively, and dipped a piece of crust in soup for Honey Bun to enjoy instead. There were no puppies in rehab, so this must not be the place.

"Look at her, just sweet as pie, like a little sentinel guarding you," Graham said, giving her scritches. "Momma's gonna love you," he told the dog.

Honey Bun nodded at him as if she knew it to be true.

25.

GRAHAM

Knowing his family would be bringing food, Graham fed Whitney something simple for lunch, encouraged him to walk around the kitchen island a few times because it was good for him, and saw him successfully into and out of the bathroom to freshen up. He got the all-clear that Whitney was up for company and then summoned the wellness wagon.

It was hard to tell who the ladies were more smitten over: the adorable puppy or a sleepy, handsome star. They were dropped off by Cousin Sage, who promised to be back in two hours. They set their supplies on the doorstep for Graham to collect without hand-to-hand contact. They sat outside the screened windows at a table set up at least six feet from Whitney. It wasn't exactly a quarantine ward, but it was what the government advised to keep COVID from spreading, so they went through the motions.

"I was listening to your mother's music since I was a little girl. Her song 'Starlight' got me through my first breakup," Cynthany said, brushing her hair back. She had dressed up to meet Whitney; Graham knew her routine for looking good. Her hair was in her best barrette, and her blouse matched the stones in her earrings, which matched her eyes, brought out their greenishness.

"I lost my virginity to 'All Right All Night,' so we both feel that connection," Tamella said, laughing at her own ribaldry.

Graham was fixin' to feel embarrassed by them, but Whitney fell into their rhythm easily.

"My mom loved hearing stories like that," he told them. "She said she hoped in heaven there would be a big web she could see connected to all the places her songs reached, who heard them and when, all the moments people remembered them or started humming. She said it made her feel like somebody to be a little part of everybody else's life."

"She did?" Cynthany asked. "That's so beautiful. Graham, isn't that the most beautiful thing you ever heard?"

"Close to it," Graham said, pulling up on the ottoman and picking up Honey Bun so the gals could coo over her. "But this guy talks like that all the time."

"Must be the poetry gene or something," Tamella said, setting her hand against the screen so the puppy could smell it. "I kid, but we wore out Willa Grace albums growing up, especially *Heather, Feathers, and Freedom.*"

"Yes, we did. It gave us a lot of courage when we needed it, like after our daddy split," Cynthany said.

"And my first pregnancy scare," Tamella said. "The second one, I call her Sage now. That was her that drove off."

"Named after ...?" Whitney began to ask, but he already knew.

"Yep, named after the song 'Sage Evergreen' because that's what I wanted for her like the song said: sacred, pure, and ever-growing."

"Always wise and ever-knowing," Cynthany said, knowing the next lyric.

"Whose ashes cleanse the winds a-blowing," Whitney finished. "We sang that one when we scattered her ashes, thought it suited the occasion."

"That's nice," Cynthany said. It was nice but sad, and knowing how Graham's cousin Sage had turned out, it was probably crossing all their minds that it would serve well at her funeral, too, should they live to see it.

Sage was doing alright the last Graham had heard, but she was having a hard pandemic, too. She didn't meet a Prince Charming like Graham did; she was still stuck at home with nothing productive to do with her hard-won sobriety. It was never the prize people promised it would be. Sage once told him that getting sober was like getting a job — she needed it, and people were proud of her, but it was still work, and she always hated it.

Whitney must have felt he was being left out of some collective family moment, so he changed the dynamic. "Would you like Willa's autograph?" Whitney asked the ladies.

"How?" Cynthany wondered. "Isn't she dead?"

"Yes, we just established that," Tamella said, patting her sister's hand. "He must mean he has one from before she passed."

"More than one," Whitney said. "Mom had stacks of signed photographs for mailing to fans, and guess who inherited them?"

Whitney gave Graham the location of the picture box, deep in the costume closet, and filed by decade. Graham used a video call to his mom to show their options, and each woman picked out a souvenir photo of Willa Grace to take home and frame, his mother a black-and-white one from her early years, and Aunt Tamella a colored photo of her in hippie beads and early-70s orange. Graham slipped their new presents through the mail slot in the front door, and they admired them in front of Whitney before thanking him profusely.

"You're just as nice as Graham said," Cynthany told him. "I was worried at first thinking I don't know what, like, 'Who is this guy, what does he want from my son, is this some kind of con or something dirty?' But you're just good country people like we are, doesn't matter that you're famous too, does it?"

"I try not to let it matter," Whitney said. "I made most of my mistakes as a young man, I'd like to think I know better by now."

"You're not that old," Tamella said. "You're younger than us at least, I swear I think everyone even five years younger than me is a baby."

"Babies don't get hernias, though," Whitney said, which started a new round of coos about how he was feeling, surgery stories the women had to share: Aunt Tamella's wisdom teeth extraction and subsequent dry socket pain, and Cynthany's prolapsed bladder from Graham's birth that was now held up with a sling made of cadaver skin.

"Sometimes new science can't improve on old science," Graham said. "I saw one patient that had metal mesh inside her that was causing her pain and could never be teased back out because it was too bound up in scar tissue. So, as gross as it sounds, they did right by my momma with her corpse pouch in there."

"I wonder what they've sewed me up with," Whitney said, moving his shirt to check out his bandage.

"Well, I was talking to your nurses, and they said — " Graham began, but Whitney reached over to touch his lips and stop him.

"I don't actually want to know," he said.

Cynthany and Aunt Tamella laughed and laughed, and started telling more tales of Graham being silly, wrong, or embarrassing.

That was a quick initiation; Whitney was part of the family already.

26.

WHITNEY

Far from being tiring, talking to Graham's family was a welcome distraction for Whitney. If he was telling them stories about his mom, he had far less headspace to focus on the itching beneath his bandage, his drained energy, and the worries that somehow his stitches would burst open, or his guts get infected.

"One time we got so lost in Cincinnati trying to find a bar she was supposed to play at that mom said, 'screw it,' and decided to just play at the first place that would let them," Whitney said. "Only one person appreciated who was playing, but luckily it was the guy behind the bar who kept me and my brother in cherry colas through the whole gig."

"Wild," Tamella said. "I bet she was a force to be reckoned with."

"Was that cherry Cokes made with the syrups? I haven't had one of those in so long," Cynthany said. "I used to do shots of the syrup when I worked at a movie theater concession stand."

"And then throw up bright red when you overdid it," Tamella added.

"That only happened once but that's so much for bringing it up," Cynthany said.

"It dyed your lips a nice color though," Tamella said. "Real cherry lipstick there." Cynthany blew her sister a kiss and then flipped her the bird.

Whitney smiled to hear them bicker, and it reminded him of another story.

"My mother always wanted a sister," he said, "and she was grand friends with my aunts on my dad's side, mostly because they often agreed that he weren't good for shit outside of a recording studio."

"We all have that complaint about men, though, don't we?" Cynthany asked Tamella, but Whitney answered her.

"Yes, we do," he said. "I've met plenty of ain't-shit men myself."

"As have I," Graham chimed in. "Present company excluded, of course," he added with a nod toward Whitney. He was distractedly digging his pinkies into Honey Bun's ears because she was loving it, absolute pudding in his hands.

"You only don't know me that well yet, is all," Whitney said, meaning it to land as good-natured self-deprecation, but Tamella didn't hear it that way.

"So long as you don't hit him, you should be fine," she said, causing a real record-scratch moment as everyone heard what she said, and Whitney was able to discern clearly that there was personal history there. Perhaps Sage's dad was more than ain't-shit, he was true shit.

"Sorry, we've had troubles is all," Cynthany said, trying to paper over the crack in the conversation, but Whitney waved away the excuse.

"No apology needed," he said, and watched everyone unclench a little with his permission. The mark of fame lingered upon him, and even Graham wanted his approval still. Whitney was a somebody, so if he approved of them, it meant something more than nothing. "Mom raised me and my brother to never hit a woman, and we never have. She'd met some real dirtbags on the road, you know, and made us promise we wouldn't be like them."

Willa Grace had solicited those promises after sending them to get hotel ice for a split lip once, courtesy of a club owner who didn't like her demands for the show. Talk about cherry lipstick.

"The opportunity doesn't really arise for you much, though," Tamella said. "You don't date women."

Graham cut in to say, "I'm a real bitch, though." It should have been funny, but the timing was off.

"I've had to deal with some real nasty women in the music industry," Whitney said, strangely insisting for some reason that the opportunity to hit women had indeed presented itself to him many times. "Divas, managers, rock stars' wives," he listed. "But my mother made it clear when we were little that if it's not okay to hit her, then it's not okay to hit any of 'em. That's how she said it, 'If it's okay to hit one woman, then it's okay to hit all of us,' and so we don't, never did."

"What a queen," Cynthany said, and Tamella nodded, liking what she'd heard.

"Aunt Tamella, you know that means that you've hit more women than we have," Graham said. "Remember that Karen at the bowling alley for Sage's birthday?"

"Oh Lord, that woman," Tamella said. "She was really asking for it."

"Literally," Cynthany explained to Whitney. "She literally kept saying, 'Hit me, skank, I dare you, hit me.' She was real drunk."

"And I didn't do anything but belly her back from us saying to get the hell out of my kid's party, until she turned to Sage and started attacking her," Tamella said. "So I hit her with cake."

"You hit her with the birthday cake?" Whitney asked, his eyebrows all the way up, shocked at the gossip.

"Just a piece!" Tamella said. "And I argued that I didn't really touch her, ya know, the cake is what touched her, I didn't even make contact, just kind of smooshed it in her face. She was drunk, we had little kids to protect, she started it and I didn't even get arrested or nothing, so it doesn't count, right?"

Whitney shrugged and asked, "What flavor was the cake?"

Tamella smirked. "Chocolate cherry."

"Beautiful," Whitney said with a grin, pleased as he always was that stories sometimes revealed the pattern of the grand design.

27.

GRAHAM

The gals stayed a solid three hours before it was time to mosey on back home. They were ready to go after two hours but spent forty minutes texting Sage to find out her ETA. The moms got to see Whitney enjoy their food, they got to pet the puppy, and they had a nice time on a sun-shiny day with someone they'd get to repeat stories about for the rest of their lives. It was a perfect afternoon of real talk, camaraderie, and was lovely right up until Sage returned in the midst of a mood.

"You didn't have to text me a million times, there was traffic, okay?" was how Sage said hello.

"You mean, 'Thanks for letting me borrow the car, mom, did you have a nice visit?'" Tamella said, picking up her bag and the folder of photos they were gifted. "We're stopping by Walmart to pick up some frames and whatever else is on the grocery list."

"When did I volunteer for that?" Sage said. "We have empty frames at the house. Hiya, Graham Cracker, and country singer guy," she said with a nod through the window at Graham and Whitney.

"S'up Sage," Graham replied. "His name is Whitney."

"Kind of a girl's name, isn't it?" she said. Graham noted that Sage's face was broken out, her hair greasy, and her nails bitten down. Signs of stress and low self-care going on there, a bad omen in someone as temperamental as his cousin, always on the edge of depression and chaotic coping mechanisms.

"It used to be a boy's name," Tamella said. "It's probably a family name, it's got old-world dignity."

"It's an old English name," Whitney confirmed, sitting up and straightening himself since he couldn't exactly escort his guests to their car in the current plague age. "It wasn't often used as a girl's name until the 60s, when actress Whitney Blake made it popular. I was named after her. Momma wanted a girl I think, but found she didn't really have to change the name after all."

"That's a riot," Cynthany said, miming a hug for Graham since they didn't want to get that close to say goodbye. "The same thing is true of Lauren Bacall, that used to be a boy's name until she made it popular for girls. It might have been Graham's name if he'd been a girl, that or Jacqueline, after Mrs. Kennedy."

"Instead, I was named after Billy Graham, boy did I lose out," Graham said, engaging in this conversation while keeping a suspicious eye on Sage. Was she using again? Was she thinking about it? Was it even fair to wonder? Since he was holding a bottle of pills he intended to hand over to his mom right about now or never, yes it was very much fair to wonder.

"That's just what we told your grandpa, I didn't name you after Billy Graham, hell no," Cynthany said. "You were named after Graham Nash if anyone, but really I just thought it was a nice name, the kind you could be a lawyer with if you wanted to, cuz it's important not to pigeon-hole kids when you name them."

"Too bad you didn't think about that, huh?" Sage said to her mom.

"You can change your name any time you want if you don't like it," Tamella said. "Lord knows I've considered it, me and Cynthany both have, obviously."

Cynthany nodded and followed Sage and Tamella down the steps of the porch. Only when they were a fair distance away did Graham and Whitney come outside to wave at them.

"That's why I was careful with your name, Sweetie, people do make assumptions," Cynthany said, opening the door to the back seat.

"Good to know I can be a lawyer any time I want," Graham said. "Thanks, ma."

"You think you'd be smart enough with that mouth of yours," Tamella told him, before saying, "Kiss kiss, thanks for having us over. Maybe someday we'll see the inside of the house, it looks real nice."

"You're welcome back anytime," Whitney said. "I'm going to have a lie-down but drive safe."

Whitney shuffled back inside and headed towards the bedroom. Graham would get back to tending him momentarily, just as soon as he saw his family off. He had a decision to make regarding the pills in his pocket.

"Hey, maybe don't go to Walmart, okay? You can order frames online just as easy and not go into a store, right? Avoid the 'rona, avoid the retail rage, and save Sage the trip," Graham said.

"It's just like the flu," Tamella said. "We don't have any pre-existing conditions, we're okay going to a store."

"No conditions that you know of," Graham said. "How'd you like to find out about them on a ventilator, alone, on the quarantine ward?"

Tamella opened her mouth to dispute Graham but was interrupted.

"Mom, I just want to go home, okay?" Sage said. "Seriously, can we check the like ba-zillion frames there first?"

"Fine," Tamella said. "I can take down one of the dusty old pictures of you stinking kids and put up this instead, good idea."

"Sounds great, Aunt Tamella, love you too," Graham said.

Sage shut the passenger door on her mother and stopped on her way to the driver's seat to chat with Graham.

"Did she behave in front of your friend?" Sage asked.

"She did, you know she's always saving her kindness for company," Graham said.

"Yeah, it'd be a shame to waste it on us." Sage sighed.

"How's your pandemic?" Graham asked.

Sage shook her head and threw up her hands. "It's going, I guess. I'm trying not to think of how much life we're all missing right now, like how long is this going to take, for real? What's the point?"

"Hmm," Graham said, taking his hand out of his pocket but leaving the pills in there. He'd have to dispose of them some other way, or hide them really good inside a lamp base or something, because Sage couldn't be near them either, couldn't know about them, not for even a second in this kind of mood. "Keep me in mind if you want to talk," he said.

"Yeah, like talking helps," Sage said, but flashed him a thumbs-up anyway before getting behind the wheel and driving away.

28.

WHITNEY

The moment the ladies left, Whitney wondered about Cousin Sage. "What's her deal?" he asked.

Graham supplied him with stories as he cleaned up, sanitized all that was touched by outsiders, and started transitioning Whitney's nest to the bedroom. Whitney was very tired and would be early to bed that night.

"Sage got a shitty boyfriend the second she got to high school," Graham said. "She's a few years older than me, so growing up she really rubbed it in that I was a baby, and she was so cool because her boyfriend had a car, and she'd had sex, and she'd done drugs."

"Sounds like a real Miss Congeniality," Whitney snarked, getting up to do some light stretches, and follow a few feet behind Graham so he wouldn't miss parts of the story.

"She actually didn't make any of it look cool," Graham said. "I wanted to get to high school, sure, but I didn't want anything to do with people like her. She was mean, kinda gothy, and when she started doing drugs all the damn time, she looked like shit. Nasty skin and hair, wearing the same stanky hoodie all the time, kept having to stay after school for punishment, and ultimately fucked up so bad she had to do summer school. I thought she was a loser, and I still kinda do, though I'm glad she's gotten her shit together a little."

"How did that happen?" Whitney asked. There was usually an

intro and an outro for addicts, the reason they got in, and then the reason they had to get out.

"She got arrested," Graham said. "She was nabbed first for being out after the town curfew at 15. Usually, that's just a call to the parents to come and get you from the police station, but it turned into a real arrest when they found drugs on her. Then her boyfriend dropped her because he was 18 or 19, I think, and she was under the 17-year-old age of consent, so people had questions about what they were doing together, and where she got the drugs."

"Too hot to handle," Whitney diagnosed.

"In a sense, yeah," Graham said, washing dishes in a daze, his mind in the past. Whitney found himself wishing he was the dishes, over there all warm and sudsy when he himself felt clammy and tacky and gross. He remembered his earlier thoughts of foot rubs and sex favors, realized his actual desire was for a washcloth, a pot of warm water, and some help for a sponge bath before bed.

"Sage got sent to summer school after that because she'd trashed her grades, screwed up summer school because her mom made her drive herself once she turned 16, which she just didn't do. Once she was expelled, she had time to find a new boyfriend, this one a low-rung dealer, and she wasn't around me for a few years there. All four years I went to high school, I only heard horror stories of what Sage was up to, was told I was a good boy but also threatened and minded extra so I wouldn't turn out like her."

"Like a younger sibling," Whitney said. He'd been infantilized a bit more than his brother because he was the younger son, but that was a small chip on his shoulder compared to all the ones related to his sexuality.

"Pretty much. I was never gonna be somebody like Sage, but I got treated like a ticking time bomb my whole life. I still hold some resentment over that," Graham said, turning off the faucet and turning towards Whitney while wiping his hands on himself rather than a dish towel.

"So, what sobered Sage up?" Whitney asked.

"A stint in jail," Graham said. "She was at risk of serving real time, like ten years minimum because she was a passenger in a car full of drugs in the trunk. The only time she got was being held before a trial that never happened. The guy driving was the one they wanted, he got bail and did an armed robbery, so when her lawyer said she was just a scared passenger, they gave her some possession charge for what was in her pockets, let her go with time served because it was nearly six months, which was the punishment limit for a first conviction anyway."

"That scared her straight?" Whitney asked. He'd had his own stomach-churning, bone-chilling brushes with severe consequences. He worried the old cold fear would return during his convalescence, but so far he was keeping that quivering dread of death and destruction away. Hopefully, his refuge would last once darkness was upon them.

"More or less," Graham said. "She got off the hard stuff with pot and pills, then ran out of money and favors for all of it and made being sober intentional. She had to get a shitty job to pay off the fine, has pretty much been trying to cobble together a life ever since."

"She doesn't like you at all, does she?" Whitney asked. "That wasn't just teasing, the name-calling?"

"She absolutely hates me, and I don't care for her either. She's pissed that I'm not a mess like her, she would love to see me fail, and I swear if she dies one day I won't care at all, except that it would upset my aunt and my mom. Harsh, but true," Graham said, coming over to check Whitney's temperature with the back of his still-damp hand. "You feeling alright? Better not worse? Not dying yet?"

Whitney smiled. It felt nice, Graham's warm, damp hands on his face and neck. He wanted that sponge bath more than ever.

Instead of asking for it outright, or answering Graham's question, he came out with a line that had been circling around his mind all day, something he read in connection to Hellboy comics, and the character Koshchei the Deathless, who was originally a figure of ancient Russian folklore, and famous for being an unkillable jerk. To gain relative immortality, Koshchei hid his soul, also called his "death," in an object off-site, specifically in a turducken type of deal under an island — in an egg in a duck in a hare in a basket in an iron chest buried under an oak upon the open sea. After he kidnapped a woman, she used her wiles to question him about the location of his death, and he said what Whitney now repeated.

"My death is far from here and hard to find."

"Well, good for you," Graham told him, before taking him straight to bed.

PART V:
RUNOFF

SEPTEMBER 18, 2020 — COVID-19 DEATHS
WORLD DAILY: 5,793 / TOTAL: 1,053,506
US DAILY: 818 / TOTAL: 208,355
LOUISIANA DAILY: 29 / TOTAL: 5,340

29.

GRAHAM

Graham didn't complain for the first week of caretaking. It used to be his job to do this stuff for strangers: bring meals, cleanse wounds, and give sponge baths (minus the happy ending he gave to Whitney). The man healed beautifully and right on schedule, but something else had happened too.

At some point, the honeymoon had ended. The fairy bubble had popped, and reality filled the space. Whitney, because he was unwell, felt leeway to mention the little irritants that before he had ignored.

"Could you not chew like that?" Whitney asked, when Graham was unaware that he was chewing in any particular way at all.

"Or I could go chew in the other room," Graham offered. He thought it was nice to join Whitney in the bedroom, have breakfast in bed together. But while Whitney enjoyed a bowl of fake-eggs, potatoes, and nutritional yeast rather than cheese, Graham was eating his too-loud chocolate crisp cereal with almond milk.

"That works," Whitney said. "It's just that gravelly sound of chewing really bothering me, thanks."

"No worries," Graham said. "It's a brain condition when you can't stand the sound of chewing and such." He left the room before he got testy by saying it was actually a form of brain *damage*. Sure, he could believe that this was some neurological condition that Whitney couldn't help, and not take it personally. Or he could remember all the things that triggered him about Whitney that he just dealt with because he was a guest in the man's house, so it was on him to do the adjusting.

Graham split the difference. He moved to finish his breakfast in the kitchen without complaint, but he brooded a bit thinking that his services as a home health aide went a pretty good way towards paying Whitney back for his generosity of abode. He was also a companion too, a sexual one during a very isolating time. Was Graham feeling *too* grateful, all things considered? He considered, ruminating over his now-soggy chocolatey crunchies, until he came to a dubious decision.

If Graham was in a mood, maybe he needed to chill out, and there was a way to do that, chemically. Those Vicodins he couldn't put into a car with Sage nor safely keep in Whitney's house ... would they not be safer slowly filtered through his body? Sure, they could be flushed or thrown out in coffee grounds or something, but Graham was raised to waste-not-want-not. Also, he wanted to take some pills. He didn't have a problem with them the way some other people did, just like he didn't mind the sound of chewing.

Graham had taken the Vicodin pills out of their prescription bottle after Whitney went to bed the first night. He'd thought of disguising them among his Tic-Tacs, but what if Whitney wanted to freshen his breath? He thought about putting the pills in some unlikely food like deep in a bag of lentils or something, but that was no guarantee that Whitney wouldn't find them. He pondered tucking them behind an outlet cover, but didn't want to have to fight to unscrew the plate with a dime each time he needed access to them.

Ultimately, Graham wrapped the pills in cellophane and stuffed them in the bottom of his push-up deodorant container. Whitney would have no reason to use that, wouldn't hear them rattle if he knocked it down, and wouldn't throw it out by accident. That's where the pills stayed for a week just in case Whitney needed them, but once he was out of the woods, Graham figured he was free to partake.

The first time he sampled them, he texted Whitney from his room saying he had some work to do, writing himself sketch scripts and such, just so Whitney would know to leave him alone and not wonder why he wasn't wandering around his usual activities. He popped two pills and got toasted listening to some classic concerts, and had a third after dinner, to watch the sunset with his feet up on the porch rail, toes luxuriating in the breeze.

When Whitney first asked him why he was sleeping and resting so much, wondering if he was feeling sick, wary of COVID-19, Graham found a perfect lie to cover what he was up to.

"Sometimes I get migraines," he said, and that kept what he was doing a secret until the day it didn't.

30.

WHITNEY

It was the migraine excuse itself that made Whitney suspicious of drug use. Migraine patients were often prescribed opioids like Vicodin, Percocet, and OxyContin for relief, if they'll take them. He'd met a fair share of junkies who started with chronic pain just like that — migraine sufferers, back injuries, and uterus-related horrors like severe periods or endometriosis. He'd met a junkie nun who'd ended up in treatment due to the uterus she'd pledged to God to not even use.

So, if Graham had occasional migraines, and Whitney had no reason to doubt his ailment, he would have wanted to keep something like a bottle of Vicodin around. Not at his mom's where it couldn't save him from an oncoming attack.

When Graham suddenly became retiring, Whitney put it together. Migraines explained why he would fill the prescription against Whitney's wishes. Maybe that had something to do with why Graham became a nurse in the first place, it made sense to him. What Whitney didn't like was being suspicious that someone he explicitly told to ditch the pills and stay sober in his house wasn't following the rules.

But he didn't want to jump to conclusions. Plenty of people had migraines but refused to touch addictive substances knowing they didn't want migraines and a habit on top. Maybe Graham got the prescription just because as a former healthcare worker, he was pretty sure he knew his patient's pain threshold better than Whitney himself did. Irritating, but not a deal breaker. Whitney had to explain to his dentist that he didn't need to be numbed for a simple cleaning, for example, so he could explain the same to Graham too. He could say it nice and slow and insistent, if that was what it took.

Whitney could tolerate a lot of pain and discomfort, he knew how to disassociate from it well enough to wait it out, or lean into it in certain circumstances (yoga poses, rough sex). He didn't take drugs to avoid pain, he took them to feel alive, it was an entirely different pathway. He was not tempted by pain meds except that they would remind him of better drugs, fond bodily memories. Aches he was accustomed to would suddenly be absent, and his thoughts would float blissfully out of his head for a time, and he would crave that chemical magic again for his preferred substances, and the cravings could get maddening.

Even years into sobriety, cravings would rear up with vengeance in surprising moments. The smell of rubbing alcohol reminded Whitney of vodka, which he linked with clubs and, of course, club drugs. A gust of fall air hit him once and reminded him of a delicious weekend he had when he was 23, fucking his then-boyfriend and drug connection all day with the window open to crisp, brisk sunlight. On the flip side, he wanted to slam into oblivion very badly when he once saw a brand of sterile wipes on someone's desk at the bank. It was the same brand used by one of the hospitals that treated him for severe dehydration and other meth-related ailments — a box of them was the only thing to look at the entire time he was there, stewing in silence because the wall-mounted TV in the room no longer worked.

That was why Whitney was militant about keeping all drugs of any kind stronger than Tylenol out of his house. He had his reasons, but he also didn't want to have to relive those reasons in explaining it to someone who should know better, someone who should just trust him even if he didn't know better, someone who was a guest in his home and shouldn't be there to antagonize him. Whitney thought that was who he had, but was he wrong?

It was hard to spot the signs in a sure way. Was Graham moving a little slower? Were his pupils pinpointed? Wouldn't a migraine do the same things to him, make him move slower, experience light sensitivity? If he was only taking one or half a pill to take the edge off a migraine, would it be enough to slur his speech? If Graham was acting a little more euphoric than usual, how could he call that a problem?

Whitney wasn't going to go snooping through his own house looking for pills he didn't want to find. He decided to just ask.

At dinner, when Graham was looking dull and distant out over his plate of chicken strips, Whitney broached the topic from a friendly angle.

"Is your head still aching?" he asked, reaching to hold Graham's hands over the table, leaving room to believe him.

"Yeah, feeling kind of crocked, but evenings are better," Graham said.

"After the sun goes down, right? Because the light hurts?" Whitney asked.

"That's right," Graham said. "They did research on it, there's a special connection activated during a migraine and light activates it and it hurts."

"That's rough," Whitney said. "Is your room dark enough?"

"The bathroom is," Graham said. "I got in the bathtub in the dark earlier today for a while, that felt better."

Whitney nodded. Presumably, that was where Graham was while Whitney was on the phone with his brother that afternoon, updating him about the hernia (Nash was irrationally worried he'd get one too — was it some genetic weakness they shared?). He'd been walking around the kitchen, cooking comfortably, feeding bits of food to Honey Bun every time she followed an instruction like "back" and "sit."

"Doesn't Vicodin work on migraines?" Whitney asked. "Maybe you should have tucked a few away for yourself."

Graham squinted and took a drink of his coffee. He looked like he was weighing different answers in his mind, playing out each draft. It put a firm crease between his strawberry-ginger eyebrows.

Graham wasn't volunteering info, so Whitney would have to be direct. "Did you keep a couple of pills tucked away for yourself?"

"What ..." Graham began, after more laborious mental deliberation, "... would it mean if I did?"

31.

GRAHAM

In his pauses, Graham was thinking about how long it would take to pack all of his shit, and what he would say to his mom was the reason he came back home. He should have known better than to try and outsmart an addict at his own game. What gave him away? Did he look foggy? He thought the migraine excuse had been such an inspired trick.

Whitney shook his head, and looked off, pressing his lips together like he was trying to keep himself from letting fly something harsh.

Graham let down his fork and remembered his other ugly break-ups. Were there ever pretty ones? Maybe in movies, with women. All of Graham's splits had been in the theme of "fuck you and the horse you rode in on." Like … your shit is in the yard, forget my name and number, and I was lying every time I was nice to you, boy bye.

Graham looked Whitney over one last time while he could, just taking a picture for the road. He was good-looking, talented, charming, came from somebodies, became somebody in his own right, and had a nice dick too, just … too good for the likes of Mr. Morrow. Graham was amazed he was ever allowed so close, but he wasn't surprised he screwed it up at the first chance.

"Guess I'll gather my stuff," Graham said, and rose to pack.

He heard Whitney clear his place at the table, and then heard him come to the door to watch Graham pack up.

"I have rules for a reason," Whitney said.

"Yes, and I should know better than most, because I was a nurse," Graham said. He knew how to pile on himself.

"You promised me you would get rid of them," Whitney said. Graham could see him in the reflection of the window. The evening light was in its lavender phase, lavender and gold and lovely. If only he had made different choices, they could be watching it together. Now Graham would have to drive home under those pretty colors.

"I couldn't hand them over to my mom with Sage around," he said. "I know that's not your problem, but it was my problem. I figured I could hide them better from you than my mom could from her, and you're in a better place than she's ever been. Had you found them, we'd be here, and this moment sucks, but had Sage found them, it'd fuck up her and my mom and my aunt, so I made the call."

"And you didn't just flush them because of your migraines?" Whitney asked.

Graham zipped up his backpack full of socks and other sundries, hoisted it to his shoulders, and turned around to face Whitney like a man.

"I don't have migraines," he fessed up. "Just needed a reason to be left alone for a few hours to feel the pills."

Whitney shook his head at Graham. "What was the point, Graham?"

"To be fair to me, at first I kept 'em because I didn't want to deal with you wanting them when the pain hit," Graham said, with a wry smile. He knew he fucked up, but sometimes you just had to smile at your own dumbass self. "And once you were out of the woods, I figured they were better off getting flushed through me and my detox organs than down the toilet."

"They can damage your liver," Whitney told him.

"Yeah, but the liver can heal," Graham said. "Flushing pills, on the other hand, means they end up in groundwater and streams and fuck up the fish ecosystem. Hormones and addictive chemicals especially, like cocaine in shrimp and stuff. Better I process it first, plus I can enjoy the high."

"Did you enjoy it?" Whitney asked.

Graham shrugged and took Whitney in again. His shirt was sleeveless showing his lean arms, currently crossed in disapproval over his chest. His shorts were the loose kind that made you think you could see up the cuff, very enticing. The light from the ceiling fan highlighted the lines on his face which beautifully framed those keen, jolly eyes of his. Graham was still doped up enough on the Vicodin that he was kind of luxuriating in the ache and pine of how much he was going to miss grabbing onto this man. Sweet like bruised fruit.

"This come-down really sucks, but ..." Graham shrugged and picked up his other bag. He was ready to get out of Whitney's life now, unceremoniously with his sad sack of shit. "I'm sorry."

"So am I," Whitney said. "This, our whole thing, was a real godsend of sorts. Not that God sent it, I mean, but meeting you at this time in this place, our circumstances lining up, this was pretty special. But it's not right that I should have to break my rules for you, I said I wouldn't."

"And I shouldn't have put you in this situation, I'm an asshole," Graham said. "Should we kiss or hug goodbye? Seems like we could have a nice separation on this one."

"Sure," Whitney said.

Graham felt a wince of sadness as he walked up to Whitney and leaned over to kiss him on the cheek. Whitney pressed his lips together as he allowed the kiss, and put a hand on Graham's shoulder, which stopped him from walking further.

"I really am sorry," Graham said. "I really care about you, and I shouldn't have ..."

"I said you'd have to get out of my house if you brought drugs in here," Whitney said, as if to remind them both that these were the rules, and regardless of nobody liking them, they had to be followed.

"I understand," Graham said, ready to go home and cry to his mommy like the loser he was.

"You don't understand," Whitney said, finally turning to look Graham square in the eye. "I consider the porch to be outside of my house."

"You ..." Graham said, wondering what the hell they were talking about now. "Okay?"

"And the porch has a hammock," Whitney said.

"Right," Graham replied, still not following.

"So, you have to get out of my house," Whitney said. "But you can stay on the hammock."

"I can stay?" Graham asked, loving this loophole, so ready to cheat this sentence on a technicality.

"I won't run you off with a gun," Whitney said with a shrug of his eyebrows.

Graham gave him a much bigger kiss, full on the lips, full of gratitude.

32.

WHITNEY

Whitney was naturally concerned that he was sabotaging himself. His sobriety should come first ahead of any man, any relationship, especially one as new and undefined as this one. But this was a new world than the one where he could do healthy activities, meet positive people, improve himself. There was nowhere to go. There was no one else to hang out with. And Graham ... he just didn't seem like he would be the one to lead Whitney back into fire and vice. He also looked so beautiful when he was sad.

Graham moved outside, and Whitney stayed in. He closed the blinds so that Graham was out of sight, but he was not out of mind. In fact, he was on the phone. Whitney put in a wireless earbud, and they talked out their new situation.

"You're kind of a fuck-up too, aren't you?" Whitney asked, finally bold enough, comfortable enough with this man who had just wronged him to speak his mind without filter. "This was so unnecessary, you didn't need the pills, and yet you got them, kept them, and took them. What is that?"

"That is a stupid self-destructive streak I have," Graham admitted, seemingly more forthright somehow when he and Whitney were not face-to-face. "Like I put so much into becoming a nurse and just quit the first time it didn't go my way. Like I'm uncomfortable with how okay I am with my comedy career being derailed by a pandemic because like ... if I fail now, I can blame the virus and it's not my fault. It's like I just want an excuse to be the fuck-up I truly am."

"Like Cousin Sage?" Whitney asked, stripping the sheets on his bed and cleaning up so he could, in a sense, sage the room of Graham's presence for now, and have a fresh space all to himself until their situation was figured out.

"Probably," Graham said. "I don't want to be that much of a fuck-up, but honestly she's the watermark in my family, so if I keep out of drug debt and out of jail, I already exceed the bare minimum."

"You're afraid you don't have the ambition to do better than the bare minimum?" Whitney asked.

"Maybe," Graham said, grunting in a way that sounded like he was trying to get into the hammock without the thing dumping him onto his tailbone.

"Do you need pillows or a blanket out there?" Whitney asked.

"No, just a hair shirt," Graham replied, referencing the uncomfortable clothes made of rough animal hair that were once worn by penitents and ascetics.

Whitney smiled as he measured soap for a load of laundry. He still found Graham funny, charming, despite his mistake. "I'm all out of hair shirts, but I can bring you a sackcloth if you like."

"Perfect," Graham said.

After a beat, Whitney said, "I'm not trying to make you do penance, to be clear. I just have to keep my boundaries, you understand?"

"You do not have to comfort me about what I did to you, man," Graham said. "I get that you have to be careful, that one lost brick could be the weak point that brings down the wall, I know you can't make exceptions for my dumbass."

"But I am making an exception," Whitney said, letting the lid on his washer fall with the sound of a gong and starting the wash cycle. "I should kick you all the way out, I should delete your number from my phone. You crossed an uncrossable line so casually, you lied to me so easily, made up a medical condition."

"I did," Graham admitted. "I can still go if you need me to go." The sound of shuffling, a jingle. "I have my keys right here, all my stuff is

with me including the pills. I'll go without complaint if you say so, but …
if you don't make me, I won't leave. If I cared for you the right way,
I would leave you alone."

Whitney felt his loins stir and cleared his throat before saying,
"You care for me?"

Graham took a deep breath. "Pretty sure I do," he said. "I think
you're so cool, so interesting, I like how I feel when I'm with you,
and you're a good lay."

Whitney laughed, and rolled his eyes at himself for leaning into
this sweet talk when he should be pulling back. "You've got some
nerve saying this stuff now."

"I know," Graham said. "The balls on me, the gall, how dare I."

"Tell me more nice things about myself," Whitney said. He could
be a pillow queen tonight, receiving without giving.

"Alright, but this is how a guy dies at the end of *The Talented Mr.
Ripley*, so I'm trusting you, okay?" Graham said. "You're definitely
talented I think, but you work harder to be good so it's earned talent,
not just natural talent, which is more admirable."

"Maybe to our Puritan work ethic," Whitney said. "I think other
cultures think natural talent is God-blessed, far more special than
those who have to grind it out."

"Oh, you want to argue about what's nice about you, I see,"
Graham said. "I'll be your huckleberry. What other heathen cultures
think doesn't matter to me, but I think it's safe to say if you work
hard to do something that comes easily to others, you've earned it
more than they have. You probably appreciate and understand it
more too."

"Probably," Whitney said.

"Other nice things about Whitney, you're precious with your
new puppy," Graham said. "When you cook, you're very neat and
fastidious about it, sweeping up little flour dustings and drips right
away, like you notice the little things. When you're being creative
like thinking of songs and stuff, you look like you're doing math,
so serious. When the radio's playing, part of you is always dancing.
You tap your fingers or feet, nod your head, if you're standing you
bounce to it."

"You noticed," Whitney said. People had seen that in him before, his mother for one, his favorite teacher in school, one of his fans who said she reminded him of her husband who'd recently passed because he always did that too.

"Of course I noticed," Graham said. "You're easy on the eyes, so what else would I be looking at?"

33.

GRAHAM

Whitney had questions about whether he was actually sexually attractive to Graham. Surely men of a certain age weren't exactly his type, right? So, what was Graham's type, he wondered, and would he have wanted to sleep with Whitney if his last name wasn't Thorn?

"My type so far has been 'available,'" Graham said. "Like, proximity and willingness have been a huge turn-on for all my live-long days."

"Who was the first guy who really turned you on though, any through-line there?" Whitney asked.

"Oh, the first time a guy gave me a boner, okay," he said, and smiled because it was one of his most cherished memories. "You'll like this."

"Go on," Whitney said.

"So, it was actually one of Sage's nasty-ass friends okay," Graham said. "He was maybe 17 and a drop-out or 19 and a full-fledged loser. He had unwashed hair, cargo shorts with chains on them, and a metal band t-shirt full of poverty holes not artfully ripped ones."

"Aw, he wore it out cuz he loved it so much, didn't he?" Whitney asked.

"Yeah, adorable, right?" Graham said, remembering that the shirt had indeed been ultra-soft and was gray instead of black after being through the wash a zillion times. "So, he was waiting for Sage to take a shower and get ready because she forgot they had plans, and the adults weren't home for whatever reason, and I was watching

TV, right, and I always mute the commercials because I hate them. I did it out of habit and suddenly it was silent with the two of us, so awkward that he had to talk to me."

"Learn anything in school today?" Whitney guessed in a mimic-y voice.

"Nah, this guy was trash," Graham said, remembering his pot funk, his lip ring, his leather bracelets. "He asked me if I was getting laid yet. Specifically, he said, 'You in high school? Had any high school pussy yet?'"

"Quite an opener," Whitney said.

"Yeah, bold," Graham said. "I was shocked, I tell you, like too surprised to be mortified because of course I hadn't gotten any pussy. I wasn't sure I ever wanted to even try any, but I also did not want to explain to him why, and I'm glad I chose dishonesty that day."

"Okay," Whitney said, following along.

"I told this guy who went by Ace, no idea if that was his real name or not, I said, 'No, the girls don't think I'm cool.' And this gentleman said, 'You know what's cool to girls? Cunnilingus, bro.'"

"Bro!" Whitney said.

"I shit you not," Graham told him, nodding even though Whitney couldn't see him, and kicking off the porch's handrail so that the hammock would start swinging. "Then he put his fingers up like a V for victory, V for peace, and stuck his tongue through."

"And that gave you a boner?" Whitney asked.

"I can hear you cringing. No, that was gross, that wasn't it," Graham said. "Next, he pestered me to do the same, like he was just trying to help a young brother out. Well, apparently, I wasn't getting it right at all, I was ignoring the clit, you see, which is the important part, and so he came over to show me."

"He did what?" Whitney asked.

Graham laughed. He had Whitney engaged now, perhaps he would have to tell this story on stage sometime for the dirtier crowds.

"He came and sat next to me and said, 'Here, gimme your hand, not the one you slobbered all over, and I'll show you.' And then he took my hand and went down on my interdigital folds."

"Bro," Whitney said, impressed this time.

"Yeah," Graham said. "And he was tender too, like teased me a little, and his lips were involved. He wasn't afraid to put his whole tongue in between my fingers. I'm talking the underside of his tongue too, all slick like dark meat turkey."

"Wow," Whitney said.

"I couldn't remember my name by the time we heard Sage turn off the shower," Graham said. "He stood up then, gave my hand back while kind of wiping it on my shirt for me, and you want to know what the best part was?"

"He gave you his number?" Whitney asked.

"Ha, no," Graham said, appreciating Whitney's zinger there. "Before he headed down the hall to find my cousin he was like, 'Don't worry, it's actually not gay to eat pussy.'"

Whitney busted out laughing so hard Graham was worried he'd pop a stitch. He was grinning at the newly risen moon thinking, if this was how it was when he was in the doghouse, maybe he should switch places with Honey Bun and be happy. They could still keep their little family together.

"Oh, that's amazing," Whitney said, panting with a light voice, probably wiping tears out of his eyes, out of breath with the laughter. "I mean that does sound pretty hot though, I get it."

"Yeah, I beat off like five times that night and probably broke some sort of record that week," Graham said. "It's still in my whack stack, to be honest. Like sometimes I'm Ace, or we're both older, or I'm older and he's still young, it's just always so hot, I wish I could send that idiot money every Christmas, I swear."

"Well, maybe we can do some role-playing when you're allowed back inside," Whitney said.

"When?" Graham asked, a stirring in his heart that was, he knew, hope, the thing with feathers that springs eternal.

"Assuming you behave out there," Whitney said. "And never lie to me about drugs again. I told you that you can do whatever you want, just not in my house."

"So, I can get wasted in your yard then?" Graham said, before adding hastily, "I'm kidding, I know that's not cool."

"If you don't mind when I turn the hose on you, have a ball out there," Whitney said, "Just don't give the neighbors a reason to call the cops, because they're all bastards."

34.

WHITNEY

Whitney stayed on the phone with Graham for hours, he was having a good time. In the forefront of his mind, he gave himself full permission for this: he'd stood his ground and kicked Graham out of the house; Graham was trying to earn back his trust and that was allowable; plus this was amusing. Graham was a professional entertainer, and tonight he was putting on a good show.

But underneath the banter, an unease was growing. By the time he was snuggled in bed listening to Graham's stories from the road.

"My worst heckler wasn't one of the drunks or homophobes, it was actually some social justice warrior who just could not take a joke about dolphin sex," Graham said. "I was like, 'Ma'am it's not my fault other people seduce dolphins,' which is a true story by the way, and that set this person off. 'First of all, I'm not a ma'am, I'm non-binary. Animals deserve our respect, I was homeless for three years and my dog was my only friend.' I asked this person, 'What were your dog's pronouns,' trying to lean into their scene, but they weren't having it. Suddenly they were yelling about how they were autistic, and queer, and a single parent, and their child was also autistic, and mixed-race on top, and basically, I was out-gunned by somebody flipping all their identity cards. It was obnoxious, but they were also so clearly unwell that I couldn't tell them to shut the fuck up or roast them without looking like the bad guy."

Silence as Graham's story closed out, and Whitney had nothing to say.

"Do you not like my take?" Graham asked. "Or have you fallen asleep?"

"I'm awake," Whitney said. "Maybe not as woke as your heckler though."

"Right? That person was a doozy. Like get your nonbinary ass some therapy, for real, because the late-night dive bar comedy show cannot help you." More silence. "Are you okay?"

"Not really," Whitney said, finally coming out with his qualms. "I've just been lied to by so many men, especially around drugs."

"I get that," Graham said. "If you want me to go, I'll go."

"I don't want to be responsible for making this decision," Whitney said, sitting up and leaning over the side of the bed, elbows resting on his knees, barfing this out. "I don't like that you've put me in this position. We were having a nice time, a summer idle, then I got sick or whatever in a way that for once in my life isn't my fault, and you bring drugs in."

Whitney got up, started pacing. He heard Graham heave a big sigh.

"Before I considered myself an addict, I was trying to walk the line," Whitney said. "I had rules about when I did and didn't get high, I had a system, I thought. Ultimately that was probably never going to work, but the guy I was seeing at the time, he didn't want to play by my rules. He didn't pay rent either, he didn't have any shows to put on, or any photo shoots to look fresh for. He had none of my obligations. But he was fun to be around, he made me feel grand. And so I let him do what he pleased in my space, on my time, even though his fun shot my resolutions and derailed my duties."

"Am I that bad?" Graham said.

"This isn't about you, not like that," Whitney said. "You're fine, my ex was fine, these are my needs and it's my job to insist on them. What is on you is that this time I was clear, because I've learned from my past mistakes, and just because you don't have that context doesn't excuse you for your part in digging up this grave again, you know? And it's especially unfair that I'm the one who has to be responsible for ending both our fun."

"I've put you in a nasty position," Graham said.

"Yes, you have," Whitney said, peeking out the window closest to Graham to see where he was now, what he was doing. Graham was sitting on the porch railing, head pressed against one of the columns holding up the roof, and tapping it slowly and regularly there, like a sleepy woodpecker.

"Your options are either shut down the party for both of us, or let me slide on a party foul knowing I might not have learned my lesson," Graham said.

"That's right," Whitney told him, and Graham must have heard him through the window, because his head snapped to look at where Whitney was standing.

Whitney adjusted the blinds so they could have a face-to-face conversation through the slats. Graham got up to come stand before him.

"Is there a way I can fix this?" Graham asked.

Whitney shrugged, but knew it was fair to shift this work onto Graham's shoulders and off of his own. "Can you prove that you've learned your lesson?"

35.

GRAHAM

Graham thought about what he could do to demonstrate regret, and only had one solid idea. It would require an assist from someone else though.

"How about we take Honey Bun for a walk?" he asked.

Whitney agreed that was a fine idea, a midnight walk to see the stars, clear the air, get out of their rut with some new scenery.

"But just to be clear," Whitney said, digging out a flashlight and the poo-bags as Graham found his shoes in the dark and met him at the door. "Taking the dog on walks will not be enough to make up for this transgression."

But that wasn't Graham's plan at all. "I know, I just want to walk with you under the moonlight."

Whitney began to sing Patsy Cline's "Walkin' After Midnight," mostly to the puppy, but Graham got to hear the performance too. They had face masks in their pockets but didn't put them on, instead got to enjoy the pollen and smell of stagnant water from the canal.

"Doesn't the sky seem bigger at night?" Graham asked, spinning time waiting for Honey Bun to find the perfect spot to take a dump — her next dump was key to his grand gesture.

"Yes, of course it does," Whitney said. "We can see farther at night."

"Right, that makes sense," Graham said. "Do you like night better than day?"

"I like what I don't get enough of," Whitney said. "If I'm working nights and don't get to see daylight, I miss it. If I don't get a night out for too long, I crave the night. I'm just perpetually dissatisfied with what I've got, no matter how good it is."

That sounded like addiction talk to Graham. They stopped on the side of the road as Honey Bun thoroughly sniffed a tuft of grass. She started to crimp up to do her business, and that was Graham's cue to make his move.

Graham grabbed a poo bag from Whitney's pocket, and another little baggie from his own: the saran-wrapped remaining Vicodin.

"Alright, ready for some magic?" Graham asked, dumping the thirteen remaining oval-shaped pills into his left hand so he could grab a handful of dog crap with the other. "I'm going to make these suckers disappear."

Whitney's face was inscrutable watching him, so Graham just blustered through his performance, palming the poop through the bag, all while Honey Bun kicked grass and dirt at his face, trying to bury her leavings.

With poo in hand, Graham stood up and tried to keep regret and nostalgia off his face as he dropped the pills in with the mess and squeezed. He really massaged around, ensuring that each pill was embedded in turds like raisins in a bundt cake, so thoroughly befouled that only the most ardent *Trainspotting*-level junkie would touch them now. He then tied off the bag in a little bow and said, "Ta-da!"

Whitney gave him a slow clap and said, "It's a start."

Graham mimed swiping sweat off his head in cartoonish "phew-whee" style. They dropped the bag of dog-doo off in the next neighbor's trash they came upon and kept walking.

Whitney started singing Patsy Cline again, and Graham joined him. Quietly, of course, because as Humphrey Bogart told some loud broad in a movie, "Honey, I have neighbors." But it was a nice moment of intimacy, one of the rare ones when Graham knew that he would remember it while he was living it. It was a real little tableau: him and his man and a loyal dog under a starry sky in the Louisiana night, singing in the dark.

Once Honey Bun had lightened her load again, it was time to head back toward the house. They crossed the street to allow the girl new things to smell and whiz on. They were halfway back in a comfortable silence when Honey Bun ventured into the shadows to get after something.

"Girl, are you deucing again?" Graham wondered, and Whitney clicked on the flashlight to see if it was so.

"Pull her back!" Whitney said, and Graham lunged for her collar before he saw what caused the alarm. There was an open-mouthed, wide-eyed raccoon face.

It would not behoove the young and naive Honey Bun to get into a fight with some dirty street ruffian like a raccoon, but that wasn't the danger tonight. Someone must have run over the critter because half its guts were all squished out and congealed around it. Honey Bun wanted a closer sniff, Graham wanted way less than the slight whiff he got.

"No you don't," he said, picking up Honey Bun entirely, and ignoring her pitiful mewls of frustrated desire.

"I know you want to roll in that, but it's not happening," Whitney told her.

"That's right, girly," Graham said, co-parenting. "That could make you sick, and it would certainly make you stinky, and then no one would let you cuddle tonight, and you'd be sad all over again."

"I think you can set her back down once we turn the corner," Whitney said. "We'll be far enough away so she won't yank the leash on me."

"Why not just gimme the leash, she can yank on me all she wants, I don't have stitches," Graham said, and was handed the reins to the dog for the rest of their walk.

Graham arrived back at the house sweatier than he meant to get with this evening jaunt. He didn't like the idea of heading back to bed on the hammock itchy with salt sweat, so he decided to ask, "Mind if I pop back in for a shower?"

Whitney stood in the glowing rectangle of the open front door and looked Graham up and down. He sighed, rolled his eyes, and said "Get your stuff and move back in."

"You're sure?" Graham asked, happy he was already back in Whitney's good graces. Perhaps his grand gesture with the pills really had done the trick, brought the issue out of the shadows, and then buried the hatchet.

"Not at all sure, but I'll allow it," Whitney said. "I just hope that rotting carcass wasn't an omen for us."

PART VI:
TURBIDITY

SEPTEMBER 21, 2020 — COVID-19 DEATHS
WORLD DAILY: 4,296 / TOTAL: 1,067,381
US DAILY: 475 / TOTAL: 209,969
LOUISIANA DAILY: 9 / TOTAL: 5,375

36.

WHITNEY

"What do you mean she can't breathe?" Graham said, on the phone with his mother the next Monday morning, not that days of the week mattered to them. "Does a cop got his knee on her neck or what?"

It turned out that Aunt Tamella had caught something, and considering the fact that she was struggling for breath, it was probably COVID-19 and not (as she had dismissed) just a bad flu.

"If you're wondering if it's bad enough to go to the hospital, the answer is yes," Graham said. "You know you wouldn't even consider it unless you were worried that it was serious, so if you're worried about that, the only way to know for sure is to go to the hospital."

Whitney was still in bed making a to-do list now that he was feeling better. Hurricane season was in full swing, and there was maintenance to be done. He had to make sure the gutters were clear and secure, needed to trim some trees, re-caulk some seals. As he wrote down things to check, he listened to Graham give an exhaustive list to convince his mother to just go to the damn hospital already.

"They can check her oxygen saturation levels and give her pure oxygen so she's not struggling," he said. "They can give drugs that'll help with the symptoms and send her right back home if she's safe enough for that." A pause before, "No, drugs like steroids and shit to help strengthen people who need some *oomph*." Another break and then, "Trust me, they don't have room to book people in who don't need to be there. If she does need a ventilator, she'll need one quick, not four hours after she's woozy and you panic-driving her and filling out forms and answering questions first."

As Graham became increasingly frustrated, pacing back and forth just outside the bedroom door, Whitney got up to comfort him.

They'd had pretty spectacular make-up sex the night of the Vicodin incident. Deliberate sex, full of eye contact, and the patience to go deep and delay gratification. It was both a sexual encounter and a therapeutic exercise to reconnect, reaffirm a level of commitment, communication, and respect. It was far better than talking it out and formally agreeing to do better, to be more cognizant of the other's needs and areas of struggle. Instead, they got naked, got intimate, and got off. Graham gave it up in a lot of ways he hadn't before.

Something about being sorry lent him some abandon in the bedroom that meant Whitney could take full control. Tell Graham to touch himself and watch him obey. Finger-fuck him and watch him squirm. Kiss him invasively, tongue fully in his mouth, and feel him take it.

Whitney himself got an aerobic cardio workout from the event, which put a full stop to the aura of feeling invalid, delicate, and old. Graham was shaky with orgasm by the time Whitney was done with him, and Whitney himself felt potent again, manly and strong. They stayed smitten through the weekend, but now Graham was getting worked up by his family over the phone.

Whitney circled behind him and started massaging his shoulders. He was hunched over the phone trying to not swear at his mother as she stonewalled his logic and facts.

Cynthany was making excuses, Whitney could hear a few words and phrases through the phone like "germs at the hospital" and "prison ward."

"Yes, quarantine sucks, but you're already trapped at home, right? And there's no ventilator there, right?" Graham sighed as she kept arguing, and leaned back until his head rested on Whitney's shoulder.

"She's putting you through the paces, huh?" Whitney murmured, but apparently he didn't speak quietly enough.

Cynthany said something else, and Graham turned to hand over the phone and relay the message, "Now she wants to talk to you."

"Yes, ma'am?" Whitney answered, expecting to be lectured too, but instead Cynthany had questions.

"You just had surgery, was it crazy in there?" she asked. "I keep seeing these videos online where people can't even come in and say goodbye when they're dying. I'm not trying to hand my sister over to some ward full of COVID and pneumonia and all that super hospital MRSA and then never see her again."

"She on about the MRSA again?" Graham said, standing right in front of Whitney, shaking his head. "Tell her any given hospital is cleaner than Tamella's funky house."

"Is he telling jokes?" Cynthany asked. "This isn't the time, we're worried over here."

"I agree with your son," Whitney said. "If you're that worried you should go, let them test you. If she doesn't have the 'rona, you don't have to worry anymore. If she does, they can send you home with medicine. If they keep her, it's because she needs the help, and going to the hospital sooner rather than later was the right thing to do, yeah? No way to lose."

Cynthany sighed, and her voice wavered when she spoke again. "But I don't want this to be happening."

Whitney felt bad for this lady, and looked at Graham with pity. "Like you said, I just had surgery, and everything was fine. A little stricter than usual but that's not a bad thing, right? They're being extra careful."

Graham took back the phone. "See, he agrees with me. MRSA was always in hospitals before, but right now they're even more careful because they know for sure everyone's contagious. No cutting corners right now. People are on the ball, by the book. It'll be okay."

Cynthany said something else, and from the way Graham's shoulders fell, the woman was finally convinced.

"I love you too, Mom," Graham said. "Love to Tamella as well, and keep me updated."

37.

GRAHAM

"I almost had pneumonia once," Whitney told Graham as they headed out to do yard work after having a thoroughly good time rubbing sunscreen on each other's bodies. "My lungs were filled with fluid just because I was in such bad shape that I was vulnerable to all kinds of shit. Body was busy fighting infections, they were hitting me with every antibiotic under the sun, and then they told me I had to breathe harder to push the fluid out, because if I got full-blown pneumonia in that state, I may not come back."

"You know they've got a vaccine for a bunch of pneumonia strains?" Graham asked. "I lied about being a smoker to get one once, because there's no reason not to. I had a friend teaching in some Asian country after college who told me about it. They got it as a perk when they were in for their flu shot. I had to beg, lie, and pay for it, but they last for ten years."

Graham climbed the ladder having volunteered for gutter cleaning so that Whitney wouldn't try it, because the scooping would cause him to torque his torso around too much. His hernia patch was mostly healed, but it wasn't completely set yet. Recovery would take about a month, even with the low invasiveness of a laparoscopic procedure. Graham, still relatively young and undamaged, would take the risk of a ladder on uneven ground while Whitney checked his list and inspected the premises.

"Maybe they'll be smart and whip those things out now that there's a lung virus going around," Whitney said, but Graham snorted in response.

"I mean, I love your optimism, but smart's got nothing to do with any decision made about healthcare in America," Graham said. "The answer is money, Honey, the almighty dollar."

"Does your mom and them have the pneumonia vaccine?" Whitney asked.

"No," Graham said, immediately pulling out his phone. "But I'll tell her about it, she can ask for it, might calm down her worries until they get all us plebs the Corona vaccine."

He had several messages already about the traffic (*Why is there so much traffic if places are locked down?*) and the waiting room (*Too many sick people here*). He texted her that pneumonia vaccines existed and that he had one himself. She responded with a picture of dust on the baseboards of the intake center saying, *Are you sure they're sterile if they're not even clean?*

Graham did not reply to that question. He put his phone back in his pocket and returned to inspecting the gutters. There was gunk enough in there that moss had grown over it.

"You know you could plant an herb garden in these right now?" he called down to Whitney.

"I imagine I could," Whitney said. "I only play a manly man on stage. I'm road trash at heart, don't know how to be responsible for a property really."

"I ain't judging," Graham told him. "I'm trailer trash myself, we do our best."

"At heart, I aspire to be river trash," Whitney said, looking out over his spot of canal. "Like Huck Finn."

"Speaking of old Huckleberry," Graham said, "do you think he was gay for Tom Sawyer?"

"Oh, one hundred percent," Whitney said, shading his eyes with a hand to look up at Graham against the morning sun. "The way Tom treated him in the books, I can easily believe he'd convince Huck to let him put it in on occasion and keep it a secret."

"Ah, he would, you're right," Graham said. "Getting all the other boys to trade their trinkets to do his damn chores? He could slip it to Huck for sure."

"That boy had daddy issues with Pap Finn," Whitney diagnosed. "He'd want Tom to boss him around a little. Tell him to take it and shut up about it and don't act like we know each other when my real friends come around."

"We know the type," Graham said. "All, 'just because I fuck men doesn't make me gay.'"

"Right," Whitney said. "Over there talking about how a warm hole is a warm hole."

"It's only gay if you're the receiver," Graham said, sticking up his finger to illustrate.

Whitney nodded. "It's only gay if you like it, otherwise it's just a bodily function, a transaction."

"It's not gay-gay, it's prison-gay," Graham agreed. "They don't *want* it, they just have no other alternative."

"Just like pirates or them Navy boys, it's not gay if you can't see land," Whitney said.

"Of course, because they've got to do it," Graham said. "Abstinence is not an option."

"Having no sex at all," Whitney said, "now that would be gay."

"Absolutely homosexual, can't have that," Graham said, and smiled as Whitney laughed.

"Speaking of huckleberries again ..." Whitney began when he got done touching his guts to check they were still sewn shut.

Graham interrupted him. "You're thinking of *Tombstone*?"

"Yeah," Whitney said, "but not Doc Holiday."

"Curly Bill," Graham said with a nod. He'd had this discussion before, very heated in a bar, as it was a hill he would die on. "Chaotic bisexual."

"Right?" Whitney said. "The way he was standing up for the pretty boy's crush on the thespian, it wasn't because he was just such a nice man."

"He was protecting his own," Graham said, nodding. "This isn't us making things up, you know. It's no *Brokeback Mountain* to be sure, but if you watch closely, before Curly Bill comes out of the opium den to fight in the street, he's gently stroking the hair of one of the oriental whore boys."

"No way," Whitney said. "How did I miss that?"

"We'll find it online tonight," Graham promised. "I've freeze-framed that scene more than conspiracy nuts do over the Zapruder tape."

"You seek the truth," Whitney said.

"I do my own research," Graham said, echoing the line used by anti-vaxxers, and pleased to hear Whitney laugh again as they went back to their chores.

38.

WHITNEY

Whitney saw Graham pause and frown after checking his phone when he came down from the gutters for the last time.

"Aunty update?" Whitney asked.

Graham typed something back and said, "Yeah. They've checked in my aunt and said no phones so now my mom can't text her."

"That's … why is that? Why can't they have phones?" Whitney asked. "I had mine in my surgery room."

"In a quarantine ward it's different," Graham said with a sigh. "Cell phones are some of the most highly-touched surfaces, they carry disease, and they're too much trouble on a ward where everyone's infected and vulnerable, nurses included."

"Seems cruel though," Whitney said. "People can't talk to anyone outside."

"It sucks, but it's the disease that's cruel, not the protocols," Graham said. "My mom's pretty upset right now, says she's going to stay in her car in the parking lot. They won't let her stay in the building cuz she's COVID-positive. She's supposed to go home and quarantine herself voluntarily, but she won't."

Whitney thought through what they would do normally for something like this, and all his ideas were kiboshed by the virus. They couldn't go to her house without risking infection. She couldn't come to them for the same reason. They could leave food out for her like a stray cat, but she was the one better at cooking.

"Can we help?" Whitney asked.

"Not really," Graham said, using the hose sprayer to rinse his hands. "I told her to go home and let the doctors do their work, it's not my fault she's wasting gas in a parking lot, they're not letting her back in unless she needs a bed too."

"Is your aunt in danger?" Whitney asked. "Do we fear for her life?"

"We do, a little," Graham said, now turning the hose so Honey Bun could nip at the spray. "She's in her late sixties, she's overweight, eats like shit, has no fitness, and she's had a stressful life. All of that plus COVID and just one other germ in that hospital, it could do her in."

"But you can't do anything about it, is that your gist?" Whitney asked.

"Yeah," Graham said, turning to look at Whitney. "Hate to have it sound like a clinical laundry list, but the amalgamation of conditions is what it is. Worrying about it won't make the difference, just add stress onto my nerves."

"Sound logic," Whitney said.

"Now, should I hose myself down for a little wet t-shirt show, or is it too early in the morning?"

With the outside of the house spruced up they moved inside, checking expiration dates in the kitchen and running a damp rag over baseboards, headboards, and ceiling fan blades. Again, Graham did all the tasks that needed a stepladder, but this time Whitney came around to kiss his belly where his shirt hiked up. It was so irresistible at the perfect height.

"Oh, hello," Graham said when he felt the attention.

"You're not so ticklish you're gonna fall, are you?" Whitney asked the belly, soft-skinned with sparse, sexy little hairs.

"I'm good," Graham said, bringing down his hands to dip his fingers into Whitney's hair.

Whitney turned his cheek to rest against Graham's body, hearing his guts swirl around as Graham's shirt came down and put him in a happy little hiding place.

Whitney closed his eyes and started to sway. Graham swayed with him and said, "Hey, put on music, what are we doing dancing in silence?"

Whitney busted out the classic vinyls. In his house, there was a mix of Granny's gospel albums, mother's country women, daddy's dirtbag folk rock, and Whitney's journey through 80s and 90s country and pop. Whitney pulled a few albums to take a journey through the ages.

First, Sister Rosetta Thorpe's *Gospel Train*, which got them toe-tapping and doing the twist as Graham took a damp sponge to every slat of the living room's blinds, and Whitney unzipped the couch cushions he could to run some laundry.

Building off the church songs, Whitney went into his mother's Tammy Wynettes and came out with *We Love to Sing About Jesus* with George Jones.

"Did you know George Jones once rode his lawn mower to the liquor store," Whitney asked Graham.

"I did, but only because they painted a mural of it in Nashville a couple years ago," Graham said.

"People called him the Possum," Whitney said.

"Well, that's possum behavior for sure, so I can understand it," Graham said, accepting his tutelage with a nod.

Next up Whitney selected Merle Haggard's *Kern River*, mostly because his name was mentioned in the title song, "… a place called Mount Whitney from where the mighty Kern River comes down."

"Mount Whitney," Graham repeated when he heard. "Don't mind if I do."

Whitney smirked as he got out the vacuum and mop. By then the surfaces and furniture were clean, and the laundry was tumbling dry. The last step to get the whole place clean was to sweep all that had fallen out the door and wipe the slate, meaning mop the floorboards.

Last on the turntable was an anthology album of the Nitty Gritty Dirt Band, and a fast agreement that the song "Fishin' in the Dark" was indeed about sex and not about fishing.

The latest update from Graham's mother was that she was cleaning out every nook and cranny of her car since she was trapped in there.

"Just gonna text her this picture of the dust pile we swept up and be like, *Same*." Graham said, typing into his phone as he spoke.

"Must be something in the air, that fall air," Whitney said, thinking they should bust out some baking pans and soak their feet on the porch while the laundry dried. Once the clean covers were back on the couch and they were rested enough to rinse off, they'd have a whole new afternoon to enjoy.

"It's crisp and light," Graham confirmed. "Fresh air makes people want to beat the dust out of carpets, that's just a fact."

39.

GRAHAM

After all their hard work in the morning, Graham and Whitney reasoned they could have pizza for lunch and dinner, especially if they made it themselves. Somehow a bread plate of sauce and cheese was infinitely healthier from your own oven than someone else's. Additional facts, science indisputable.

He did his best to distract his mom from her worries as the day went by, sending her images and status updates of everything they did: a POV shot of the foot bath soak; pizza before and after baking shots; puppy after puppy picture because who didn't love those? Only heathens and serial killers.

But the puppy pictures could only do so much good against the progressively bad news from the hospital frontline.

A text came in saying, *I think it's bad news, need to call you.* Graham made his excuses to Whitney and took the call on the porch. Despite the weather finally easing below 80 degrees, the trees were still in ripe summer colors, bright and green.

"What happened, Momma?" he asked when she picked up.

"They told me Tamella's been intubated," she said. "That's a tube, right?"

"Yes, it's a tube down her throat," Grahams said. "It means she's on a ventilator."

"She can't breathe on her own?" Cynthany asked.

"Not well," Graham said. "The ventilator pushes air in and she breathes it back out."

"Does it hurt?" Cynthany wondered. Her voice was smaller this time.

"It's not comfortable, but it's better than gasping for air," Graham said. "And they might have knocked her out for it, so if they did, she's just sleeping."

"A coma isn't sleeping," Cynthany said, trying not to cry.

"It's really common though, they put people under and on ventilators all the time for surgery," Graham reassured her. "Whitney just came out of one and he's fine, more than fine, doing great."

"Yeah, but he's him, and this is my sister," Cynthany said.

There was no disputing that. Graham could offer only cold comfort. "Just focus on what you can do for her when she gets out," Graham said. "When, not if, okay? Maybe clean up her house or something so she comes home to clean sheets, or get your place ready for her so you can take care of her on your turf and not Sage's. How does that sound?"

"Oh, I forgot about Sage," Cynthany said. "She barely even knows about this, I've only been telling you."

"I'll call her for you, give her the update," Graham said, wanting to save her that chore at least. "Just text me what hospital Tamella's at so I can give Sage the number in case she wants to hear about it straight from the source."

"Okay, yeah, thanks," Cynthany said, then sighed. "So, I shouldn't just sit here, I should go home."

"Correct," Graham said. "Do some more cleaning if you need to do something, that'll help later. But if you're too tired, especially if you start getting symptoms, sit the hell down, okay? Take care of yourself. You know you want to skip the hospital if you can."

"Okay," Cynthany said, and Graham heard her start the car. "I gotta go now, gotta drive. You call Sage."

"I'll do it the second we hang up and text you when it's done," Graham said. "Love you, Momma. Love Aunt Tamella too."

The call with Sage was a lot less tender. Graham texted her that there was family drama, so she'd pick up his call, but when she found the drama was illness and not a scandal, she was unimpressed.

"So, she's sick, it got her. It'll get us all eventually, right?" Sage asked. "I live with her, probably have it too, and I'm fine, but she's just old so it's hitting her harder."

"Young people are dying too," Graham said.

"It's like flu, dangerous for old people, and immuno-whatevers, and babies mostly," Sage said.

"It's a luck-of-the-draw thing, and your mom isn't lucky right now, and you have her DNA," Graham said.

"Well, I feel fine," she said, cocky.

"You've got to stay away from people for two weeks starting now," Graham said. He cared less about her health than he did about keeping her from infecting others. "Not trying to boss you, I'm just saying that's the rule, and if you infect other people and they die, their family could sue."

"*Pff*, they can try, but they won't win, it's not like I'm spitting on people," Sage said.

"Where are you?" Graham asked. There was an electronic murmur over the line.

"Just picking up food and heading home, I guess, since I'm radioactive," Sage said.

"The old and the sick and the babies salute you," Graham said. "Heads up, my mom might go over there to clean up a little so Aunt Tam doesn't come home to chores." Sage could help, but if Graham suggested it, she wouldn't.

"Mom would like to walk in and see those nice vacuum lines in the carpet," Sage said. "Get a fresh whiff of Febreze."

"If she doesn't lose her sense of smell for a while, or forever," Graham said. "The long-term side effects are still a mystery."

"Gotcha, well thanks for the update," and that was that. No questions about the whole ventilator thing, serious though it was. No questions about visiting, but Sage and Tamella were always on prickly terms, as much as they loved and needed each other.

The sun was going down, and the temperature with it. Graham gave the blushing sky a once-over, and went inside to stay warm.

40.

WHITNEY

With the evening upon them, Whitney and Graham fulfilled the morning's promise to themselves to watch *Tombstone* once again. Both had seen it multiple times, but both were also shocked by how gay and women's-libby it was too.

"I swear it's like all my trashiest friends love this movie, but they skip over all that freedom talk and just focus in on the guns and the fighting," Graham said as he closed his laptop on the credits, and shifted down on the couch so he could lay his head in Whitney's lap to pontificate up at him. "Like the West was actually made of women running their own whorehouses and saloons, cowboys who were black and brown, but they miss all that to gobble the knobs of sheriff deputies when they definitely hate to see a cop at a party."

"They probably just like the outfits and the authority," Whitney said, as he released curls from Graham's hair that were still in damp clumps after his shower. "Your friends just want a big hat, some boots, and for people to either admire them or clear out of their way when they plod down Main Street."

"Probably," Graham said. "I was right about Curly Bill though, wasn't I? He'd fuck anything living and most things dead."

"I can't wait to ruin my brother's day with the update," Whitney said. "Once I came out and started realizing I had a community, like a historic community, he complained that I was being irrational, trying to make everything gay just because I was."

"He did? Tell him to take it up with history, LOL," Graham said, text-speak part of his language as a digital native far younger than Whitney. For a moment Whitney fretted that Graham was seeing him from a bad angle, all wrinkles and turkey wattle double chin. He shoved the thought away from his consciousness — it was there to darken and sabotage a nice moment. Graham helped dispel it by reaching up to play with his man's ear.

Whitney continued his point. "I showed him an article about how many men President Lincoln slept with, he really hated that."

"Oh, I saw that one. So many men in his bed, in his nightshirts, but only one woman because he had to get married for a political career," Graham said.

"He was sick with having to do it, too. Marriage to a woman broke up him and his boyfriend Joshua Speed," Whitney said.

"Who among us hasn't experienced a love for a Josh of our own, only to watch that guy square up and marry some lady when he was done with us," Graham said, shaking his head which caused it to rock pleasingly back and forth on Whitney's lap. "I feel bad for the Joshuas of the world."

"I feel bad for their ladies," Whitney said. "At least guys like us know the deal and move on to better pastures."

"Right, lucky us," Graham said. "You should tell your brother about Lawrence of Arabia's hobbies next. Dude hired soldiers to come whip him while he exercised naked, that's like so many fetishes in one."

"Masochist, was he?" Whitney asked. "That helps explain why he liked the punishing desert so much. Not what Peter O'Toole said in the movie, 'It's clean,' but because it's painful, and he likes it."

Graham giggled, boyish in the delight of talking about smutty things. "We should watch that movie next, there's hardly a woman in it and none of them speak."

"Like an exact zero on the Bechdel Test," Whitney said. "It's hard enough to find a movie where women speak about anything but men, and yet there are some where they do not speak at all, amazing."

"Yeah, a total sausage fest," Graham said. "Just war and fashion, the two gayest and most cut-throat occupations."

"You think war is gay?" Whitney asked.

"The same way sports are pretty gay, they're just an excuse for manly men to scrutinize and admire each other," Graham said. "You should hear what Ernst Rohm said about gay soldiers."

"The Nazi?" Whitney asked, almost scandalized.

"No, the other Ernst Rohm, of the New Orleans Saints," Graham said with a sarcastic eyebrow raised. "Of course, the Nazi! He was of the opinion that gay men were hyper-masculine and would be especially well-suited for Nazi work because they weren't tied to wives, children, or families that could soften and humanize them."

"I mean, it's an arguable point that detached groups of men have done just about every cruel thing in human history," Whitney said, trying to think of that one time a cabal of women did any mass genocides, and coming up empty.

"Hitler agreed, to an extent," Graham said. "At least he realized that married and family men wouldn't be any good for street fighting, because they had people to live for and protect."

"To be fair to us, if men weren't around to oppress women, maybe they'd get the industry and capital together to start decimating other tribes," Whitney said.

"You'd like to think it's a flaw of human nature to be vicious, not just us men?" Graham asked.

"Yes, apparently. Can you blame me?" Whitney asked.

"Nah, I hope women are down in the mud with us too, I'm a feminist like that," Graham said, which made Whitney laugh, which bumped Graham's head off his lap.

"Don't tell your brother about Rohm, he doesn't help the cause," Graham said as he sat up.

"No need to air our dirty laundry," Whitney said.

"That's right," Graham said, pulling his phone out of his pocket, but cutting his eyes at Whitney for his last piece of advice. "If your brother's churchy, ask him if he knows what's gay about the King James Bible, then tell him it's King James, but that's only the first answer."

It took Whitney damn-near a full minute to recover from laughing, but when he did, he asked, "Speaking of women, how's your mom, your aunt? Any news?"

"Catching up on the texts she sent during the movie," Graham said. "She cleaned up her house, packed some supplies to head over to Tamella's." Scroll, scroll. "Oh shit, she said the house was wrecked, robbed."

"What?" Whitney asked, leaning to look over Graham's shoulder, not that he could read the tiny text at the speed Graham was swiping through it. "Is your cousin okay? Sage?"

Graham looked back at Whitney again, his eyes much darker and harder now, showing the cruel and ruthless soldier latent within.

Graham gave it to Whitney straight: "If money's gone and Sage is gone at the same time, it's because Sage took it."

41.

GRAHAM

Graham got on the phone with his mother for half an hour, pacing outside in the dark at first, but then back inside to start writing down important details. Soon after, it stopped being a private call, and instead he was updating Whitney with every new twist and turn.

Long story short: Cynthany arrived at her hospitalized sister's house and put her key in an unlocked front door. She didn't notice it much at the time, the lack of thunk when the deadbolt threw back, but she would remember it later.

She walked in and thought the living room was cleaner than usual, with fewer shoes piled at the door and not so many clothes laying around the couch either (neither shed dirty ones nor folded clean ones in stacks). But then she found the kitchen with its cabinet doors left open. Not just one door askew, but nearly all of them. She looked closer: the good silverware drawer was missing its contents, and the jar of loose change was gone.

Cynthany assumed the house must have been robbed. She pulled out her phone and tapped 911 but did not hit send. She went quietly through the halls, door to door, to see the extent of the theft, wary that someone might have heard her arrive and was hiding to attack her. She cleared the bathroom and towel closet first, then her sister's room. The jewelry box was dumped out with anything shiny gone, and one drawer from her dresser was pulled out and flipped over. Just one.

Cynthany approached Sage's bedroom last, the room at the back of the house, always out of the sun the way Sage said she preferred.

Sage's room was gutted. The closet empty, the drawers evacuated, and the surfaces cleared leaving only the dusty outline of the keepsakes that used to be there. Cynthany sat on the edge of Sage's bed and understood: Sage had heard her mother was hospitalized, came home to grab all the family cash and valuables, packed her stuff, and disappeared.

That was when the 911 call was canceled, and Graham started getting texts and pictures. Messages like, *Tamella was robbed*, and *Look what happened*, and *What about my house, should I go check?* Several just said, *Call me please*, or *Need a call back*, and finally, *Son, please call*.

Graham was filled with a cold rage as he heard his mom describe all this in a shaky voice. She was trying not to cry, but she was already on edge on the day she saw her sister disappear into the caverns of a quarantine ward. She was trying to stay strong because Tamella was having the worse day; alone, sick, and afraid. Cynthany was trying to hold it together, had come to the house specifically to push back panic with productivity. Right in this vulnerable moment, she found out that someone else who should have been helping had chosen selfishness instead.

"What should I do?" Cynthany asked. "Should I clean up this mess?"

"No, Momma," Graham said. "Don't worry, Tamella won't have to see it like that, I'll go over and clean up myself before that happens."

"And I'll help," Whitney said, leaning closer so that Cynthany might hear.

"What a sweet man," Cynthany said, though she sounded miserable as she said it. "Tell him thanks."

Graham mouthed the words "thank you" at Whitney and carried on talking to his mom. "We gotta report what she did to the cops first thing tomorrow, she can't get away with this crap anymore."

"Don't be mad, her mother's sick, she probably just wants drugs," Cynthany said.

"Of course she just wants drugs, but this is still wrong," Graham said. "If she's worried, she could turn to you, if she's sick of all the stress, she could take solace in a quiet house knowing her mother's got the help she needs. Instead, she robs the woman. How's Aunt Tam supposed to feel when she wakes up and finds out her savings are gone and her daughter's back on the junk again, or even OD'd? That happens a lot when people relapse, they take the shot they were used to when their tolerance was high, and kaput, they're done."

"Don't say that, Graham, I can't even think of it," Cynthany said.

"Okay, I won't," Graham promised. "But go home, you don't have to clean up after her. Don't touch anything, lock up, and go home to make sure she doesn't rob us too on her way to hell."

"Alright, I'll just go home and ... go to bed?" Cynthany asked. "What else can I do?"

"I wish I could be there with you, Momma," Graham said before they exchanged goodbyes, though he was glad he didn't have to sit vigil with her all night over something they couldn't change. Graham could compartmentalize useless worrying about that, most of the time. He'd learned to do it, practiced it, he had to or else his natural anxiety would overwhelm him for a thousand things he had no control over.

Graham had been like this since he was a teenager, fastidious about what was worthy of worry and what was not. It made him come off as uncaring sometimes, but it was an asset while nursing. You don't have time to fret over the patients you can't help, so focus on helping the ones you can, and take care of yourself in between.

All of that was true, but also Graham knew he would not sleep very well that night either.

42.

WHITNEY

The news of Sage's supposed spree was familiar to Whitney. He didn't know her, but he knew exactly what went through her mind when she found out her mother was in the hospital.

First, she realized she had the house to herself and was relieved. Part of her surely wished her mother a speedy recovery, but being a known addict in someone else's house was like being imprisoned in a panopticon: you felt watched at all times. So hooray for Sage, she could finally do whatever she wanted.

Second, she wondered, what was it she wanted to do? Maybe on a different day in another year she would have wanted a bath and pizza delivery, or a cheesecake and a movie marathon, but this was the pandemic year. After so much time in lockdown with her mother hovering over her, and no ability to get a job and get back out on her own, the urge was not to stay home, it was to wile out and get high.

Third, she knew her aunt was on the way. Graham told her that his mother would come to her house to clean, and that would mean someone else watching her, possibly judging her for not being the person who thought to clean first and relax later. She might insist that Sage help clean, criticize her for letting the house get in such disarray in the first place, and ruin her night of peace lest she start a fight by throwing Aunt Cynthany out or barring her from the premises. Time was running out to do something for herself with this window of freedom.

So finally, Sage decided to go for broke. Get home, grab the money, and get gone. This would likely mean severe consequences later, but so what? After all the minding she'd tolerated from her mother, maybe Sage didn't want to be on the hook for her post-COVID care anyway, and if that meant she was barred from ever coming home again, was that so bad? Maybe part of her problem was having a place to fail back to, maybe she needed to have nowhere to go back to before she could move forward.

Whitney kept all of this speculation to himself, because Graham was aflame with outrage and wouldn't want to hear it. Whitney's projections on Sage were one thing, because he remembered all of his jailbreak moments well. The freedom of them, the fuck-you of them, they gave a gambler's high just in the endorphin reward of cutting loose and going for broke.

On the other hand, Whitney also understood the frustration of dealing with addicts because he'd known many himself throughout the years. He understood why people never trust him for example, especially after he'd lied right to their face before. He understood why people hid their money and silver away before he stayed the night, because sometimes seeing a big enough easy score would trigger the old latent pathways of addiction and need. He understood the frustration of giving a person chance after chance, watching them get clean and productive and happy again, only to watch them backslide into an ugly activity they knew good and goddamn well would wreck everything once again.

The problem with addicts is the Dr. Jekyll and Mr. Hyde conundrum. Mr. Hyde had nothing of value, no friends, no good looks, and no purpose. Meanwhile the accomplished, respected, and comfortably wealthy Dr. Jekyll had everything anyone could possibly want … except for the freedom to be Hyde. That was the catch-22 of addiction: Jekyll longed to be Hyde, and Hyde was content as a despised ruffian in a hovel, and society just could not abide such as him.

It remained true that when people like Graham said, "I would never rob my own mother for a temporary high," they knew not of what they spoke. They did not know the high of Hyde, because if they did, they wouldn't boast so boldly about what they would never, ever do under any circumstances.

Whitney let Graham go off though. That night was not the place to play devil's advocate. He agreed that this was a turd cherry on top of a trash sundae, that Cynthany didn't deserve any of this, that Sage had better stay gone if this was how she chose to leave when times got tough.

Graham finally cussed himself to exhaustion. They got confirmation that Sage didn't knock over Cynthany's house too, so the damage was contained for now. The men took and sent multiple pictures of Honey Bun to take the edge off a hard day for Cynthany, but the day was not done.

Graham made sure his phone's sound was on, plus the vibrate, in case his mother had more news throughout the night. In the hushed dark, Whitney was curled against Graham in a way that he could smell his hair while he drifted off to sleep. Nothing against bald men, but Whitney did love the mix of shampoo, scalp, and sweat that perfumed men's hair, the pheromones embedded in their pillows. He was at the bottom edge of pleasantly nodding out when Graham's phone jumped, and he lunged for it, clearly not feeling restful at all.

Whitney could see Graham's face in the dark, lit up by his phone. He was frowning, and then he shook his head. That shake had a lot of quit in it.

"What happened?" Whitney asked quietly.

"Mom's asking me, *What does a pulmonary embolism mean?*" he said, and then began to type back to her.

"That a blood clot in the lungs?" Whitney asked, sitting up.

"Yes," Graham said, "and it means Aunt Tamella's going to die."

PART VII:
RIVERBED

SEPTEMBER 28, 2020 — COVID-19 DEATHS
WORLD DAILY: 4,078 / TOTAL: 1,103,562
US DAILY: 528 / TOTAL: 215,220
LOUISIANA DAILY: 15 / TOTAL: 5,480

43.

GRAHAM

It was a full week between when Tamella's machine turned off and the day of her funeral. During that time, California was getting eaten up by wildfires and so-called firenadoes, a new zealot of the female variety was nominated for the vacant position on the Supreme Court, and someone had done the math to realize that the 200,000 dead Americans from COVID-19 topped the amount of U.S. battle-killed soldiers in the five most recent wars combined (Persian Gulf, Afghanistan, Iraq, Vietnam, and Korea in reverse order). Tamella was only one of them, and Cynthany was currently trying to keep herself from becoming the next, but it was hard.

"I'll never be okay again," was the first thing she said to her son after she got the news that her sister was gone.

Graham couldn't tell her that wasn't true. The woman she was talking to that morning, the one she had known every single day of her life? That person didn't exist anymore. Cynthany couldn't even see her sister's body to say goodbye because she, and it, were contagious.

Graham listened to his mother say everything she had to say the night the embolism took Tamella. He heard her journey through shock, from disbelief saying how it couldn't be true even though it was, how it didn't feel real, but she'd known it was coming for hours somehow. A stark, horrible acceptance finally arrived after midnight.

"I didn't know how I was going to tell her about Sage, but I guess I don't have to now," Cynthany said.

"Well, that's something, Momma," Graham said, after clearing his voice so he wouldn't cry because this wasn't his party to cry at. "Tamella never has to hear any bad news ever again. We're hurting right now, but she's not, and that's something."

"I guess it is," Cynthany said. She decided when she couldn't talk to Graham anymore because she was just too tired. She told him she loved him very much, that he better not try to come comfort her in person because he couldn't get the virus too, she just couldn't handle that. Graham promised to do what he could.

"I'll take care of the phone calls," he told her. "I'll figure out the hospital stuff, the funeral stuff, you can just … do whatever you want to do, like take care of her favorite things. You know she'd trust no one else."

And that's what happened. Cynthany went and got anything cherished, pretty, or high-quality out of her sister's house and consigned the rest of it to Goodwill. Tamella and Sage rented, and it was closer to the end of September than the start of it, and no one would be paying rent for October, so there was no time to waste in clearing out.

Whatever Sage left behind that her aunt didn't find precious was put with the junk. Cynthany kept the baby albums she and Tamella had lovingly created with their own hands and scrapbooking kits. But boxes of Sage's school stuff, her stuffed animals, her childhood furniture and keepsakes? Cynthany had no energy to recover them. Graham agreed with her.

"Sage forfeited her stuff when she took off. Her mom might have come home from the hospital and thrown them out herself, so it was only what she bargained for," he said as he and Whitney did the second pass at Aunt Tamella's to check for any remaining valuables.

Whitney didn't respond, just kept sorting things by type for Graham to review behind him.

"Do you disagree?" Graham asked Whitney. He wasn't trying to pick a fight exactly, but he wasn't preventing himself from approaching the edge either. Whitney never took his bait.

"She knew she'd have to live with the consequences," Whitney told him in Tamella's former living room. He spoke carefully like that, in vague fortunes and platitudes, waiting for Graham to reach an even emotional state again.

It took a few days, days in which Tamella was moved to a crematorium and her body scheduled for incineration. Days in which they decided if Cynthany couldn't attend a funeral while COVID-positive, they just wouldn't have one. The whole tragedy felt unfinished no matter how many chores they crossed from the list: canceling subscriptions, notifying banks, getting confirmations from the hospital, the landlord, the county. Cynthany said the moment they had her ashes, she wanted Graham to let them go.

"Just pick a spot on the river," she said, her breath labored though she was still well enough to stay home and be sick on her own recognizance. "Can't rest ... until she's ... at rest."

So then it was just a matter of waiting for the pickup day, because the crematoriums and funeral homes and mortuaries, they were all backed up. Big cities had refrigerated trucks outside of hospitals for the overflow of dead, mass graves were back, the carnage was real. But still, people didn't see it on TV, so they were still spitting and snotting on employees at the stores that remained open, angry that someone making minimum wage would dare tell them to wear a mask.

The whole time Whitney helped. He handled any tasks that didn't need personal information, he did the heavy lifting to move the dusty crap of somebody else's aunt. He had nothing to say that wasn't agreeable, heartfelt, or an offer of food. Finally, Graham took time to recognize that behavior for what it was.

The night before they would drive to pick up Tamella's ashes and drop her off in the river, Graham found himself sitting in Whitney's bed, with all his things on the nightstand. At some point, he had moved almost entirely out of the guest room except to use it as a wardrobe and office for any work that needed his full focus. Graham realized how kind it was that Whitney had made room for him, literally cleared the nightstand of his own stuff so that Graham could take over, which he did in the moment without comment, though it was well past time to acknowledge it now.

Whitney was closing the rest of the house, checking locks and stove knobs, and turning off lights. When he returned to the bedroom and got under the covers, Graham got on top of him and held his face between both hands.

He had planned to say something. He wanted to say thank you, tell Whitney that he was so kind, so patient, that he was the greatest man to have ever given him the time of day in the first place, let alone gone the extra mile to help out with miserable family garbage like an older lady's funeral.

But Whitney didn't need to hear it. He saw what Graham wanted to say written all over his face, smiled at him, and nodded. They kissed themselves to sleep on the eve of a very long day.

44.

WHITNEY

Whitney awoke at the sound of his alarm clock, a rare noise during lockdown for him, only needed previously on the day of his surgery. He got dressed in silence, putting on a funeral suit of sorts, not all black, but not really the sort of thing you'd wear to anything joyous either. Funerals, a tax audit meeting, court if you messed up but not if you were getting married.

Graham looked haggard, shoulders drooping and defeated, eyes in a watery wince like there was a migraine behind them. He didn't say anything as they dressed and ate oatmeal, so Whitney didn't speak either.

Whitney assumed he would do the driving that day, and Graham didn't contradict him. First stop was the funeral home just over the state line in Mississippi, where a simple cremation and what the person they spoke to called a "plain Jane" urn cost over $3,000 dollars. It was an ugly little place with somber furniture offset by glaring fluorescent lights. Whitney had been to a few court-ordered Narcotics Anonymous meetings in places like that, bingo-hall-type spots where the carpet had always been flat. The chairs were cloth, and so smelled musty after a while. The art, mirrors, and certificates on the walls were all hung unevenly with no eye for balance. The cords to speakers, air conditioning units, and lamps were all exposed, either taped down to the floor to reduce the risk of tripping, or dangling against the bare portions of beige walls.

At least that was what the interior looked like in pictures online, they would not be walking into the establishment. Only the previously-held body of Ms. Tamella Clare Kincaid was to enter, and someone would meet them outside with the jar of her ashes once they texted their arrival.

In the parking lot, on a day so sunny it seemed fake as if the daylight came from a lamp, they sat in silence. Graham rolled down the window after the quiet became too much, and took a deep breath of late-September air. Not exactly autumn in the South yet, but certainly thinking about it. It was a balmy 64 degrees that morning. The high of the day would only just touch 80.

No radio this morning, no music. Whitney snapped it off the second he started the engine out of a personal fear that any song he heard today would forever remind him and Graham of the events, places, sights, and smells. He had learned to prevent triggers from forming, basically, having developed so many in his time on the earth.

Whitney shifted and remembered his surgery scar, so took off his seatbelt since they weren't moving anyway. The skin was healed over, but his worry for the area had not, he still considered it weaker and more vulnerable. It would need a few more weeks to fully heal under the surface, and he didn't want to squeeze it if he didn't have to. He was rubbing the spot in blood-flow-stimulating circles when Graham finally had something to say.

"Why are you doing this for me? If you don't mind me asking," Graham said.

"Why wouldn't I? You've already done plenty for me," Whitney said, pointing at the scar he was fretting over. "In fact, so did Tamella, didn't she? So, I'm doing it out of respect for her too."

"I don't just mean today," Graham said. "Or even helping clean out her house, which was extra. I mean this whole time letting me just share what you've got. I mean I know there's an age difference here but I'm no sugar baby, and yet you've been babying me."

Whitney had been a sugar baby more times than he'd been any sort of daddy or even mentor. He knew why people did it with him: because he was a sexy young thing once, and because he knew a few famous names, and because they thought they could make him more like them and thus take credit for whatever Whitney eventually became. That was true in the sense that he became a drug addict, they could see the mark of their own fingerprints there. But anything that Whitney was proud to have become had nothing to do with them, had more to do with his family, and the friends who came around even when he was broke and ugly.

So why was he doing all this for Graham, what was he getting out of it? At first amusement and affection, sure, but what was keeping him in for the broken and ugly?

"I'm doing all this with you because ... it just feels right," Whitney said. "I meet you at an illegal show, I either invite you home or I don't, and the invitation feels right. I find out you're living cramped with your mother while I'm in a big house all alone, I either move you in or I don't, and the move feels right. You lose somebody who was kind to me, and your mother is so sick she needs help, tell me ... am I supposed to sit that out while you go off and deal with it alone?"

"You could've," Graham said. "It would have been fine enough to just kiss me goodbye in the mornings and wish me luck and be nice to me when I got back all sweaty and sad."

"But it wouldn't have felt right," Whitney said.

That was the long and the short of it. The work wasn't fun, but if Graham was picking through a dead woman's things all by himself, Whitney couldn't exactly enjoy his own leisure. Had he been a different kind of person, a bigger bastard, maybe such behavior wouldn't have shadowed his relaxation, but being who he was, and with the debts he felt still weighted against him on a soul level, Whitney couldn't resist doing the right thing when it plopped in his lap like that. There was still an element of vanity to it even as he did for others, perhaps. But it was the actions that mattered most, that's what all the good preachers said.

Graham got the text that his aunt's ashes were ready, and he showed it to Whitney. It also asked could he please come to the front of the building masked and stand at the table being set out for him. Upon looking up they confirmed: someone was unfolding the legs of a card table and setting a clipboard and pen on it before retreating inside.

Graham put on a surgical mask and went to sign for the ashes alone. Graham watched him do-si-do with the woman at the door, who apparently asked him to step back six feet to a place marked off with tape before she came to collect the paperwork. She then brought out the ashes, which were in a bag in an urn in a box.

Whitney remembered Koshchei the Deathless, with his soul in an egg in a basket in a chest buried at sea. He said his death was far away and hard to find, and yet someone found it, and brought it right back home to him.

45.

GRAHAM

As Graham Googled around for local crematoriums and mortuaries, he came across articles lamenting the dying of the "deathcare" business during the pandemic. Even though people were dying in droves, business was apparently not a-booming. They couldn't hold big in-person funerals, viewings could only be held in intervals of ten people at a time, and people weren't spending money on lavish flowers for the event. When half a family got wiped out at once, no one had the cash for an ornate tombstone, basically.

Graham felt no sympathy for the industry. He'd never buried anyone himself before, but he had a fair understanding of the uselessness of the big, expensive, luxurious coffins for corpses, covers embroidered for viewing but forever sideways for the stiff in the box. The articles talked of the lack of "pre-need" plot sales because people weren't coming in for the sales pitch of buying their own graves anymore. Funeral homes could hold that money and invest with it from the day a person forked it over to the day they died, and now their money wasn't coming in anymore, boo hoo.

Maybe big families needed a catering service to get together, maybe rich people needed an event to mourn when everyone else just went to church and then to the widow's kitchen for a potluck. It didn't mean he cared that up-selling death merchants were feeling the pinch during a global plague, just like everybody else.

Whitney said he knew a few spots along the Mississippi that were pretty enough to stop and have a picnic at. The plan was to tour them until they found one without onlookers, but the first they came to was vacant and available. Lucky them.

The sky was clear, the water murky. Graham took a deep breath of the air, a little ripe with the smell of the water, but lighter than the air in the car for sure. His face mask was off for now, but he had it ready to go for when it came time to scatter the ashes. Just in case the breeze tossed the cremains back at them, at least they wouldn't have to swallow Aunt Tamella. As with household cleaning, now that face masks were an option in the USA, Graham would never be without them again in some situations. They were a must-have for scattering ashes.

Cynthany couldn't get out of bed, but until she was critical, she would absolutely not submit herself to the hospital. Plenty of people were sick enough to get admitted but there wasn't space, so they prioritized people healthy enough to survive on the few ventilators available and asked the old and infirm to go home to die on their own. It sounded cruel, but Graham thought they should do that more often. Dying in hospitals is bleak, bright, noisy, and impersonal. Dying in your own bed is a relative delight if you've got to do it one way or the other.

But Cynthany wasn't dying, at least they didn't think so. She was struggling, she was breathing in shallow, quick breaths, but she was expected to limp through it. Graham called her on an electronic tablet so they could be face-to-face at a distance for her sister's last goodbye. He offered to wait for her to get better so she could participate, but Cynthany said she couldn't get better if the first thing she had to look forward to was a misery. Graham would bring her back to this spot later if she wanted that, a place where she could stand and think and say something to the dead if she wished.

"Hey, Momma," he said to her. "No issues this morning. They gave us Aunt Tamella's ashes very respectfully, and we're dressed nice, and the weather's good."

"The trees across from here bloom in the spring," Whitney said, having unboxed the urn and checked that the ashes were indeed ashes and not sand or kitty litter. "It's a very nice place to stand all year, and they can't tear down the Mississippi, so it'll always be here."

"That's true," Cynthany said. "Nothing hurts that river."

Graham put a wireless earbud in one of his ears so he could hear his mother over the distance for this business. He gave Whitney the other earbud. He told his mother the plan.

"You can hear me? And Whitney?" Cynthany nodded, and Graham nodded back. "Okay, that's good. I'm going to do the scattering, and Whitney's going to hold the iPad here so you can see. Whitney also offered to sing if you like?"

"That's a nice idea," Cynthany said. "What song?"

It was Alison Krauss's "Down To The River To Pray" since Cynthany and Tamella both liked her, thought her voice sounded like clear water. And the sentiment was right, would fit the time, the place, the occasion.

As Whitney started singing, Graham got started, opening the bag of cremains like a blooming petal so that it wrapped around the urn's rim. He knew this wouldn't last longer than two, three minutes tops, and got to it, tossing the urn without dropping it into the wind four, five, six times and watching the dust hover in small clouds before dissipating. Ashes to air, earth, and water.

Fortunately, nothing significant blew back on him, which was good luck because it would have stuck right to the tears that fell from his eyes. Instead, the paper face mask caught his tears, a mask that the scientists said could have prevented this virus from reaching his aunt at the wrong time and causing all of this heartache.

Graham snapped the mask off and let it rise into the wind too, so that when he turned around, no one would see the darker spots caused by his crying. That was more "Tears of a Clown," and they weren't singing that one today, no matter how well it suited Graham this and every damn day of his life.

46.

WHITNEY

Whitney finished singing his song and handed Cynthany back to Graham for their goodbye, giving them a little space as the grieving family. He took the urn back to the car wondering if it would become a vase just like the others in his house. By the time his grandmother left him the house, there wasn't a vase in it that hadn't first been an urn.

When Graham joined him again, they quickly decided it was time to eat. In late September of 2020, only a scant few restaurants were open.

Of course, some food joints that closed for six months in lockdown would never open again. Even in good times keeping restaurants open and profitable was a struggle on a prayer, but after sending people home and selling supplies in pre-made kits, plenty of them weren't going to have the money or the will to come back, especially if it meant fighting with ornery locals who didn't want to wear their masks between bites.

Just last week Whitney had shown Graham a new report from *Morbidity and Mortality Weekly*, mostly because he thought the name of such a publication would amuse him (and it did). It said that since eateries were allowed to open again, those testing positive for COVID were two and a half times more likely to have recently dined out, and four times more likely to have visited a bar. Basically, the people getting sick next week would be the people having a sit-down lunch today, so Whitney and Graham wouldn't chance it.

They went to a drive-thru for comfort food: fried chicken, biscuits, and gravy. They got three kinds of potatoes for sides: mashed, tot, and hash. It was that kind of day, the sort where you ate your feelings without shame, because there was no better way to process them as quickly as they needed to be dealt with.

Not ready to go back inside yet, Whitney went to one of the other pretty river spots he'd had in mind for spreading ashes, and they ate their food on the hood of the car, squinting in the sunlight and using their drinks to pin down the wrappers before the wind could snatch them away. Other than that, the breeze was nice. It ruffled their hair but didn't throw sand in their food. Weather-wise it was the perfect day, but considering the occasion that brought them outside, it was more like Lou Reed's "Perfect Day."

In between fries, Graham had something to say.

"You know, I'm really grateful for you," Graham said. "I don't know if I could have lived through all this on my own, and the only reason I'm not on my own is you. You're kind of a blessing to me, and I just hope I'm not a burden on you in return."

Graham kept eating like what he said was no more profound than saying, "I think it's going to freeze tonight." In a way, it was that simple a statement, just as plain and regular as the forecast.

"I know exactly when I felt the same way about you," Whitney said. "That day I dropped the mason jar of chia seeds, remember? It was before my surgery, and you were sitting with Honey Bun in your lap like a toddler, and I had my earbuds in so maybe you thought I wasn't listening, and I mostly wasn't but then there was a long silent tail on the end of one song, and I heard what you were saying to her."

"Oh yeah?" Graham said. "I was just telling her about how fine her daddy is."

"That's right," Whitney said. "There you were, cozy in my house, whispering sweet nothings to my dog about all the wonderful things you thought about me. That I was handsome, and talented, and that I loved her very much, and I thought … how the fuck did I ever get so lucky, that this was a day in my life? I was so glad none of my ODs ever took, so glad I had lived so long and in the exact way that I did it, if all of that meant having such a moment with you. I felt so blessed I accidentally dropped what I was holding."

"The jar of chia seeds," Graham said, nodding, remembering.

"Maybe if they'd only have knocked over on the counter instead of shattered on the floor I'd have said as much to you right then," Whitney said.

"Right, because it's not that much of a blessing when we're still finding those chia seeds on the bottoms of our feet."

Whitney smiled, shook his head. "Maybe I should have said it then anyway, after you finished up telling the dog, 'He's a ten but he's a clumsy sommabitch,' but I missed the window."

Graham smiled now with the sun and the wind and his hair in his eyes. "You didn't miss the window," he said. "This was the exact right time I needed to hear it."

Whitney reached over and grasped Graham's shoulder, then placed his palm against Graham's cheek. For his next breath, Whitney swore he could taste the sunlight on the air. They held for a beat, before both looked back out at the water. They'd said something important today, something good, but it was also unsurprising, and once said, changed nothing except what they were calling the feelings that had long been present.

Graham washed down his last bite of food with the last slurp of his soda. Whitney wiped his hands on his pants, ignoring the napkins he then folded up with the wrappers and other trash. Graham hopped down from the hood of the car and stretched his legs.

"Do you want to go home after this?" Whitney asked. "Or stay out in the sunshine as long as possible, maybe go for a hike?"

Graham thought for a moment and asked, "Honestly?"

"Of course," Whitney said. They were one-and-oh for honesty today, one-and-only, they were winning with honesty.

"I want to go home and fuck in the sunshine," Graham said. "All afternoon, if possible."

Whitney wanted that too.

47.

GRAHAM

On the drive home, Graham thought about how sex was a reaffirmation of life. It was inherently a life-affirming thing because it only existed, evolutionarily, for reproduction, but even sex that had no hope of seeding new life still proved to people: *I am potent, productive, vigorous, vital, alive.*

He'd seen a documentary years ago, *Paragraph 175*, named after the anti-sodomy provision of the German penal code that made gay men subject to arrest and deportation to the death camps under the Nazis. In an interview with a homosexual Holocaust survivor, the man described being herded into train cars, cattle cars. Knowing that their destination would be a new kind of torment, rather than pray, or mourn, or be consumed by fear, he said that a "closeness" developed between the men. What he meant was that he and the others got their rocks off with the random strangers who were along for the ride.

The interviewer was shocked. They were standing on a train to help really summon the trauma, tap into that sensory experience, but who was disturbed now, huh? Graham loved that. He loved that the interviewer, a gay man himself, was seemingly more floored by a hand job than the gas chambers at that point, like … what else was a fellow condemned to die supposed to do? Was it rude to defile the death train? Was the man wrong to want to get his cock out one last time before being exterminated? Graham treasured that man so much, who knew that he had to enjoy every second of life he had left, and didn't let the bastards get him down even in that darkest hour when the forces of evil had won. Had Graham been at all a man of faith, he'd be saying a prayer for that fucker every night of his life.

But probably an afternoon of sex was as fine a way to honor him as any other. Achieve orgasm to appreciate the life he still had, knowing exactly how temporary it was, and how quickly it could be snatched away.

Graham wasn't kidding about wanting to fuck in the sunshine; he moved Whitney's bed over to the sunny window in his room so they could bask in nude comfort. He put on a trance playlist he had, songs without lyrics that were all five minutes long or more, songs good for staring into the middle distance and letting one's mind go blank, like white noise but with a string accompaniment.

Whitney gave the dog a chew bone to make sure she didn't feel neglected while the grown-ups played, and went to the bathroom to prepare. Graham got completely nude and did some limbering stretches. He started with toe touches, to feel the tendons that ran through the backs of his legs like bow strings. He then reached for the sky to feel his blood go somersaulting out of his head and make him forget which direction the ground was for a second. Next, he put his arms out in a T shape, crucifix-style, to make the small circles his elementary school gym teachers taught him, and to give his rib cage as much room as possible so that his lungs could fill to the max for that natural oxygen high.

Whitney opened the bathroom door again, equally nude. He leaned in the frame, striking a pose as he stroked himself firmer and firmer. They smiled, because it was almost funny, but didn't quite merit laughter.

Graham unfurled an arm from shoulder to fingertips, an invitation to dance. Whitney accepted, and moved in a slow twirl on his way to Graham's arms. They were still half-smiling as they started to sway.

A slow rhythm, rubbing tummies together, getting used to really touching each other. After weeks and months in the same house, many nights in the same bed, touching insides with outsides, there were still places unfondled, underappreciated.

Graham started at the top and intended to feel his way down: hands up through Whitney's hair, draw the whorl of his ears, feel the pulse in his neck. A nibble of collar bone, a sniff of underarms, a kiss on the thin-skinned spots at his elbows and wrists where needles had punctured before.

Graham took one knee and then the other, looked closely at Whitney's bellybutton as though it were a peephole. He had never really noticed it before and felt that he should — this is the spot where the man before him first grew in the womb, and this and all of him wouldn't be here forever. None of them would.

A wave of fatalism hit Graham, but he just hugged Whitney's waist until it passed, rocking his head side to side against his underbelly. *No no no* to thoughts of entropy, futility, and death. These attentions stimulated Whitney enough that his engorged shaft rose up to meet Graham's lips. *Kiss kiss kiss* until Graham reached the lips that parted down below, then looked up to see the lips that parted above.

Before Whitney could think to speak and break the meditation Graham wanted this to be, he started to suck, remembering the sensual bits of Walt Whitman's poetry he'd done an uncharacteristic amount of reading to unearth and understand because it was the gayest thing in his backwater library, hidden under the rich Americana of the man's legend:

> *I mind how once we lay such a transparent summer morning,*
> *How you settled your head athwart my hips and gently turn'd*
> *over upon me,*
> *And parted the shirt from my bosom-bone, and plunged your*
> *tongue to my bare-stript heart,*
> *And reach'd till you felt my beard, and reach'd till you held my feet.*

If that wasn't the kind of fellatio that could spin a world on the axis of the male member, his bare-stript heart, Graham just didn't know the meaning of life and never would.

He fluffed Whitney to the next threshold of arousal, then took him to bed. He was there to roll across the sheets, feel them cool in the shade and warm under the sun. He wanted to lay atop Whitney and then flip to feel weighed down by him. He wanted to spend hours there if he could, luxuriating, edging, delaying gratification. Today was about being tantric, less about penetrating and more about inhabiting.

They didn't need to speak, so they said nothing. They didn't need to stop, so they kept going. The magic held until the sky changed shades, and the dog needed them back again. Graham almost cried when he came, but didn't.

48.

WHITNEY

Whitney spent the rest of his day after their tantric sex-perience cuddling on the couch with Honey Bun in his arms. Graham asked to be left alone for a while, first splayed out on the bed in the sun, and then as he talked with his mother over the phone, telling his own stories of Tamella and then listening to hers. There was a lot of sniffling and comforting going on that felt private, so Whitney stayed out of it.

Whitney couldn't help but remember the other funerals he'd attended for women who'd loved him. He whispered some of it into the velvety earflaps of his puppy.

"My mother's funeral was gross," he told her. "Family that didn't approve of her, industry people who were never her friends, fans who didn't know her at all. Her own mother skipped it because that was the right call, but me and my brother went because ... I dunno, we thought we had to?"

Honey Bun gazed back up with placid devotion, and Whitney kissed her forehead a few times in the center spot where there was a divot perfectly sized for human kisses.

"Now Granny's funeral was much nicer, almost too nice," Whitney said. "Like how is the finest, bloomin'-est spring day that ever was supposed to be sad?"

Honey Bun heard the question's intonation and cocked her head. Whitney started massaging both ears in a way that made her tail thump happily against the couch cushions. Graham was right: dogs were too good for the likes of man. The way she was conforming to fit him, every sound he made, every face he pulled, that overwhelming and obedient devotion. What had he ever done to deserve such love? Nothing. He had been stumbling-high at his grandmother's nice funeral, and she had left him this house to give him a chance to get right. It had worked, or at least it had helped, but he hardly deserved it.

Graham was feeling grateful for Whitney's help today at least, so perhaps Whitney had paid his grandmother's good grace forward. Today he was the steady one so that other people could grieve and be messy if they needed to be. If there was a heaven, Whitney's dead women were probably nodding in approval down from one of the highest clouds today. Their boy was doing right at the moment.

In another week, Graham's mother would hopefully be cured of COVID-19 and out of quarantine. At that point, Graham would have to be the steady one again, with Whitney but a bit player in another family's drama.

"We have other things to worry about, don't we?" Whitney asked Honey Bun. Though she hadn't been privy to his internal logic, she was still in total agreement with whatever he was proposing now. "We gotta make sure Granny's house don't get ate up by the hurricanes, yeah?"

Honey Bun was in, ready to rock and roll. Whitney pulled his phone out to check the internet, see what was brewing and possibly heading their way.

The year's hurricane names were being taken from the Greek alphabet, the one that gave us the very word "alphabet" in that it went Alpha, Beta, Gamma, Delta, and so on. So far Alpha and Beta tropical storms had come and gone without bother, but any one of them might ramp up into a full hurricane and wreak havoc.

"You name a storm after the fraternity letters, you're bound to get some messy ones," Whitney mused.

Honey Bun was falling asleep now that Whitney was distracted by his phone, and only blinked in acknowledgment of his insight.

Whitney wondered if it wasn't a good time for a nap himself, but hardly had the thought before Graham emerged from the bedroom to join him in the big chair. Whitney remembered the first night they met, when he'd been kissing Graham in that chair. And then the way Graham tended to Whitney in that very same chair when he came home from his hernia surgery. Granny's old Bible-reading chair sure was seeing some interesting sights these days.

Whitney craned his neck so he could see Graham without disturbing the sleeping pooch by his side. "How's your mother?" he asked softly.

"I should be jealous, you two look so in love over there," Graham said, before answering, "Mom's as good as she can be. Breathing's still hard, she's got no one but me to talk to now and I'm not her friend like her sister was, I never will be. She's got a couple of other old gal pal friends but it's been years since she talked to them and she won't reach out until she can actually speak without gasping."

"That could be good," Whitney said. "Reaching out like that I mean, sometimes old friends aren't estranged, they're just on ice until you need them." Whitney had a few like that, not a word or a card for years until something serious happened and someone called to catch up. Then suddenly you're on the phone for hours, vomiting up traumas and gashing open old wounds just to let them breathe. It didn't seem like it should be healthy but it was. Venting was an antiseptic that kept misery from becoming toxic.

"Yeah," Graham said. "I think she'll be alright in the end, but that's not what she thinks, and her opinion matters more for whether she'll actually get better. The first thing she told me this afternoon was, 'I'll never be okay again,' and I can't exactly argue with her. Tamella wasn't supposed to die now, they were supposed to always have each other, but there's no fixing it, no way to make it right."

Graham's voice quavered at the end of that pronouncement, and he took a big, shaky breath trying to keep back tears. Whitney tensed, ready to get up and go to him, but Graham held out one hand and used the other to pinch between his eyes.

"Don't you dare wake up that sleeping angel on my account," Graham said, which made them both look down at their doggy daughter and smile to see her chasing rabbits in her sleep.

49.

GRAHAM

Graham thought his day was over. It was one of the longest days of his life, right up there with every other demolishing disappointment, like getting kicked out of the nursing job he thought would be his forever career, his whole identity. It was like three days in one already: sending Aunt Tamella back home to the God some people believed in; reviving himself with Whitney; and then comforting his mother until she was tired enough to rest. On top of all this personal tragedy, his mother was also despondent. She just wanted to sleep until this day was over, and Graham talked to her until she was tired enough to try.

But after all that, Graham's work still wasn't done.

While Whitney was moving the bedroom back in place, and the sun was about to go down, Graham got a call from a number he didn't recognize. Like most of his friends and fellow Millennials, Graham never picked up his phone for an unknown number. He didn't know how they did political polls with the likes of him, and assumed the phone scammers cursed the whole generation of them for having phones in their hands all day and every day, but never picking up.

However, today was an outlier. It could be someone calling about Tamella's property, some bill they didn't cancel, some confirmation still needed. So he lifted up one buttcheek from the good chair to dig his phone out of his pocket, and he answered.

"Hello, this is Graham Morrow," like he was the secretary of his own life and existence.

"Oh, Graham, thank God you answered, buddy." It was Sage. Of all people on the planet, it was Sage. "I got arrested for some bullshit, being in the wrong guy's house. Nothing's gonna stick, but I need someone to call my lawyer and post bail, and I can't get ahold of my mom. Is she still in the hospital or something?"

Graham could hardly believe what he was hearing. Of course, Sage didn't know what had happened. She had gone off the radar before Tamella had given up the ghost, so she had the audacity to call Graham thinking everything was still as she had left it, that she could still come home, make her excuses, and be let back in.

"Hello? Graham, I'm on limited time here, are we still connected?"

Graham didn't know what to say for a moment, frozen with outrage, wanting to lash out, or just hang up and let Sage stew in her ignorance for as long as possible. But he didn't do either when he spoke. A calm, mature voice of seriousness took hold, and just let out the facts.

"Sage, after you took your mom's money and left, she died," Graham said. Sage was silent, but he could still hear the hustle and bustle of whatever jail she was calling from in the background. "Aunt Tamella never knew that you stole from her, which I'm glad about, for her sake, but she's gone. You meant so much to her, and you weren't even around to hear about it."

"What happened?" Sage asked. "She was healthy, did the hospital fuck up?"

Graham wondered if Sage was already thinking about bringing a malpractice suit. Not a second of mourning before she was trying to make this tragedy work for her. But he didn't make any accusations, he didn't have the energy for it. Sage didn't deserve his curses even, he owed nothing to her but this last bit of information.

"I won't be calling anyone for you," Graham said. "With Tamella gone, you don't have a family anymore, not in me or in Cynthany, you hear that? I'm going to block your number from my phone after this, and if you come near my mom's house, we'll call the police with suspicion that you're trying to rob us too. We already filed a report saying what you took from your dying mother, so if they don't get you for whatever it is you did when you left, you'll absolutely be in trouble for that."

"Are you serious?" Sage said, her voice getting shrill in Graham's ear. This was about to make her hysterically angry, but let her fume — it didn't shake Graham's resolve at all. "You're just going to abandon me after my mother died?"

Graham's lip twitched in a sneer. That was when Whitney leaned around the corner. He'd been listening.

It was time to say goodbye to Sage. "Her funeral was today, you missed it. We scattered her ashes in the Mississippi. Tell your problems to the river from now on."

Graham hung up before he could hear what else Sage had to say. He blocked the police station's number and her cellphone, then deleted her from his phone's contacts. Graham tossed the phone on the coffee table, and looked up at Whitney, ready to defend himself.

"You think I was too harsh?" Graham asked. "Is that a shitty thing to do to an addict, drop-kick them when they're down?"

Whitney came forward and knelt in front of Graham, leaned in between his knees, and kissed him before speaking. "You're not responsible for her choices, only your own. There are some people who used to be in my life who never will be again because of how we left off when I was high or jonesing. Do I wish they'd come back? Sometimes, but sometimes I think it's better this way. There's no fixing what happened, and if you try to force a present connection, the past can't die."

"Let the dead lie?" Graham asked.

"It's fair," Whitney said. "I'm certainly not offended, and I didn't even like your cousin."

Graham smiled. He realized he had wanted Whitney's permission to cut Sage off, and now he had it, and a burden was lifted. He didn't have to feel guilty, Whitney said so, and as a former addict himself, he had the authority to grant absolution as far as Graham was concerned.

"You know something? I never liked her either." Graham scooted forward to give Whitney a fierce, back-cracking kind of hug.

They were in a good place that night. In the next week, they would learn that their good place was in the direct path of Hurricane Delta.

PART VIII:
AUGEAN

OCTOBER 9, 2020 — COVID-19 DEATHS
WORLD DAILY: 5,990 / TOTAL: 1,164,986
US DAILY: 879 / TOTAL: 223,737
LOUISIANA DAILY: 26 / TOTAL: 5,604

50.

WHITNEY

Whitney was usually well-prepared for a storm on most days, and never had to enter into panic-buying. He certainly would have imagined it would be worse during COVID lockdowns. Scarcity was a little more real because of supply chain delays, and people were a lot more desperate. Whitney had cans of water in his pantry (not plastic because the chemicals leech) that could last decades. He had two backup packs of batteries for every one device he might need: a camp lamp, a technology charger, a portable radio. He never expected to be standing on a dot in a socially-distanced line out the door and around the side of the Walmart to get what he was allowed to buy this year or any year while he maintained a sound mind. But he was shopping for someone else for this storm: Graham's mother.

Whitney would have rather given her half of his supplies and hoped for the best, but Graham was worried they wouldn't have enough. Cynthany was still struggling with what they were calling "long COVID" symptoms, meaning even though her body was just about done with the live virus, she was still having trouble breathing. Her thinking was still sluggish, and her body still ached. Those symptoms could last weeks or months or longer, nobody knew for sure at this point. In someone as old as Cynthany, they could plague her for the rest of her life.

So when Graham said he was going over to board up his mother's windows against the storm, and asked Whitney if he could go pick up what he could from a store, Whitney couldn't say no. Not without hating himself at least, because a no then would have wounded Graham, and the sight of that sting would have made Whitney feel ill, so there he was.

In front of Whitney was a mother trying to hold onto her sanity and an antsy toddler at the same time, a dangerously precarious balance. A man just behind him was wearing a red MAGA hat and a bullish look on his face like he would just love for someone to say something about it, because he was itching to fight or rant or both. Whitney was in short sleeves, and despite being plenty warm in this temperate Southern October weather, he was hugging his arms trying to stay away from the air, which could carry disease.

Once inside, Whitney was only able to get the pre-portioned amount of certain storm staples. Just two jugs of water per person, one large or two small packs of toilet paper, and just one container of bleach or disinfecting wipes while supplies lasted. Whitney skipped the bleach in favor of vinegar instead since it too had disinfecting properties. He got what he could in toilet paper and canned soup. The water and batteries were conveniently taped together because the store knew why they were selling what they were selling and made it easier for everyone. Not that this got them any better treatment from people who were harried, offended, and in need.

Transaction complete, Whitney stood in the parking lot and sprayed his packages and the exposed parts of himself down with a mix of vinegar and water he already had in his car. This was done in an attempt to sanitize it all to the best of his ability before loading up the items and hopping behind the driver's seat once more. He thought when he first took this task that he would hit both the Walmart and the Target to get double supplies, really make an effort on behalf of his man, but once safely locked in his vehicle, Whitney found himself the coward. He didn't want to do that again, and he didn't have to, and no one but him would know he ever had the thought to be more kind, more generous, and he would just eat that thought and swallow it down with his other secrets. Whitney had some real bruisers in the Secrets Jail — this wimp of a regret would be disappeared by the big thugs in due time.

As he arrived at Cynthany's house and found Graham fighting with a drill as he held up a window-covering board on his own, Whitney flashed briefly over the memories of people who had done this for him before: got him groceries, cleaned up his place, made repairs on his behalf. His efforts today had already tapped him out, and Graham and his kind, sick, grieving mother were far more worthy of the help. Whitney turned off the engine and was frozen by the thought: *Why had anyone ever helped him?* This was the first time he was doing the same for someone else in years, decades even. It was a wonder that he hadn't been left to his own devices since they were all he deserved.

"A little help, my dude?" Graham called out as the board in his grasp threatened to wobble over and possibly amputate one of his toes if it landed on his foot.

"Yeah," Whitney said, though Graham couldn't hear him in the car. A little help was about all he could offer, and he snapped out of his memories to give it.

51.

GRAHAM

Graham hugged Whitney as soon as they were done securing the window. He was sweaty from laboring for the past hour and Whitney was potentially contaminated from the interactions at the grocery store, but some things just couldn't be sterile. Someone once told him that if sex was safe, you were doing it wrong; probably that applied to love and family too.

"You smell like salt and vinegar chips," Graham said, because it was true, and he was hungry.

"I already wiped down all the stuff I got, should we haul it in for her?" Whitney asked.

"I would, but she's still in quarantine and says the house isn't safe and we better not come in," Graham said. He was allowed to get the window covers out of the garage and was told to help himself to the hose for water because even her glasses she felt were too radioactive to touch.

"Porch drop it is, then," Whitney said, before lowering his voice to ask, "How's she doing?"

"It hurts to hear her breathe," Graham said. She'd had to speak to him through the phone even though he was right outside her windows because she didn't have the lung strength to project. It was like being 9 years old again, told to play outside and stay outside until the streetlights came on because the adults had had their fill of childish things and needed a break all day and every day. Summers were always like that, and after school throughout the rest of the year. Graham tried not to feel resentful as he helped his mother, though part of him did acknowledge that all those years of neglect could be paid back now, if he wanted to be petty. But then life was being cruel enough to Cynthany at the moment, and she had let him come to stay with her indefinitely before Whitney plucked him away, and what one put out to others would invariably come back ten-fold later, so Graham simply did his best to avoid splinters and tried to think of this task as a free workout instead of chores.

Whitney helped him finish the front windows, and then they piled the fresh supplies on the patio chairs.

"Momma, you come get this stuff while we clean up the yard, okay?" Graham called out. "Because then we need to put these chairs in the garage."

Cynthany's reply came as a thumbs-up emoji text. Graham and Whitney started a search pattern around the house looking for anything problematic in the grass. They found a rusted pair of hedge clippers long ago abandoned under a wildly unpruned bush. There were a few pieces of trash that had blown in like a plastic water bottle and a styrofoam plate that they just left until the inevitable post-storm cleanup. At the end of their trek, Graham disconnected the hose he'd drunk from earlier to tuck it safely in the garage too, while Whitney observed Cynthany on the porch taking in supplies one by one because it was all she had the energy for. Once clear, they each took one of the two porch chairs to safe storage.

"We're gonna head out now, stay safe, okay?" Graham shouted through the door before joining Whitney back at the car. The reply he got via text was worrisome, *Take care of each other.* Graham typed a message promising to do so while shaking his head.

"It's gonna be dark in there," Whitney said as he backed out of Cynthany's driveway.

"I assume so, what with Tamella gone and mom all by herself," Graham said.

"Oh," Whitney replied. "I just meant literally dark if the power goes out, but spiritually dark too, yes."

"Right, it's already spiritually pitch black for her tonight. Am I doing enough for her?"

Whitney drove through two turns before he gave an answer.

"I think if you tried to do more, you'd just start a fight."

"Yeah," Graham said. "Maybe it would be a fight worth having though, to not leave her alone right now. She's supposed to stay in quarantine for two weeks, but she's been testing negative, but she's still sick. I think I just know myself well enough to know some easy excuses when I see them."

"You mean you're too happy to stay away?" Whitney asked.

"Yeah," Graham confessed. "I'm over here trying to pretend like, 'Oh no, I can't nurse my mom because she's in quarantine technically? Well, twist my arm, rats, too bad,' when I didn't want to anyway. Maybe I shouldn't let that be the excuse, you know?"

"You suspect yourself of taking the easy way out too fast?"

"Yes, that's it," Graham said. "You know me pretty well, too."

"I just know self-sabotaging thoughts when I hear them," he said. "You're trying to feel bad about a good deal, even though if the circumstances were different, you'd follow through on the bad deal."

"Like if I was still living at home, I'd be doing all the same stuff, just on top of mom and getting on her nerves, is that it?"

"You know yourself so well," Whitney said with a smiling glance at the passenger seat. "What do you think?"

Graham thought that sounded about right. Maybe it was fair to have what he wanted and enjoy it. He read it in a book somewhere once and could almost accept it as true: *Nice things were nicer than nasty ones.*

52.

WHITNEY

Back at the house, Whitney and Graham settled in to learn some fun facts from the news about this particular hurricane.

Hurricane Delta was the fourth one to make landfall in Louisiana that year, a mere seven weeks after Hurricane Laura touched down.

"Aw, does that mean we've been together for over seven weeks?" Graham asked. "Proud of us." This made Whitney laugh, first because the time was so short, and then again because it was actually a pretty decent record considering some of the other times he'd flamed out in cohabitating.

Hurricane Delta was the first of the Greek-named storms to hit the mainland. They only brought out the Greek letters after exhausting the alphabetical list of twenty-one names. They skipped the letters Q, U, X, Y, and Z because those didn't have enough first-name variety.

"Guess that explains why we've had no Hurricane Xena," Whitney said. "Tragic."

Hurricane Delta was a record-setting tenth named storm to hit the United States in 2020, breaking a century-old streak of Not That Many.

"Sure, it seems like climate change, but why does it still snow in winter?" Graham asked sarcastically.

"You should make a character out of that type of guy," Whitney said, which started the invariable brainstorm.

"Yeah, the guy who's like, 'Sure they say we evolved from apes, but no one can explain to my dumbass why other monkeys still exist so I refuse to believe it.' Just need another example to hit the golden rule of three."

"It'll come to us," Whitney said. "Maybe a flat-earth conspiracy even though the moon is round?"

"You mean that moon we never actually landed on because how come the flag was all ripply when there's no wind in space?" Graham asked.

"You may have something there."

"It's not because they forgot to pack starch on the rocket because what kind of communist would do that?" Graham said. He opened his laptop to take and save some notes, and then backed it all up on a hard drive he kept in a waterproof baggy in case both hell and high water came.

When the water came, however, it was not floodwater from the ground up, but a terrible rain from above that leaked through the roof.

Graham and Whitney stayed up as late as 11 PM waiting for the storm, but it wouldn't arrive over their heads directly until roughly 1 AM. They agreed they might as well sleep while they could in case the howling winds woke them up, or the howling Honey Bun. Instead, it was the sound of licking that roused them, as Honey Bun was happily drinking water that was weeping down the wall of the bedroom and puddling under the window.

"Not good," was Graham's sleep-addled assessment. Whitney could only gape at the mess.

Immediately his mind went to homeowner hell. When was the roof last worked on? Where would that paperwork be? Would this be considered flood damage or wind damage or what according to his insurance company? How long would repairs take and where were they going to stay while the work was getting done? Was the water coming creating a danger with the electrical outlet on that wall?

"Grab Honey Bun," Whitney said. "I'm going to shut off the power."

And thus, they chose darkness in the middle of the night. They shut the doors to the master bedroom and moved to Graham's bed to make poor attempts at sleep until the sun came up and the storm had passed. In the drab, moist early light of Saturday, they discussed their options.

"You know I can go back to my mom's and take Honey Bun if you need the space to deal with repairs," Graham offered. "Or we could all go to my mom's, she likes you."

"And if the repairs take weeks?" Whitney asked. "Lotta people are going to need repairs after the storm, and you said you and your mom were stepping all over each other before."

"Right, that's how we met, isn't it?" Graham asked. "But you saw her, she's barely stepping at all. And maybe the repairs won't last so long before we can at least move back and sleep here. And maybe it's better that she can't say no to company, so we can like ... bring some noise and some energy to her house. I think the dog alone could give her a new lease on life, don't you?"

Whitney sighed, looking up at the guest room ceiling as pale as cereal milk in the overcast dawn. He could let Graham take Honey Bun to his mom and get a hotel room for himself if he wanted, beg off saying there wasn't enough room for two grown men to be added to Cynthany's tiny house, or that as a 50-year-old former junkie, he couldn't risk even the whiff of COVID. But as he pictured solitude, Graham touched his face.

"Eyelash," he said, explaining the caress. "Want to wish on it?"

Whitney looked at Graham's fingertip and thought, *Let me keep this guy; I promise to take care of him.* He blew the eyelash away, and the decision was made.

"You said your mom's testing negative?" Graham nodded. "Then if she'll have us, we'll use her house as a base."

Graham smiled and gave Whitney a big kiss. It was clear he hadn't made peace with leaving Cynthany alone and was happier to have a reason to go back than to stay away.

"We can make it fun. We'll watch movies, and she can teach me how to make a few of her old recipes. She's always wanted to teach me, and at this point watching you cook when I barely know how to crack an egg makes me feel more emasculated than putting on mom's apron strings, so ..."

Whitney stopped the rush of mania with another kiss, one that got so sloppy and enthusiastic that the dog wanted in on it.

"Oh, whoa," Whitney said, as Honey Bun clambered over them and started throwing her tongue in the mix too.

"Are you excited to go see Momma?" Graham asked her as he overwhelmed her back with scritches and hugs. "Ooh, she's gonna spoil you rotten, just putrid, just you wait and see."

53.

GRAHAM

Graham got permission from his mother to crash at her place with his new boyfriend and that guy's dog. Whitney packed up valuables he wanted to keep with him and locked up the rest where workers couldn't find and be tempted by them. They arrived at Cynthany's house for lunch with everything that would otherwise spoil from Whitney's kitchen. They put Honey Bun's crate in the garage with some food and water until they could get the house prepared for her safe entry (poisonous or choking hazards secured and valuable leathers placed out of reach). They crossed the threshold into Casa COVID and hoped they'd be safe.

The place was dark and dank, it smelled like a sick house. Nothing vomitous, just stuffy and sour with hints of astringent antiseptics. It also felt smaller than it had ever seemed to Graham before, as if he had grown two feet since he'd last been inside. He didn't mind the burrow feel himself, but with both men suddenly crammed together in this smaller place after the architecturally pleasing roominess of Whitney's house, he worried that it would create tensions. Like two grown men trying to dine at a kids' table with one little gal trying to have a tiny delicate tea party.

Graham hugged and kissed his mother as soon as he set down his bags and told her, "Let me get Whitney settled in my room and then I'll come sit with you, yeah? What're we watching?"

"I want to watch something with Timothy Olyphant," she said. "I just love him."

"So do we," Whitney said. Graham was unclear if he meant him and Graham, or just all the gays in general.

Graham's childhood room was messier than he left it, as Cynthany had been piling clothes on the bed to either hem, darn, or donate, and moving junk onto the floor and surfaces. There was an old toaster, presumably broken, and plastic bags full of coupon mail, and boxes from Tamella's house that were stashed unopened for now.

"Make yourself at home, I guess," Graham said. "Sorry it's such a wreck."

"I've seen far worse," Whitney said. "Want me to just stack these boxes out of the way so we can clear the bed, and you go tend to your mom?"

"Yeah, if you don't mind," Graham said. "I know this isn't ideal, but ..."

Whitney caught Graham's eye and shook his head as he found a spot for his suitcase. "I've met so many people who could never bring a man to stay in their mother's house, couldn't go back themselves once they came out. A lot of those people were in bad shape when they met me, homeless, junkies. This is all actually very ideal."

Graham nodded, schooled again by Whitney's hard-won zen. "I'll go thank my mom for having us then."

"Sounds good," Whitney said. "You've got a good mother, she makes me miss my own. And she's got a good son, better than my mom had. Thank her for me too."

"Will do." Graham was going to say that exact thing to Cynthany, whisper it in her ear. Not the bit about himself being a good son — they both knew too well he could do better — but that she made Whitney miss his mom, Willa Grace. That would mean the world to her.

"What's the damage ... on Whitney's house?" Cynthany asked when Graham returned to the living room.

"Roof was leaking on us in the bedroom," he told her, mindful of how special it was indeed to be able to talk to his mom about sharing his bed with another man. He'd gotten used to her acceptance because he'd come to expect it from everyone his age or younger, but it really was no guarantee. He'd had her and Aunt Tamella accept him for who he was without any hemming or hawing, without internal turmoil or a struggle to swallow it down. It really was something to value and appreciate.

"Seemed like a pretty sturdy house," Cynthany said. "Well-built. Hope the repairs are simple."

"So do I," Whitney said, joining them in the laundry chair after moving the basket of to-be-folded clothes to the floor. "My guy will give me a quote as soon as he can, but his own place has a downed tree somewhere on the property, so it'll be a bit. Thank you for inviting me to stay here."

"You're most welcome," Cynthany said. "I wish I could have … hosted better, but … that's just not the year we're having."

"No, it is not," Graham said. "Now about that Timothy Olyphant, I assume everyone here agrees we can just put on *Justified* and let it ride?"

That was indeed suitable to all. Whatever problems Graham had with "copaganda" shows took a backseat to watching a pretty, charming man in a cowboy hat do anything.

As the show played, Graham and Whitney started cleaning as subtly as they could. They agreed on the ride over that it would be hurtful to have people come in and, before even sitting down, start cleaning up everything they could see as if it offended them, so they kept it subtle.

Graham offered to get everyone drinks, and while in the kitchen got the dishwasher going. Whitney volunteered to start folding the clothes he'd found, which sparked a friendly round of argument about the proper way to fold shirts (store display style or regular?) and whether underwear should be folded at all (they decided boxers yes since they were as good as shorts, but briefs and other undies like thongs no, unless they were granny-panties for full coverage — it was a matter of fabric yardage).

When Cynthany showed signs of flagging energy, Graham suggested a nap and accompanied her to her room to switch her sheets to the spare set. He promised to do laundry while she was down, just a good son keeping on top of his chores.

Cynthany changed into a nicer set of fresh pajamas and got into bed. "I'm sorry about Whitney's house," pause for gasp, "but I'm glad you boys are here."

"I'm glad we're here too. I know it was smart to stay away and not spread the virus and all, but it didn't feel right, did it?" Cynthany shook her head and closed her eyes. Graham brushed her hair away from her face where it lay on her pillow. "I love you so much, and I'm glad you're still here. You make Whitney miss his momma too, because you're that wonderful."

Cynthany's response to that was tears, leaking from under her eyelids, spotting her pillow with droplets. "You're sweet boys," she said.

Graham hadn't meant to make her cry, but he wasn't going to stop her from doing it like it was wrong. She was just missing her sister and crying because she was so un-used to hearing nice things about herself that it overwhelmed her. Graham kissed her forehead and let her rest.

54.

WHITNEY

Once Cynthany was asleep, Whitney got the tour of Graham's house, feeling the full circle closure of it all, as it wasn't even two months ago that Whitney first showed Graham through his home.

"Here we have a state-of-the-art kitchen experience," Graham said quietly, maestroing around with mock grandiosity. "Late-century modern American design, with the original particle board cabinets. See the grain detail here on this part where the laminate has chipped off? That's just a hair over the strength of corrugated cardboard, these are truly delicate but remarkably well-preserved examples of the period."

Whitney stifled his giggles, knowing they must be quiet lest they disturb Cynthany. "What about the bathrooms?"

"Ah, well, this home has a luxurious one-and-a-half bathroom, for just behind this wall next to the kitchen plumbing is another sink and a toilet. Now, you can't run the dishwasher and get good pressure in here at the same time, and if the dishwasher ever clogs and backs up, you'll find peas and carrots erupting from the sink, but that's just a novelty add-on, we weren't even charged for that when we moved in."

"It's like a fountain when you think about it," Whitney said.

"It is, I agree. Dishwashers aren't really necessary if you plan to raise children either, as my father and his father before him made clear that I was the dishwasher under their roof. 'Dishwasher' is actually my middle name."

Whitney snorted. "I was the lawn mower whenever we lived in a house with a yard."

Graham nodded his head wisely. "Children are such a blessing. Now, you've already seen the living room, so you've probably noted it's classically claustrophobic and cozy instead of those dated styles of spacious and breathable. It's something we call Claustro-cozy™ and it's a registered trademark of the industry."

"Amazing," Whitney said.

"The master bedroom is occupied right now, but it has the full bathroom and tub. Does that mean that young Graham had the delight of showering in his parents' bathroom during his formative masturbatory years? Yes, as a young master that was the custom in this house. He learned to take rag baths in the guest sink instead, which is a water-conserving method his parents appreciated because it kept the utility bill down."

"So considerate of him."

"He thanks you for noticing," Graham said. "This last room? To quote Madonna, this used to be his playground, the place he dreamed all his childhood dreams. Behind this framed copy of his Tae Kwon Do certificate is a hole he punched after a fight with his grandpa about whether a goth music concert was too Satanic to attend with his friends."

"The devil worms in through the tiniest of holes," Whitney said. He'd had a few of those lectures himself, not from his parents but from church-affiliated sobriety organizations.

"Little did the man know the concert was just a cover story for Graham to go and do drugs with his friends. This is where Graham learned to lie better, so good in fact that he ultimately gave up a useful career to make up crap on a stage."

"So, it was worth it in the end?" Whitney asked.

"I'll tell you when I get to the end," Graham said, before at last giving up the performance and sitting down on his bed. He patted the mattress next to him so Whitney would join and pulled him back so they could lay side by side and stare up at the ceiling. "I used to try and follow the ceiling fan blades to hypnotize myself for sleep."

Whitney tried to do the same, but it immediately threatened to give him a headache, so he stopped. "Did that work for sleep?"

"Nope, it only stirred my brain up worse." Graham sat up and flipped over the top of Whitney, pressing down on him until they were eye to eye. "I like you here. It feels wholesome."

Whitney closed his eyes as Graham kissed him, happy to be an addition to the memories of Graham's past.

"What's the plan for today?"

"I'm going to get this place as clean as it should be for all of us, and I imagine you have some pain-in-the-ass phone calls to make," Graham said.

"Ugh, thanks for the reminder," Whitney said. He'd have to call his backup contractor to see who was available and when, and how low a priority Whitney's leaky roof was compared to neighboring damage. He'd have to call his utility company for water and electricity to have both paused possibly, depending on how long this was estimated to take. He'd have to check in on the couple of neighbors he had phone numbers for to see if their homes were okay and to be on the lookout for anything hinky at his place while it was vacant. This would be an ongoing fret for days, possibly weeks. It was an Augean task, formidable and distasteful, not unlike Cynthany's grief or Graham's coming work of nursing her through long-COVID symptoms. It was called "Augean" because of King Augeas, a figure in Greek myth whose stables were so big and so dirty they were impossible to clean, until Hercules was set the task and diverted two rivers through them to wash the filth away. Whitney was no Hercules, but his task wasn't quite so difficult. He just needed to compartmentalize and deal with it. Today, he only had to make phone calls.

"I'll let you know when the place is fit to let Honey Bun in," Graham said, standing up. "If we stay busy until then, meet me back here for abominations at sundown."

Whitney smiled at Graham's retreating back. *Will do*, he thought, a common phrase of Graham's that had crept into Whitney's speech patterns.

55.

GRAHAM

Graham left Whitney in the bedroom to make his calls, snoop around, and get settled while Graham finally tackled the rest of the house. He started with the quick stuff, picking up laundry and wiping down surfaces. He would have vacuumed but for the noise of their old beastly machine, so that would have to wait until his mother was awake again. He did creep past her to do a cursory wipe-down of the bathroom mirror and counter, and dropped some bleach in the toilet bowl for a quick swish with the scrubber. He collected her laundry hamper before skedaddling back out.

After that was the wet stuff, washing dishes and cleaning the guest bathroom thoroughly and putting out fresh hand and dish towels. He started a load of laundry in the garage once he'd been through each room, which was where he finally stopped to cop a squat and chat with Honey Bun.

"Are you just out here being an angel?" he asked her. She thumped her tail in response, *Yes yes, very much an angel, the best angel.* "Not even a whimper, huh? You trust us to come right back out here to get you, don't you?" Graham washed his hands in laundry soap and laundry water before closing the lid. He needed a clean hand to stick in Honey Bun's crate.

She sniffed the new smells of his fingers and then forced her head under them for pats and scritches. Graham was smiling, feeling the endorphins release in him as this adorable creature loved him for free. Underneath that smile was a lot of sloshing darkness, a pit of sorrow and fret that had no bottom. But smiling at the dog was the flimsy well cover keeping a cap on it, for now.

"You know, if my mother dies, that makes me an orphan," he told her quietly, whispering. "An adult orphan hits different, I get that, but an orphan all the same, all alone. I'd have to deal with this house, which I was never happy in, the whole family wasn't happy in. Around every corner is an ugly memory of Sage, of Grandpa, of death."

Literally just around the corner outside the garage door, in the alley between the house and the neighbor's fence, Sage had given some loser a handjob for a hit of something. The front door still had a dent from Grandpa's boot when he was strong enough to kick up a fit about how much he hated his son's choices, his son's family, and the people like Sage and Tamella that came with it. He had a few happy memories too, like his own first handjob during a sleepover, that was dope. He remembered his parents being sweet to each other when the world was battering them down. But the bad memories outnumbered the good two-to-one, it wasn't a place worth wallowing in.

"Without mom here this is a hateful place, I'd have to sell it," Graham explained to Honey Bun, who'd turned her rear towards Graham to get scritches above her tail. "But who's buying right now? If I can't sell this place, there are taxes to pay every year, and I'm not making money, I'm a kept boy right now. How cute is that going to be when I'm 40, huh? This gig isn't going to last much longer, it can't possibly. Whitney's money is for him to grow old on, I'm a bad bet."

Maybe he'd keep the house because he'd need someplace to get mail, to land between tours. Maybe he could rent it out, become a slumlord, that would suit him just as well as any other kind of income. Maybe he should stop worrying about what he had to do with a house that wouldn't be his unless his mother died when she was only sleeping a few rooms away.

Graham sighed. He had one last rhetorical question for the dog. "There ain't a river so long it doesn't contain a bend, huh?"

Honey Bun, topped off for affection, left Graham hanging with that philosophical inquiry, and curled back up in her bed. She looked just like the golden buns she was named for, so cute it made Graham's heartache. He sighed and let a feeling of longing roll through him. Oh, to be a pampered puppy in this cruel and bureaucratic world. He then hoisted up to get back to his chores.

Whitney had emerged and was unpacking the cooler of food from his house to fit it into Cynthany's freezer and fridge. He updated Graham on dinner options.

"Your mom's got some frozen meals that'll do for dinner if we don't want to make an effort, or I could make dinner burritos for everybody, there's tortillas, beans, cheese, salsa, and saffron rice in the cabinet."

"That's the best option, if you don't mind," Graham said.

"Not at all," Whitney told him.

Even though Whitney had already agreed, Graham felt the need to explain further. "It's just those frozen meals, like the family-sized ones? Those mom and Aunt Tamella shared on Sundays, it was like their church. Go to the other one's house, bake up a tray of chicken parm or a skillet bag, and just split it in two to share and indulge while they caught up and gossiped."

"I won't bother those then," Whitney reaffirmed.

"It's just, it meant something very specific to her and it might trigger a lot of feelings if we served that up the wrong way, since Tamella just died," Graham said. It was upsetting him even though it wasn't happening, wasn't going to happen.

"Graham, I heard you," Whitney said, closing the freezer and frowning at Graham, likely wondering what his problem was.

"It was just really special, you know? Like what a precious thing to do with your sister, when so many siblings hate each other, like me and Sage. We're family, but we ain't friends at all. And my mom had that, and now she just doesn't. It's just gone, her big sister's gone."

Graham didn't realize he was crying until Whitney was holding him, using his shirt to wipe Graham's tears away.

56.

WHITNEY

By the time Cynthany woke up, Graham had pulled himself together and dinner was ready. They put on a season of *Justified* and grazed idly, informally, buffet-style. There was a lot unsaid all evening, and Whitney felt like they were all three waiting for the day to end. Nothing more could progress until tomorrow, nothing could start, and there was nothing to even plan until they knew more about how long this stay would be, and who all would get sick.

That was the part that kept Whitney quiet, trying to double-think away the very real possibility that by staying here with a COVID-19 patient he could get it, and it would really hurt him, possibly kill him in some unexpected way. All that meth, those close calls he'd had.

There was one time when his heart stopped for more than thirty seconds until the guy who'd shot him up pounded his chest in desperation. There was that hospital stay when his lungs were full of fluid because his body was busier fighting C. diff bacteria in his guts, and they almost didn't clear themselves before he got pneumonia on top. There was a worrying two-day stay in the ICU when his white blood cell count kept mysteriously going up and up until at the eleventh hour it sorted out whatever infection his body had found and plummeted back down.

How much unseen damage had been done with those scares? Had the seed of his death already been planted? He managed to avoid HIV, but he was feeling today the same uneasiness he knew when waiting for test results after an indiscriminate bender of drugs and sex partners. As he sat next to the wheezing mother of his latest boyfriend, was it already too late?

He had survived earlier brushes with death largely due to his youth. A doctor dispassionately told him straight to his face, "If you had been this sick at 40, you'd be dead." At 25 he was lucky, but another quarter-century later, at 50? His luck was dwindling along with his bone density, his muscle mass, his reflex speed, his collagen, and the pigment in his hair. Something like COVID could easily knock him out.

And yet Whitney agreed to come to this sick house, agreed to stay. He didn't want to be alone in a hotel room even if it was safer in the long run. He *felt* safer here, comforted and cared for, part of a little cocoon. If he did get sick, he knew that Graham would care for him, and perhaps it would be a relief to catch the 'rona and be done with it, gain whatever natural immunity that could engender.

Whitney had heard about bug chasers, had someone point out a guy at a party and ID him as one. Those were gay men who sought out unprotected sex for the explicit purpose of catching HIV. They wanted to get it over with, wanted to be part of the special club of select few who were more valuable because they could die at any moment. It was perverse, but Whitney understood the twists of logic. He was breathing possible plague air right then, not because he wanted to die, but because he wanted to be in this particular inner circle, regardless of the risk.

When Cynthany started falling asleep, Graham took her to get tucked in. Whitney washed the dishes, and knew Graham had returned when someone else's arms circled his waist at the sink.

Whitney finished rinsing and shut off the faucet but stayed standing there seeing his face reflected in the window. Graham was pressed against his back, rocking him gently side to side.

"I'm so tired," Graham said. "How'd your contractor stuff go?"

"I'm on the list to check out and quote a price. I'll need to go back as soon as possible and take pictures of any damage for insurance."

"Oh, I'm even more tired now just hearing that," Graham said.

Whitney smiled at his reflection. "I have to call insurance tomorrow too, the phones were busy today."

"No, stop, you're killing me," Graham said.

"And possibly I'll need to hire a lawyer who can hound them on my behalf."

"Mercy, mercy," Graham pleaded.

Whitney relinquished and turned around to catch his drooping fella. "Your mom okay?"

"She seems tired for real, like almost too tired like something's draining from her. But I guess that's to be expected, right, battling a virus? It seems worse than I've ever seen her before, but maybe COVID is that bad."

"Maybe it's being sick and being sad at the same time," Whitney said. He knew that being stressed and depressed made people more vulnerable to opportunistic illnesses ... pairing a pandemic-strength virus with the greatest loss of her life was most assuredly putting Cynthany through the wringer.

Whitney, on the other hand, was having one of the best years, the best summers, of his whole damn life. Perhaps the good of his mood would counteract the strength of the virus, or perhaps this was one of the kinder last hurrahs people were allotted when their number was about to come up.

Whatever would come, Whitney had made his choice, thrown dice with death. Had he placed a bet on who would get the sickest by the end of this stay, he would have been wrong for each and every one of them.

PART IX:
STORMSURGE

OCTOBER 23, 2020 — COVID-19 DEATHS
WORLD DAILY: 6,693 / TOTAL: 1,245,781
US DAILY: 857 / TOTAL: 234,752
LOUISIANA DAILY: 21 / TOTAL: 5,820

57.

GRAHAM

By the end of the week, it was Graham who got sick, not Whitney. Perhaps it was because Whitney spent more time away from Cynthany dealing with his house, or because he didn't get as close to her when he returned. Graham was checking his mom's vitals twice a day, brushing her hair up nice, and sharing meals face-to-face. He was the one who caught symptoms, and Whitney didn't.

"That's how some people survived AIDS, isn't it?" Graham asked, when it was his turn to be put to bed and waited upon. "Freakishly. They just somehow did not catch what was going around."

"Or if they did catch it, they didn't go full-blown," Whitney said, tucking Graham in, neither of them knowing how long Graham would stay in his old bed, or how much would be changed by the time he left it once and for all.

"Maybe I'm one of them lucky ones," Whitney said. "I've avoided far more bugs than I've taken home."

"Until you met me, right?" Graham said. It was his last joke before the fever took him.

Being sick and knowing the only way out was through, Graham leaned into his fever detachment. He couldn't smell anything, couldn't taste, and so all that sensory input was void. He soon got a little delirious as the chills kicked in. He knew what they were up to, knew that so-called "chills" happened when the body rapidly contracted and relaxed muscles because it was actually trying to heat up. If it were cold, it would do this for warmth, but with a fever it was done to burn out the intruding virus. Brain said to germs, *This body can survive at 110 degrees if need be ... can you?* Chills helped cook the offending bug.

Graham stared at the ceiling, his old friend. He couldn't think, so entertainment was moot, no TV series or podcast could be followed, and no book could be read. He distracted himself from his body aches by focusing on his lungs and how shallow they felt with COVID clogging them up or whatever was happening in the chemistry set of his cells. He was tired enough from the energy being burned over the battle within to sleep.

He slept for days on and off, noticing the daylight when it was around but hardly able to discern dawn from dusk. He tried to eat what was placed before him, but just didn't see the point of chewing, so mostly took in liquids and sauces and lickable things like mashed potatoes. With such a lack of input, Graham had very little output, needing no trips to the bathroom as his body used every bit it was given to ward off starvation, dehydration, and defeat.

Whitney sang to him. He was perhaps sleeping on the couch or driving the distance back to his house each night, Graham was already aware that his sick bed was a solo one. Whitney would come to serenade a song or two, and once told Graham he was writing a song about him, unless that was part of a fever dream.

Cynthany petted him. Her full personality was still on mute, but she was up and about, clearly feeling physically better. She told him things she remembered about growing up with Tamella. The things she described filtered into his dreams — tire swing summers, bracing winters, school milestones like graduations and homecomings and proms. Graham thought it would be very cozy to be a sister, have a sister. He resisted thinking of what it would feel like to lose that.

He didn't notice what was happening around him until it was too late. While Whitney was gone during the day running his own errands and tending to his house, Cynthany was preparing for something. She got out her best stationery and all her private papers. She wrote letters and made lists and apportionments for all her closest friends and noted down their most recent contact info. She wrote out all her bank passcodes and security question answers. She saved up her pain medication until she knew she wouldn't underdose.

She didn't plan to leave without saying goodbye, but she also didn't want anyone to stop her. So while Whitney was gone and her son was asleep, Cynthany unlocked Graham's phone using his sleeping face to bypass the PIN, and recorded a video there as her suicide note.

"Hi Graham, my sweet son. I'm sorry about this for you, but I think it's right for me. I've done what I was meant to do on this earth. I had my husband, he's gone. I had my son, he's grown. I had my sister, but now I'm alone. I'm not sad, or at least I don't feel sad. I think this is okay. More time would have been nice, but I got more than a lot of people do. I don't see the point in working one more day, trying to stay healthy, just to stick around and see what happens. I already know what happens. You turn out great because you're already great. You get older and I get old. Then I die anyway of something else. So, I'll go now, and you'll be okay, you'll have the house. I love you."

She put the phone back in Graham's room and gave him a kiss he wouldn't remember later. She left a note to Whitney on her door so he wouldn't come looking for her (*Taking a melatonin gummy to sleep sound, need the rest, do not disturb please*), then took a week's worth of Oxy and slept.

Graham wouldn't know she was gone for a full day after she'd departed, when he was finally feeling better enough to sit up and call for a mother who would not come.

58.

WHITNEY

While Graham was down and out, Whitney and Cynthany were cordial enough. Without Graham as a buffer, or even a topic of conversation since they knew exactly where he was and what he was up to, they hardly spoke at all.

Whitney would update Cynthany on when he was preparing to leave and when he planned to be back, so she'd know when this practical stranger was coming and going from her house. In turn, Cynthany would tell Whitney about the weather forecast for his travels. "Should be an easy drive tomorrow, sunny and dry," or, "Might rain tomorrow afternoon, you may want to be off the road when that happens." One evening he helped her pick out picture frames that would best match the signed pictures of Willa Grace he had given her. That felt strangely significant, helping Graham's mother honor his mother, but he couldn't put his finger on why in the moment, and didn't think of it again until after Cynthany was dead.

It was Whitney who first discovered she was gone, but it took him a while. He came back from his errands to the ghostly empty living room and kitchen, the strange feeling of vacant rooms in what he knew was a full house. He peeked in on Graham who was breathing the open-mouthed sleep of someone stuffed up and saw the note on Cynthany's door. It said she was going to bed early, didn't want to be disturbed, and Whitney respected her wishes and went about his evening untroubled. He microwaved a breakfast bowl for dinner while her organs shut down. He turned the TV volume down low out of consideration for two people who were either dead or dead to the world. He did the quiet work of reviewing his receipts of the day: a morning coffee and burrito, large trash bags for the lawn cleanup he worked on while the professionals repaired his roof, and a newly released digital album from a friend of his to do his part in boosting their sales. Before the evening was too far gone, he shared the link of the album's single saying it was "fire" with three emojis of flames. He hadn't even heard it yet, but he could say nothing else about a friend's music, so that was his truth regardless. Whitney made plans for the next day that he would not be able to accomplish.

"Momma?" Graham called out the next morning. "Whitney? Anybody home?"

Whitney was awake, laying on the couch hoping his house would be livable before the next hurricane came through. After nearly two weeks in someone else's house, he wanted his own space back. More than that, he wanted his house leak-proof before another storm, not after getting an extra helping of damage. There was a new tropical storm on the horizon, the twenty-eighth of the season, and its name was Zeta, on a pale horse perhaps. The end of the alphabet, the alpha and the omega storm.

When Graham called out for him, Whitney got up to find Graham alive again, upright, looking thin but vastly improved. His eyes were curious, his movements were cautious but deliberate. He was disentangling himself from the bedclothes and ready to catch back up to life.

"You might want to pipe down," Whitney said, smiling from the doorway to give Graham the space to pick himself up. "Your mom is still sleeping."

Graham checked the clock, swore it was too late for his mother to still be sleeping. To prove she was asleep and not gone, Whitney knocked on her door. Without an answer, he let himself in. By himself, he discovered that Cynthany would never wake up again.

She had a note pinned to her nightgown that said: *DNR. Message for Graham on his phone. Be happy. Love, Cynthany.*

Whitney unpinned the note but touched nothing else. He wondered if it was his job to keep this scene from Graham, protect him from the sight of it. Cynthany looked unnatural, the way she was positioned in a slump. There was a bucket-like trash can by the bed that didn't usually stand there, perhaps it was there in case she felt sick. Whitney wanted to move her into a more comfortable presentation, wanted to hide the bucket, but was unsure if that was even legal now that someone had died, apparently intentionally. If anyone was going to restage the scene, it had to be Graham's choice.

Graham had emerged from his room and was headed down the hall saying, "I want nothing more than a bath right now, so make way."

Whitney quickly decided it was his duty to get out of the way and let Graham handle this on his own terms. He nodded at Cynthany's corpse, a sign of respect, did an about-face, and showed Graham the note first so he'd understand what he was about to walk in on.

"Something happened to your mom last night," he said, not knowing that what happened had begun yesterday morning. Whitney had nothing else to say.

Instead of explaining, Whitney took Graham by the shoulders to get his attention, handed him the note, and then walked down the hall to face the living room. The early light was coming in like cream through water. He heard Graham go still, make one small noise as if to dispute what was already decided, and then push through the bedroom door for the final revelation.

Whitney waited for the next sound, predicting a shout, a moan, a whimper. But instead, the next noise that came was the sound of the shower being turned on.

Whitney went back to the bedroom to find the bathroom door closed and the bedsheets pulled up. Graham had tucked his mother in one last time.

59.

GRAHAM

Graham took a shower in a remarkably numb state. Part of it was his remaining sickness, that ethereal, head-on-a-balloon-string feeling of being stuffed up and spacey. The majority was the stark reality that his mother was dead, and he was in a whole new parallel reality to the world he went to sleep in.

It made sense, as horrifying as it was, and Graham couldn't blame her. He'd never had a friend or family member as close as his momma had her sister. Living wasn't that damn enjoyable, and after a loss like that, why not shuffle off? Graham could be feeling sorry for himself, but mostly he only wished he could call Cynthany in the afterlife and tell her, "Yeah, I get it, you do what you gotta do."

Graham got out of the shower, wrapped a towel around his waist, and headed back to his own room without stopping to linger over Cynthany's body. She wasn't there anymore, he could feel her absence, and her body had very little significance without her spirit in it.

Graham checked his phone for the goodbye she left. No text, no email, but he finally found her video. He nodded at her through the screen, everything she said made sense, she just ... hadn't needed Graham's permission to believe it, apparently. Graham made sure he saved the video to his computer and then a flash drive so he could safely take it off his phone. In case someone came investigating, he didn't want anyone else to see what was meant for him alone. He took her last post-it note and tucked it safely in his wallet.

Whitney popped up from the couch when Graham came back out of his room dressed in clean clothes. He didn't seem to know what to do with his hands or with Graham, so Graham let him know what he was thinking.

"I wouldn't mind a hug if you want to give one, but I also understand if you don't want to get too close to me since I might still be infectious ..."

Whitney got him in a hug before he was finished talking, and that felt nice, even through the numbness.

Whitney kissed his temple before spitting out a lot of information. "I have to go meet with my contractor in an hour, but I've done some Googling about what to do next. Best first thing is to call 911 and say someone has passed, and they'll send out a medic or coroner or something to officially declare what happened and transport her to where she needs to be. Probably the same place as your aunt, right? I can help as soon as I get back, we can wait to call I think, because it's not like this is a crime scene."

"Isn't it? She did kill herself, and that's not allowed."

Again, Graham wasn't offended or angry, didn't feel cheated or wronged. He mostly felt nothing, but intellectually he always thought laws against suicide could fuck off. What right had any government to tell a person they couldn't take their own life? Maybe the state felt it had the right to use your death more effectively to its own ends, but that was man's law flying directly in the face of the laws of the universe. Graham reserved the right to off himself if life ever got too brutal to bear, and he certainly would not begrudge his own momma the same privilege.

"Those may have been the old laws," Whitney said, "but suicide now seems to be more a public health risk, kind of like, you know ..."

"The pandemic that led to this suicide, yeah." Graham sighed, and considered Whitney before him, beautifully alive after seeing an off-color, clay-like corpse. Graham grasped his man's shoulders and called the shots for the day. "You go to your appointment, I can handle making some phone calls here. In case it comes up, let's pretend like we don't know how she died. Like if they figure out it's an overdose, that's news to us. We found no note, so maybe it was accidental, and if they don't look too hard and chalk it up to COVID, that's fine too."

"Alright, whatever you want," Whitney said. "I'll be back as soon as I can, I promise."

"And I promise I won't be dead when you get here," Graham said. He hadn't expected he'd be in a joking mood, but his comedy always came out of a place of darkness, an endlessly deep pit that just got deeper, darker, wider.

"Is that … should I be worried?" Whitney asked.

Graham brought him back into a hug. "Ignore the sarcasm, I can't help that. I'm not teasing you, and you don't have to worry, and I will be here when you return. Keep texting me if you want reassurance and I'll keep messaging you back, okay?"

"Okay, maybe I will," Whitney said, checking his watch and aware that he'd have to hit the road ASAP to get to his meeting. "As much for you as for me. It's been a disturbing week."

"That it has," Graham said. Everything was upside down and wrong, but still they had to keep appointments, make phone calls, and be about the business of life in these surreal and apocalyptic times.

Whitney left reluctantly. Honey Bun joined Graham on the couch as he looked up numbers and started making calls. Her kind eyes and sweet face gazed up lovingly at Graham, resting on his chest right over his heart as he laid down to work. He was still not at 100% and was feeling fatigued, woozy. He knew he should eat but wanted to set some wheels in motion first.

The paramedics would come by before end of day, whenever they had time. They recommended having the deceased person's social security number and date of birth ready to go. Was the person positive for COVID-19 before they died? Yes, the whole house was lousy with it, so they would come in masked and gloved to take the contaminated body away.

The funeral home was an easier call, said they were ready whenever the dead woman was, basically. The receptionist gave him a very human response by saying, "Mr. Morrow, weren't you just here for somebody?" Yes, he was. "That's just not right, baby, I'm so sorry. We'll do what we can to make this as easy as possible."

Graham thanked her, hung up, and then started to cry. Something about a stranger being so sweet, so offended on his behalf that he was dealing with death again, was just too beautiful to stand for such a sad circumstance.

Honey Bun came to lick up his tears before they dried.

60.

WHITNEY

Whitney was both relieved and reluctant to leave Graham, but good or bad, it was happening regardless. His repairs were complete; he had to come by and sign off on them, make the final payment, and resume liability again. He intended to move back in with Graham as soon as this day arrived, but would it happen now? Maybe Graham needed to stay at home, maybe he'd want to, so he could have his own space.

Or maybe he wouldn't, maybe he would need companionship more than ever now that he was orphaned from family entirely. Whitney remembered the day when both his parents were gone, and he was left on his own. It was a disturbing realization that he was the adult now, that no one who knew better could help him anymore, not with experience, stability, money, nothing. He remembered who he called for reassurance that day, and he wondered if she was available again now.

Lexi Bellerose was not her original name, she was born Alexander something near New York City, which was where Whitney met her. She was a drug counselor by the time he knew her, not his sponsor officially, but she never really turned it off, so he got counseled all the same. He called her whenever he thought he was having a bad day because she'd had worse and could make that clear without it turning into a contest. He also made a point to call her every year on her Lexi birthday, which was the day she got her gender-affirming top surgery, and tell her he was glad she was still alive.

That was a long-running phrase that came from a very serious talk about suicide they once had. In NYC, in the late 90s, Whitney had failed at his first solo attempt at sobriety, and he was mad at himself. He thought it was true that he could quit if he wanted, and he didn't like being proved wrong. After the anger faded though, he was tired, mortally tired. He had enough drugs left over to maybe overdose, and he was thinking about it. He knew if he told Lexi about this urge, she wouldn't make a big deal out of it, but she would stop him. She came over when he called, and criticized the shit out of his apartment first, to break the ice, dispel the tension.

"Why is everything so white?" she asked with an exaggerated sneer. "You aren't white enough yourself, you gotta look at it too?"

Her handbag was the same candy green as her false nails, and Whitney wanted to touch them both to appreciate how smooth they were — he got his hands on the bag first, and Lexi didn't side-eye him about it because she never carried anything worth stealing in her bag. Her valuables were tucked on her person, always.

She finally got done dressing down the place and then sat across from him on his white bar stools at his white marble countertop. That was when Whitney got to touch her nails, stroking them gently one by one. She asked what his problem was, and he told her.

"I don't want to die, but I also don't want to keep living," he told her. "I'm so tired. Just sitting still, being sober, it seems exhausting, and to have to do it for the next fifty years or more?"

Whitney sighed, and Lexi who was only four years older than him but infinitely wiser, managed not to roll her eyes.

"You don't have to kill yourself to die," she told him. "You just have to wait long enough. If you wait, this feeling will pass, and you'll be glad you were alive to feel something else."

Lexi had been imprisoned, hospitalized, assaulted in her life. She'd been beaten, turned out, used. She'd been so sick when she was cold and homeless one year that she nearly died for real, and still had a spot on her cheek that was dead from frostbite that she disguised as a beauty mark. She shouldn't have had any sympathy for Whitney's problems of too much good fortune too soon, but she did. She'd survived so much she could sympathize with anybody, it's what made her such a fine counselor and better friend.

The plan on that day was for Whitney to do at least one thing towards living each day he could text or tell Lexi about. *Lexi I took a hot shower. Lexi I sent my tax receipts to the accountant. Lexi I bought groceries.* After two weeks it turned into a weekly update, then monthly, and now when she called him around Pride each year, he updated her still. This year the call would have to come early though. He texted her before getting out of his car to shake hands with the contractor and finish up their business.

Lexi I have a boyfriend, and his mother just killed herself. Time for a call tonight?

He wasn't out of his seatbelt before she messaged him back. *Just name a time, handsome, I'll be here.*

He sent back heart emojis. They did not at all encompass how grateful he was that she always made time for him, but they'd do in a pinch.

61.

GRAHAM

"You don't know me, but I know Whitney," Lexi said as an introduction to Graham.

After a day spent in hideous silence waiting for the medics to come take the body and give him some paperwork to do, Graham was somewhat mystified by this request that he talk with a counselor. Like did he need to be handled by a therapist, really? But Whitney insisted this wasn't so much a therapy session but just a wise old friend of his who'd helped him before and could help Graham too.

"Hi," Graham said to Whitney's phone as Whitney waved goodbye from the front door. He was going to take Honey Bun for a walk so Graham could have some privacy. "I'm not sure what to say."

"If you start talking about anything, what needs to be said will bubble up eventually," Lexi told him. "How about starting with something pleasant you like talking about? Got a favorite band or any hot goss about Whitney he wouldn't want you to share with me?"

"Oh," Graham said, with his first smile of the day at the delightful idea of embarrassing his man. "Well, he took me to an orgy as a first date."

"What? They have orgies out there in the sticks?" Lexi asked.

"It was an online orgy," Graham clarified, and then described the hilarity of it — the regular flab on the bodies, the inartful camera angles, the constant refrain of "please mute" from the orgy master, another one of Whitney's colorful friends. "To be honest, it took the squeamishness out of going all the way the first time because we were performing. We were out of our own heads and putting on a show, and the show must go on."

"Hmm, you are both stage acts, I wonder if that wasn't an innate understanding of the situation you each had that made it a matter of course," Lexi suggested.

"Maybe," Graham said. "I never really thought about it like that, but when in the moment I'm definitely one to carry through, come what may. Like if you flub a line, no you didn't, and you barrel through until your scene is over."

"Yes, Honey," Lexi said, and he heard her snap through the phone. Graham imagined she had long nails but somehow could still always snap her fingers, open a soda can, and type proficiently. "I have put on some shows myself, lip-syncing and costumes, and you better believe I don't fall down and crawl off if I break a heel."

"Right? Like, okay so something hit a sour note, jammed the wrong spot, dance through it and you'll fall back in step eventually."

"Yes, that's true," Lexi said. "You got jammed in the wrong spot pretty hard today, though, didn't you?"

Graham raised his eyebrows, impressed. Lexi sounded like a drag performer, but was there a magic component in her act? Because that was some damn-fine sleight of hand she just pulled.

"I did get jammed hard today," Graham told her. "My mother died. And she didn't just die, she killed herself."

"Does that make a difference?" Lexi asked.

"Yes," Graham said without hesitation. He hadn't articulated it yet, but he did have strong feelings about it. "I mean I think she had the right to take her own life, I think we all do, but I also think this wasn't the time. I was right down the hall, and I just ... I wouldn't have done that to her, I don't care how bad I felt. And now I know for sure that she would do this to me. And maybe that's selfish, because I know she was in serious pain. Did Whitney tell you about my mom's situation at all?"

"I know the gist, that she lost her sister," Lexi confirmed.

"Right, well ... I get wanting to die after that, I really do, but on the other hand, was there no reason to want to live? I feel like there was enough time for her to be happy again and not leave me here all alone. Is that self-centered?"

"In a way, yes, but everybody is self-centered, it's how we're wired," Lexi said. "And to be fair to you, life is hard, and you're the one still living it. For better or worse, your mother never has to deal with heartache again, but you do, because of her choice, for the rest of your life."

"But I'm not mad at her," Graham insisted, wandering into Cynthany's room as he said this, talking to the spot on the bed where she took her last breath, as if he could talk to her spirit. "Or at least I think I already forgive her as much as I have the right to."

"You gotta stop thinking about feelings you're 'allowed' to have, there's no authority that grants permission to feel what you feel, it's just the hand you're dealt. If you don't like your feelings, you can work through and change them, but you can't deny them, they don't listen."

"Yeah, feelings are rude like that," Graham said, stroking his mother's pillow. "Pushy bastards just waltz right on into your house."

Lexi laughed, and Graham smiled, because he always felt a win when he made a stranger laugh. "I can tell you from my personal experience that people who really want to go do it like your mother did, without telling anyone. If they tell you, they want to be stopped, or they just want attention and know this threat makes people jump. Most people at least, Lexi don't play that dying swan bullshit but once, she won't get used twice."

"And here I am taking up your time," Graham said.

"No, no," Lexi said, "Whitney is taking up my time asking me to talk with you, and I love that boy, so I help him out by chatting with you. You're funny, you earn your keep."

"How does Whitney earn his, with music?"

"Not for me, I hate that country shit. How does he get an accent when he sings that he doesn't have when he talks, what is that? Twangy yokel stuff, no thank you. Whitney gets Lexi's attention because he used to bend over every time I asked him to pick something up, so I could see that ass in his jeans."

Now Graham was laughing. "Tell me this was a game you played, like 52-card pickup. You just throwing down cards and making him go fetch."

"Close, but I didn't need the cards, I just had him come over and pick up around my apartment so I wouldn't have to break a sweat. It's too unladylike."

That was sound logic to Graham, as wise as everything else Lexi had said.

62.

WHITNEY

When Whitney returned home, the conversation with Lexi was over, and Graham appeared in better spirits. He wasn't happy per se, but he was more relaxed.

"How was Lexi?" Whitney asked, as Honey Bun barreled into Graham for wiggly kisses and butt scratches.

"Yeah? Did you have a nice walk?" Graham asked the dog first, before answering Whitney with, "Lexi was a trip. Nice of her to take the time for me."

"I made a donation in your name to the homeless fund she runs for street kids, for her time and efforts," Whitney said, kicking his shoes off and joining Graham and Honey Bun on the couch. He put his arm around Graham and found him receptive, then noticed what he was doing.

"Your mom's paperwork?" Whitney asked.

"Yeah, since it's all mine now," Graham said. "This is the important stuff. Her clothes can all go to donation so long as I check the pockets first because she forgets — forgot — stuff in there all the time. If you're down to help, you could sort the food in the house, basically anything we'd eat we can pack up and take back to yours, the rest if unexpired can go to a shelter too."

"Speaking of my place, we can move back in tomorrow," Whitney said. They were both on the same page there without having to discuss it: Whitney's house was their house, and Graham's house was something to be dealt with. "There's some paint drying right now, the fumes are kinda strong, but we could probably sleep in the second bedroom tonight if you didn't want to stay here?"

"There's work to be done here," Graham said. "Want to pull an all-nighter with me?"

Whitney was willing. He handled the pantry and fridge first, then emptied the crawl space of boxes with holiday decorations. Graham would probably need a few things out of there, special Christmas tree ornaments or embroidered stockings or whatever he grew up with. He disgorged the cabinets and drawers of the house and sorted what they held into like piles so Graham could handle them in batches. He'd cleaned out houses of the dead before, he knew what would help without needing instruction for a while.

They reunited for dinner, and shared a somber frozen lasagna, one of the two-person meals that Cynthany once shared with Tamella, and now were available for anyone who happened along. They clinked soda cans on the couch with the cowboy marshal show still playing endlessly. They made inane small talk about how that Timothy Olyphant guy seemed like one of the truly lucky ones, a Vanderbilt descendant with good looks and talent who was seemingly genuinely sweet. They speculated that he probably had a soothing singing voice and a huge dick too, just one of the blessed.

When they finished eating, they got out the garbage bags and started packing and labeling the contents: clothes, trash, linens, donate, and keep. Graham was all business, staying busy until exhaustion took hold, and he could fall asleep easily, most likely. He didn't set aside much for sentimental value besides old family albums and things custom-made, things that were irreplaceable. He called them to bed after midnight and told Whitney to take the first shower. When Whitney reemerged is when the dam broke.

Whitney came out of the master bathroom and found Graham sitting at his mother's vanity. In the middle of putting used makeups and lipsticks in the trash, he'd spotted the picture of Willa Grace, recently gifted and framed and placed beside the mirror Cynthany saw every day. Graham was hugging the face of the photo to his chest. He wasn't crying but he looked like he was about to.

Whitney knelt behind the little vanity bench and put his arms around Graham, watched his face through the mirror. Graham didn't move, just sat for a moment until he had something to say.

"She was just here," he said. "She had just put this up, decorating like she meant to stick around. When did she change her mind?"

"I can't answer that," Whitney whispered.

"Oh, I know that," Graham said, finally coming out of his stupor enough to move, to react to Whitney, touch his hand. "I just can't believe it, like I know she's gone but it's like my body doesn't feel it yet, and I don't know when that'll happen, but I know it's going to be horrible."

"Lexi says you can't control stuff like that," Whitney said, remembering that she said as much to him when he felt numb to the world and dead inside and was incredibly skeptical about the promise that his sensation would return. "You don't have to want it or work for it or qualify for it, the feelings will come when they come, and you just have to deal with them as best you can."

"I get why she left," Graham said, before coming alive and turning to face Whitney. "But why are you still here?"

Whitney assumed it was because he loved Graham. Not so much in love with him, because they were too friendly for that, and not so much like an elder loved a younger either, as a teacher or parent. Whatever advanced knowledge Whitney had he'd only gained from the reality of more years spent screwing around, he had no extra wisdom to impart that he wasn't parroting from someone else who had mentored him. But it was love all the same, a kinship or camaraderie of a sort, and it compelled him to stay.

"There's nowhere else I'd rather be," was the best way Whitney knew how to describe it. Graham nodded as if he understood.

63.

GRAHAM

Graham was bone-tired, but knew he'd have a hard time falling asleep once he was showered and spooning with Whitney in the dark of his room. His mind was awake yet blank, like a broken TV set that still buzzed because it was turned on, but showed nothing on the screen.

Whitney started singing and humming a kind of lullaby about tired horses that turned out to be some lesser-known Bob Dylan song when Graham asked. It was soothing enough to help Whitney fall asleep at least. There he lay, silver and serene, where Graham left him. He decided to quit fretting in bed and got up to fret on his feet instead.

His first order of business was to drink a cup of his mother's sleepy tea which only triggered his ragweed allergies and made him sneeze. Graham next looked up where the word "fret" came from and how it came to mean both worries and guitar string things. The first meaning was from an Old English word, *freton*, which was to eat up, devour. When one fretted in the mind, one was being ate up by worry, a fitting descriptor.

Frets for guitars came from a different and far more mysterious source, perhaps the German *feggara* to fetter or shackle, or the French *fetur* for laced, latticed things like a trellis, or Old English again but the word *freten* for fastening, binding. Frets used to be fashioned by tying a guitar's neck at intervals, preventing the string from sounding too long.

Graham looked up from his phone wiser in a sense, and at long last a little more tired. Instead of returning to try and sleep beside Whitney, he vowed to bore him with his new knowledge of frets tomorrow and went to rest on his mom's deathbed.

So, this was the last ceiling Cynthany saw, he thought. Did that hold any significance? Not really, but it was true, nonetheless. Would Graham ever forget that fact as long as he lived in this house? No, he would not. Was that healthy? Hell no, but he would have to do a lot to remove it from his life. Was that smart? Man in his thirties inherits a home, the one vehicle to American middle-class stability, undersells it to ensure future homelessness, and shacks up with a boyfriend instead. Would Whitney go along with that? The invite to stay at his place was predicated on everyone being in lockdown and Graham stuck with his mom, but now mom was gone, and though he and Whitney had history at that point, history was in the past. Would he soon be part of Whitney's past? The man had history with his brother, with his orgy buddy Lyle or Kyle or whatever, with Lexi. Maybe Graham was just the newest on that list of people who used to be close with Whitney, but ultimately became a twice-a-year phone call friend.

Graham's frets eventually turned into extremely literal dreams about trying to clear a house that kept filling up. Whitney found him in the morning, and Graham opened his arms so that Whitney would join him in bed for some calming kisses until the sun was too high and the work left undone too pressing to linger any longer. By noon, Graham had found some clarity and made a decision.

"I don't want to spend another night in this house," he told Whitney. "So, if it's agreeable to you, let me pack up the essentials to take to my room at your house, and only come back here to clear the rest of the junk in stages."

"That works for me," Whitney told him, standing and wiping his brow after he tied off another trash bag of packed linens. It was cool weather but hot work as the day wore on. "Are you going to sell the place?"

"I think I have to," Graham told him. "I can't be coming back to all the dark memories here forever, but it may take a while. Although with all the hurricane damage, who knows — people need new houses, don't they?"

"They do," Whitney confirmed. "Speaking of, you'll have to lock this place down in your absence, there's another storm on the way."

Graham sighed. "Ain't that always true."

Graham sent Whitney with a box of photo albums, keepsakes, and paperwork to his place to ready it for their return. Graham would follow with the usable groceries after doing all he could to batten down the abode. How long Graham would just loaf at Whitney's without any declared relationship status or plan to vacate would continue to linger like a white cloud above them.

He set three full bags of trash on the curb after confirming that trash pickup was back on after the storm. He cleared drawers but left furniture for the movers he would hire to cart it all out. He'd be driving his mom's car back to Whitney's with the groceries, and remembered he'd have to sell that too, or if it was in newer and better condition than his own vehicle (as he suspected it would be), sell his ride and upgrade to hers. Graham assumed he would be back again in the coming days before Hurricane Zeta came through, but that would not be the case.

A minor Category 1 for most of its life, Hurricane Zeta would only kill a few people. One man would die by electrocution from a downed power line, another would drown, and a few more would suffer fatally from the usual post-storm misfortunes like carbon monoxide poisoning from generators or clean-up-related accidents. Several of those died when a tree fell on their house or trailer, including a young couple in their twenties who were killed together in their bed.

Still, Zeta would rise to just shy of the top ten Louisiana storms since 1950 in cost of damages. A portion of that damage would be Cynthany's former home and all that was left in it by her son that late-October day.

What Graham got out of his mother's house on first exit was all that he would inherit. A few chores, a few trinkets, and a slow-moving insurance payout that would ensure his financial security for a few years. Just long enough to get a career going, he predicted. Lucky in loss.

PART X:
HEADWATERS

NOVEMBER 5, 2020 — COVID-19 DEATHS
WORLD DAILY: 9,440 / TOTAL: 1,339,045
US DAILY: 1,344 / TOTAL: 247,411
LOUISIANA DAILY: 20 / TOTAL: 5,995

64.

WHITNEY

Whitney's house was unbothered by Hurricane Zeta, and his relationship with Graham was somehow unchanged by the man's multiple bereavements. The only difference was in Graham himself, who checked his phone less frequently because who was calling him now? No one needed him anymore.

They passed Halloween pleasantly, splitting a bag of candy while watching *The Rocky Horror Picture Show*. They voted on November 3rd with no hope or energy, but logged their Blue and Green choices in Red-as-hell Louisiana, and were unsurprised to be in the minority. It appeared that nothing else would happen until the vaccine rollout, which wouldn't be until the next year. Besides a couple's Christmas, which Whitney was looking forward to already, the only event interrupting their days of walks with the dog and making dinner was a birthday. Specifically, Whitney's sobriety birthday.

Eleven years. Eleven dull but relatively painless years compared to the punishing excitement of his twenties and thirties. He spent his forties patching back together his body and mind, doing atonement, earning paychecks, and fulfilling his duties rather than pursuing pleasures. This time last year, pre-pandemic, he thought that hitting the decade milestone would free him to seek enjoyment again. Ten years was solid, you could trust someone ten years sober, they'd almost reset to a normal person again. He thought maybe he could start exploring legal hemp products without becoming a junkie again. He thought he could date, perhaps even go dancing in clubs, without it feeling too dangerous to be around the sights and smells of a bar. All those temptations were snatched from him once lockdown started, however. The fact that Whitney still found a date regardless still made him happy.

"It's my sober birthday tomorrow," Whitney told Graham after they woke up to the news they needed about the presidency.

"Fifth of November? Guy Fawkes Day, nice," Graham said before quoting the nursery rhyme about the Guy. "Gunpowder, treason, and plot."

"That's about how it went down," Whitney said.

"How should we celebrate?" Graham asked. "Naturally you can't buy a round of shots for a sober birthday, and that's the end of my creativity. Wait, let me check the internet."

"Feel free."

They were both slumped on living room furniture. Graham lay with his bare feet up on the back of the couch, leaving a tent for Honey Bun to nap beneath. Whitney watched from the armchair, jouncing one foot on the opposite knee to the beat of some song not yet written. Now that the hurricanes had left them high and dry, it was time to think about making something with the rest of the time they had in isolation. With light at the end of the tunnel in the form of an approaching vaccine, there was a flicker of optimism again, was there not? Something worth singing about.

"My guy, this is bleak," Graham concluded after scrolling. "How are you supposed to stop doing the highest heights of deep, dark drugs, come out of it alive, and the best idea for your victory celebration is *bowling*? These em-effers suggest bowling, laser tag, paintball ... are these sober 8-year-olds we're talking about? A spa day and a murder mystery dinner, because you're *Murder, She Wrote*? Or take a sky-diving or trapeze class in case you miss the death-defying most of all. What is this garbage?"

Whitney smiled. "Sober positivity," he explained. "It's so good because you did so good, good for you, you goody-good."

"One suggestion is to thank your family and friends who helped get you sober, I mean ... I'd rather get wrecked. Don't mean to be flippant. I get that it's hard and people really do help, but how hokey can people stand being?"

"That's why I order my anniversary chips online," Whitney said. "I don't want to go to a meeting, not all of us need the meetings. I have music to catch my complaints."

"Hell yeah, you do, that's how country music was invented. A little blues, a little bluegrass, a lot of things to cuss about, and a lot of Jesus to make up for all that cussing."

"Beautifully put," Whitney said. "I haven't ordered this year's chip yet, maybe you can help me pick out the design."

"Hold up," Graham said, sitting up with elaborate care so as not to disturb the dog. "You can just buy 'em, don't have to like, earn 'em?"

Whitney clapped his thighs and said, "Come and see."

On a shelf deep in his costume closet, in a slim case designed for AA tokens, slipped among other personal records like baby books, yearbooks, and photo albums, Whitney kept his tiny medals. He didn't like to look at them out on display, but just like old photos, he couldn't throw away such personal things. He brought them to the kitchen table so Graham could examine them under the light.

"They look like poker chips," Graham said. "Or Pogs, remember Pogs? Or is that just some 90s kid thing like watching Nickelodeon with jelly glitter sandals on? Don't listen to me, I just mean these fancier ones, these are actually kinda rad."

"So, the first few, those I got the old-fashioned way from meetings, and the colors go with the specific anniversary," Whitney explained. "White the first one for purity or renewal I think, just for showing up. Silver for the first full twenty-four hours sober, then red and gold and green, and so on and so forth for each month, until you hit bronze for the first year, and then they can get creative. These are AA chips, not NA. I quit both, and AA groups were easier to find back then."

"Are the NA ones different colors? This is like karate belts, all these colors," Graham said, hefting each medallion and stacking them like quarters.

"My family got me a special one for my one-year milestone, bronze but with gold glitter as you can see. I've treated myself to the rest of them to match my tastes at the time." Whitney started pointing out some of his favorites. "Got this rhinestone rainbow one for the year I was sober and getting sex urges again, really renewed my pride. Got this tree of life one the year Gran died and left me this house, a new beginning. The one with the guitar player was for when I put out my first album since cleaning up."

"That was a good album," Graham said. "I forget that I know that guy now, but I loved your *Can't A While* so much I wore it out for like a whole summer."

"Glad you liked it," Whitney said. It was always nice to hear, to remember, that he had fans.

Graham seemed mesmerized by the coins, the clink and weight and candy color of them. "Can I get you one? The coin for this year? As a gift?"

65.

GRAHAM

Graham didn't know if he was out over his skis or what, so he kept babbling. "Are sober birthday presents customary, or no? Is it a *faux pas* to buy a guy a custom coin? A fox pause, as they say? Assuming I know you well enough to get the right design, is that a thing that you would appreciate?"

"Sure," Whitney said. "You were most of what happened this year, so go for it."

That gave Graham a task he didn't understand the magnitude of for the rest of the day. How to encapsulate 2020, the year of race riots and plague and recession, in a positive way? Sure, Graham and Whitney had found a good thing in each other, but they hadn't even reached their three-month hookup anniversary yet. It just felt like a long courtship because real life had stormed into their oasis hard and fast.

A lot of the AA chips available for purchase looked very cultish. Graham searched "sober medallions" far and wide on his laptop, skipping the ones that looked like some Harry Potter business with triangles and wands, and resisting the urge to Google whether that mess was Masonic in origin or what. There was diverse representation at least in special designs: Veterans, Bikers, African and Native Americans, all the minorities. There were a lot of faith-based ones with crosses and Stars of David. Or was it Star of Davids? Graham didn't need to know that either, so he kept on keeping on.

The gay chips were too gay, and the ones with real silver and gold were too gauche, and while the Narcotics Anonymous ones looked cool because they had diamonds on them, Whitney said all his chips were on the Alcohol side of the divide, and Graham wanted the set to match. What else did he know about Whitney, really? Graham didn't know the man's favorite color, couldn't name a food of special significance, and Whitney already had a music coin. What else was left? He could get a medallion with a coffee pot or cup on it, a sailboat, planets, mountains, roses, and animals like a camel, a butterfly, or an eagle. The worst of the lot were coins with the faces of the AA founders rising up like presidents on money. Graham was about to give up and just select one with holding hands — that sort of represented their relationship, a little? Until the right animal arrived and made the choice clear.

Honey Bun slithered into his lap, trying to displace the laptop. What was this warm object getting all the attention when Honey Bun should have scritches instead? When her head noodled up through the gap at his crotch and the dog started invading his spot, Graham laughed because he knew what the coin should be now: dog, duh.

Graham considered a medallion for the Chinese Year of the Dog, since regardless of Asian calendars this was Whitney's Year of the Honey Bun. In the end, he decided not to overthink it, and went with a simple bronze coin not unlike the ID tag on Honey Bun's collar, and the same color as her golden fur. It had a four-toed paw print on it: plain yet pretty, just like her.

Graham opted for expedited shipping for the next day just in case it worked, but with the storms throwing a wrench into everything, he wouldn't hold his breath. He wanted to show Whitney he found the perfect present and was toying with ruining the surprise.

"Should I tell him?" he asked the curious limpid eyes of Honey Bun. "He's gonna love it because it'll remind him of you."

Graham got a notification on his phone that he assumed would be the order confirmation with a picture of the present. He opened it fast thinking he could give the dog a peek, but then saw what it really was: an email alert that his mother's remains were ready for pickup.

He had forgotten. For a blissful hour or so he had forgotten. Now he remembered he had to repeat the same goodbye he'd said to his aunt and scatter his mother's ashes in the same spot. Talk about sobering.

Honey Bun bestowed a burp upon him and then left Graham's lap. He called her a stinker and went in search of fresher air, and Whitney. He found the man squinting at his phone in bed.

"Candy Crush or porn?" Graham asked, slithering up into Whitney's space the same way Honey Bun had recently encroached upon him. "If it's porn, you should share."

"Just a text from my brother asking if we're running low on anything because of the hurricanes that he can send from his area," Whitney said. "Although I did get something spicy from Lyle this morning, a sort of sexy-gram for the next Zoom orgy if we want in."

"I mean, maybe," Graham said. "It's more fun than raking leaves, ain't it? Or picking up my mom's ashes, which I guess I'll have to do tomorrow, even though it's your birthday."

"That's okay. I'll go with you, same as last time," Whitney said.

"I found the perfect coin though," Graham said, scooching himself up Whitney's chest and nuzzling in at his side. "Medallions, sober chips, whatever they're called."

"Tokens to ride the sober rails," Whitney said with a sigh, stroking Graham's head as he came into petting distance.

Graham closed in for a kiss. "Congrats on your passage."

66.

WHITNEY

Whitney set his phone aside to turn and face Graham. It was time for some pillow talk.

"Sober birthdays aren't that special to me," Whitney began, "so we can do whatever we need to do about your mom. Half the time I hate these anniversaries and don't want to remember that I'm sober, or why it's so important, or all the people I should feel grateful towards, one of which is my brother. He always kind of expects me to thank him every year when he wishes me well. It's not like I don't appreciate his help, I do ..."

"Right, like it's nice to offer to send supplies or whatever, to look out for you," Graham said. They were face to face on the bed, aligned to one another while the room looked sideways around them.

"It is, very nice," Whitney agreed. "But it's also a reminder every time that no matter how long I've stayed sober, there's always a chance that I'll slip. Like I can feel him thinking, 'Uh oh, Whitney has to deal with hurricanes? Better keep an eye on him, just in case.'"

"The only way out of recovery is death, isn't it?" Graham said. "I mean, they talk about it like cancer, you're never what you used to be again, always in recovery, in remission, which means you're actively hoping the bad thing doesn't rise up to get you again, always guarded against it to the end. It sounds exhausting."

"You've got the right idea," Whitney said. "They don't paint too rosy a picture of it even when they're trying to sell you on it. It's work, it's penance, it's amends, forever."

"And wheat bran and church service, sounds like being on parole," Graham said, then pivoted topics slightly. "How would it work if I wanted to get fucked up sometime? I'm not saying I want to now or even soon; it's peaceful here, me and you in lockdown. But someday this will end, and non-lockdown Graham drinks, but I can't do that in your house, and coming home shitfaced is just as bad as getting drunk on the premises, isn't it?"

"That's true," Whitney told him. "I have a system on the road, I can hang out with people as they party and just go back to my hotel when I need to, but … I don't know, you don't fit into any of my patterns or systems. If it's any consolation to me and to us, I think everyone's going to be out of sorts after this pandemic stuff. Some jobs won't come back, and some industries won't ever be the same again, and people are living in towns they never chose."

"Maybe we'll have our fun on the road, and meet back home to be wholesome," Graham suggested.

"Maybe," Whitney said, though truly he had never thought about what happened after this. He wouldn't have guessed that Graham, in the prime of his thirties, would want to stick around with him after he was allowed to wander free again. He still wouldn't bet on him wanting to play house for the long game, but it was awfully precious that he was thinking about it.

"Hey, lemme see that dirty picture," Graham said, reaching to stroke Whitney's chest, his belly. "I think we could fool around right now, it's feeling like fool-around o'clock."

Whitney brought his phone back. "Is it that time already? Well, yes, it is, feels like it comes earlier in the winter, doesn't it?"

He pulled up the text from Lyle with a digital flyer of a guy making an 'O' face as he buried a dildo inside himself. It was right on the line where if you weren't horny, it'd be funny, but if you were even a little bit feisty, you couldn't help but think that looked like a good idea. Feeling uptight? How about a surefire way to loosen up, let free some of those orgasmic endorphins.

As they looked at the image, Graham's hand traveled to Whitney's lower abdomen, and he felt a stir. Whitney's body was ready to be rearranged in there.

Graham borrowed his phone to visit a porn site, a quick fix for a hard dick. Whitney got out of his clothes and into position, occasionally tweaking Graham's nipples, flicking his tongue on his ear lobe, sucking a finger. When Graham was firmed up, he flipped on top of Whitney, kissing him to distract him from the insertion that nevertheless still had him clutching the comforter.

Oh, but Whitney loved it ever so much, the feel of another man's invasion. There was nothing else like it, and it drove every other thought from his mind. He found it tragic that some straight men never experienced this or anything like it, not even with their girlfriends, not even in solo curiosity, just depths unplumbed.

As Graham went to work, Whitney bit at his beard, licked one bead of sweat from his face before it dripped, and felt Graham moan in response. He found that place — harder to trek to without the drugs but still accessible with effort — where his body and mind were so blissed out together that they didn't feel separate. An orgasm like a hum of light, even though light and sound were two different things.

In the euphoria, Graham gave a few final thrusts before collapsing into Whitney's embrace. When their breathing even back out, Whitney put his lips to Graham's ear and asked him a question.

"Want to stay up late and have birthday cake with me, to celebrate?"

Graham lifted up on one hand and combed his hair back with the other. Damp with sweat, it held the shape of his fingers afterward in even furrows.

"There's cake in this house I didn't know about?"

67.

GRAHAM

Whitney had a box of cake mix and a magic trick to show Graham with a simple can of soda.

"So this is an old Weight Watchers tip, apparently, something Granny taught me," Whitney said as he cracked open a Diet Coke with its pleasing tsk and hiss sound of carbonation. "You can make this cake without all the oil and eggs and butter that adds calories, just dump one can of soda in the mix, stir, and bake."

Whitney demonstrated as he spoke: dumping, stirring, and turning the oven on for the baking bit.

Graham nodded appreciatively. "I did hear those additions of eggs and oil and stuff were listed on the back of the box because housewives felt too useless without adding extra ingredients. They gave them the whole easy mix, and these good Puritan women, they just couldn't stand not having work to do and wanted it back, it was their whole purpose."

"I mean if those cake mixes were anything like these, that might be true," Whitney said, dipping one fingertip in the cake batter mix to boop Graham on the nose with it. "It just needs water, and there's water in soda. In diet soda, no extra calories, and with flavored diet soda, fancy."

"Ooh, you mean like getting a cream soda or something to add extra sweetness?" Graham asked, liking the idea even as it disgusted him. "I mean like they're obviously sweet enough already, but I see the potential."

"Vanilla cake is good for letting the soda flavor show out," Whitney said. "I made one with an orange soda once that was really tasty, and you can mix and match flavors like get a blueberry cake mix and a lemon-lime soda, or for the chocolate cakes, add cherry cola or root beer, which gives it a syrupy taste."

"Oh, damn, you could make a Mountain Dew cake and embrace death," Graham said. "That would be such a hit at the trailer park, I'll have to tell my trashier friends about that."

"Before Granny went to Weight Watchers, she'd make her own frosting for cakes out of butter and powdered sugar only, just mashed together and spread on top," Whitney said. "But when she got diabetes, you know, had to knock that off."

"Ugh," Graham said, imagining eating sugared butter straight. "That reminds me of watching white people make recipes on these apps, people making salad with mayonnaise and practically drinking sour cream. It makes my guts clench just looking at it, that's too much dairy for real."

"For real," Whitney agreed, popping the cake tin in the oven and turning to face Graham with both hands on the counter, like the proprietor of a saloon. He looked Graham up and down where he sat on a bar stool before telling him, "This is nice."

Graham came around the kitchen island to join him for a hug and felt the warmth coming from the oven and agreed. "This is very nice, cozy with you."

"I was just thinking, this pandemic could have been so much worse," Whitney said, before pulling back from their snuggly little hug to look Graham in the eye and clarify. "I know it's bad for you, I don't mean to complain about my hangnail in the burn ward, I just mean … if this had happened in a different year for me, an addicted year, I probably would have killed myself after a few weeks. Overdosed, or the withdrawal if I couldn't get the shit, or a tainted batch cut with who knows what because you know supply is in high demand right now, and the supply chain is stressed for criminals and drug mules too, and I just … it's scary to think about. Makes me truly happy to be clean when most years I'm more grudgingly glad."

"'Grudgingly Glad' sounds like the title of your next hit single," Graham said with a smirk. "I know what you mean about this being a better year for bad news. I mean it was the exact wrong year for my little comedy career, but if this pandemic had happened while I was still in nursing, or in school, or when I was living at home as a teen with both parents? Mom might still be dead, just from a murder instead. One of us would have snapped and murder-suicided the rest of the unit."

Whitney nodded. "A better year for it, and we found each other."

"And we found each other," Graham agreed. "Lucky us."

68.

WHITNEY

After cake, the house was sleepy. Warm and full, Graham was ready for bed, and Whitney tucked him in saying he wanted to cross midnight before joining him. He had something he wanted to do alone.

This year, Whitney was glad to be sober. He felt healthy, clean, and at peace in mind and body. Many of his sober anniversaries had not been like this. Even though his skin wasn't sallow, and his body didn't hurt, and his genitals and asshole were in functioning working order, his mind was unimpressed. What was the body for if not to use for pleasure? What was the point of a fastidious, early-to-bed, early-to-bran-muffin life if it had no thrill?

Whitney was still relatively certain that if he found out he had some terminal disease, he'd go back to getting fucked up for the last few months. But today, perhaps because of his mature age, he was content with a quiet, painless, dignified life. Maybe having a boyfriend made the difference.

Another important bit was missing though, had been MIA during the lockdown months: his creativity, his art, and that drive not unlike an addiction to have it seen and to perform it.

Whitney decided that was how he would pass the time until midnight turned on a new year of clean living: composing. He took his guitar (named Jubilee) out to the porch, after dusting her off which was a shame to have to do at all.

Whitney went through the meditative act of tuning it by ear. This was something his brother was never able to do, despite having laid his hands on dozens of instruments throughout his formative years growing up in their musical family. Nash often insisted he had an ear for good music, but stupid fingers that did not listen to his brain as well as Whitney's did. It added a special element of disgust to how Nash saw Whitney's drug use. He even said it outright in an intervention-style letter: there was Whitney so blessed to be the baby, the pretty one, the talented one who carried the gene for the family pride of making sweet music, and that wasn't enough for him? Whitney got a record contract, concert opportunities, he showed up brand-spanking-new to the scene and found he already had friends in the music business who did favors for him on the reputation of his parents alone, and he found life hard? Whitney had young money once, had weeks off between tours like summer vacation for adults, had been getting laid hand over fist in a man's most lustful years, and he still needed to snort meth to feel good? It was offensive.

With his chords tuned, Whitney started plucking Bob Dylan's "Tomorrow Is a Long Time" to loosen up his fingers. He remembered how he tried to argue back against Nash's points, saying that as an openly gay man and all, it's not like *everything* was easy for him. But his heart hadn't been in his own defense. It wasn't that hard to be a gay white man in pop country territory, nor was it a flirtation with death to be promiscuous in the 1990s after AIDS was understood and genuinely avoidable. When half the dancers and choreographers and hairdressers backstage were gay too, Whitney wasn't that oppressed, and he knew it. A little othered, but honestly just enough to give him access to an outsider's perspective, something many an artist treasured as the source of their purpose. Nash said a normal life, a non-blessed life with average abilities would hurt Whitney way more than a little bit of chosen hardship with drugs. He said it would be like Johnny Cash regretting his misdemeanors when whose actions put him in trouble, huh? And didn't the experience of a few nights in jail help build his legend? Everyone had bad days and rough nights, but not everyone got a national tour deal out of them, basically.

Whitney started humming. He didn't want to write a song about this stuff, he had a whole album of woe-is-Whitney ballads already. But he did have to sort through these thoughts before they'd clear his mind. It was like clearing an inbox before starting the day's work at the office. Whitney's office was this peaceful porch, these beckoning pines, the smell of wood and dirt and playful wintery night air. Blessed again, wasn't he?

Whitney stood up and started to sway to match the motion of the trees. He danced a little, quietly, with his old D-35 Martin as his partner, speaking of Mr. Cash for whom it was specially designed. Whitney smiled remembering another perk of being himself was he had rhythm enough to dance with. In a gay club it wasn't so much, like he would be trounced trying to vogue, but at a hoedown or hootenanny? The ability to move his body to the beat without becoming confused and dancing to the lyrics instead was impressive. On a stage with singer-songwriters, there was no guarantee that they could use their bodies as well as they could operate their voices.

At last, Whitney was warmed up, feeling loose and unburdened, and for his subject, or perhaps his object of address, there was Graham. He knew he'd have to write some sort of song about this particular man in his life, but didn't know what it would be. Short and sweet? Sad and mournful? A song of love and lust? A song of friendship and optimism? He would have to tinker around and find out.

Whitney knew one thing for sure: Graham's last name Morrow would have to be involved as a play on the word morrow. Sorrow, borrow, tomorrow, there was something to figure out in all those meanings, something that would be a nice gift to Graham, for however they would end up after this sick and solitary season was behind them.

As Whitney swayed and heard the boards of the porch rock beneath him, he was feeling hopeful. In the house behind him, Graham and Honey Bun were sleeping. In the world before him, though these were trying times, the greenery was still green and the woods still calm. For all the sadness, it was easy to set it aside, wave it away, or waive it for now, to be dealt with later, on the morrow.

It was coming together, the occasion for this song, the point of it. Whitney was so engaged trying to work out the mathematics of its structure, the meaning of its theme, that he did not notice when the clock ticked past midnight, and a new day had begun.

69.

GRAHAM

Graham was on autopilot the next morning, just running through all that he knew he should do while thinking of it as little as possible. He took his morning piss, brushed his teeth, drank a meal replacement shake rather than eat solids so he wouldn't have to do the mental and physical labor of preparing, cooking, or chewing anything. He wanted to get to the other side of scattering his mom's ashes ASAP, and was ready at the front door with his shoes on before Whitney knew what hit him.

"Guess I should get the lead out," he commented, but Graham assured him he was all good, no rush. He'd take the dog for a morning walk to burn off some energy.

In the time it took Graham to complete their bright morning jaunt, a package was delivered to Whitney's front door. Addressed to Graham, it was the first thing that made him smile on a day he thought would be nothing but a grind. It was the AA chip, delivered with shocking speed, and pocketed by Graham for whenever the right moment arrived.

They drove quietly to the funeral home again, where Graham received a box of ashes once more. They told him they were so sorry to see him back so soon, perhaps the only business that could say such a thing with kindness.

Before uniting Cynthany with Tamella in the murky Mississippi for all time, they treated themselves to lunch for the sake of Whitney's sober birthday. They went to the Takery, a takeaway bakery that handed them their order and sent them on their way. They stopped at the closest park, clinked cupcakes, and dug into the same tub of chicken salad with two spoons, lovers' style.

"Lexi found some of your little skits online," Whitney said after a sip of latte. "Sketches I mean, excuse me. She thinks you're funny, says you've got a front-row fan next time you're in the city."

"In New York City? Who knows when that'll be, we can't even get into the Applebees, let alone, you know, the Big Apple."

"Funny, you," Whitney said with a soft smirk. Graham could still perform his little dumb-dumb jokes for his audience of one. He reached over to wipe a little cupcake frosting off of Whitney's cheek and tasted it. Oreo frosting, not bad.

The silence between them was cozy, calm. Graham knew it wasn't always like this, that some people were together and in love and everything, but they had to work at it every day, had to plan for it, set time aside to discuss it with each other, therapists, other family members. In this hard year, hanging out with Whitney was the easiest thing of all. It was harder falling asleep some nights than just sharing space with him.

Graham went for their food bag looking for a handy-wipe or something, and noticed the box of ashes on the floor at his feet. He nudged it with his toe, and wondered how long he would get to know Whitney before something like this separated them, too.

"I'm still not feeling it," Graham said, wiping his fingers clean before going for the crackers and pimento cheese dip. "The loss of Momma. Like I can feel it in me, the sadness, but it hasn't cracked open. Like that thing you said about whatever myth dude, it's in an egg in a box all chained up at the bottom of the well."

"I get it," Whitney said. "Delayed emotional response, dissociation, classic PTSD stuff."

"Yeah. Honestly feels like an emotional shit I wish would just crest already, but that's not how it works."

A beat of silence, and then Whitney snorted and started laughing. "I'm sorry," he wheezed, breathless. "It's just … 'emotional shit' is too good, whoo."

Whitney was wiping his eyes, holding his side, at complete mercy to a fit of the giggles. Watching him struggle got Graham going too, and suddenly they were laughing their fool heads off on what should have been a sober, somber morning.

"You know something?" Graham asked. "I fucking love you. You're just a wonderful man and I love you."

Whitney's laughing lapsed into a smile. He took a deep breath, then took Graham's hand in his.

"I feel it, too, I love you. I'm glad you said it first, though, I wasn't prepared to hold my breath hoping a fine young thing like you would fall for this old road dog."

"Old road dogs are hot as hell, what are you talking about?" Graham asked.

"Skin a sickening shade of worm-pale, wrinkly like crumpled trash," Whitney said.

"Wrinkly like an old map to legendary places they have stories from," Graham countered.

"Stories of all the places I've thrown up?"

"And all the talented people who saw you do it, yeah," Graham said. "Sounds like every episode of *Behind the Music* to me, don't tell me it ain't cool."

"Cooler than comedians?" Whitney asked. "They're road dogs too, right?"

"Nobody's throwing panties at the stage over a good joke," Graham said. "Just because a man might prefer tighty-whities doesn't mean a thong slingshotted at your feet isn't one of the highest honors in the biz."

"I got roped by a bra once, does that count?"

Graham scoffed. "You have to ask? Guess you're too pretty to be smart."

"What does that make you if you love me so much?" Whitney asked.

"Too smart for my own good."

70.

WHITNEY

After lunch was licked from their fingers, Whitney drove them back to the outlook spot where Tamella had been scattered. He worried for a moment because someone else was there this time, some woman repacking her car before carrying on down the road. She was likely moving to a new place because it looked like her whole life was piled up in the backseat — another reminder that the pandemic was happening to everyone, separately and individually, but also together.

With a full-bodied shove to close the overstuffed door, the woman resumed her trip, and the spot was clear for their little ceremony. Graham got out cradling the box of ashes, and Whitney had an idea of how he could help his guy get through this.

"I was thinking I could sing another song just like I did for your aunt," Whitney said, as Graham broke his heart by peeling back the box's tape slowly, like he was opening a present. "One that would match, another Alison Krauss?"

"Momma would like that," Graham said, raising the ash bag and looking out at the edge, the drop, and the mighty Mississippi. "I'm going to go over there, and you can stay here and sing if that's cool?"

Whitney nodded and cleared his throat. Once Graham's back was to him, he started singing about heaven's bright shore, on which there was no death, no graves, and no more goodbyes.

Whitney sang the whole song, all four stanzas, to give Graham time to open the bag, court a favorable wind, and let his mother go bit by bit. When Graham shook out the bag and turned back around, his face was changed, but not in the direction Whitney was expecting.

Graham was smiling from ear to ear. "This feels happy somehow," he said with a baffled laugh. "I know it's sad, too, but all things considered, this feels right. Momma and her sister, they're together again, you know? That's how it should be, even if this is not the way it was supposed to happen."

"That's beautiful," Whitney said. He was about to cry himself, it was so painfully touching, but he didn't want to pop Graham's bubble of euphoria. If only everyone could have such a revelation at a funeral. People feared death, loathed it, but it was a truly unifying part of everyone's life in a sense, and the place where they all belonged in the end. "It's like how Whitney Houston put it, 'It's not right, but it's okay.'"

"The other singing Whitney," Graham said. He rolled his eyes, but then shook his head in pleasant wonderment. He folded up the ash bag small enough to fit in his pocket. They'd take it home, turn it inside out, and hose any leftover residue off onto the same tree in Whitney's backyard where Tamella's final dust landed, and Whitney's old dog Sugar Bear was buried.

In cramming the ash bag into his pocket, Graham found something else that made him even happier. "Oh, this is for you. Happy birthday, Whitney."

Whitney looked down to see what Graham was holding in his palm: a sober medallion with a paw print on it.

"It's perfect! For Honey Bun." He picked up the coin, then grasped Graham's hand to pull him in for a kiss. "You nailed it."

"I know, right?" Kiss, kiss. "Took some searching, but as soon as I saw it, I knew there was no other."

"I have something for you, too — hold on." Whitney had brought ol' Jubilee with them just in case the occasion arose to distract Graham with the song he inspired. It was feeling less like a distraction and more like just one more affirmation of life.

When Graham saw Whitney strap on his guitar, he guessed what was happening. "You wrote me a song? Goddamn finally, I've been sleeping with you for months, been waitin' for my song already."

Whitney laughed as he got a pick out of a pocket in the guitar case so this could sound crisp. "Now this isn't finished yet, and it's not polished either, but I've got the gist."

"Wait, before you start, what's it called?" Graham asked as he sat on the hood of Whitney's car to watch the show. "Something about me being a life-changing piece of ass?"

"Something about 'Tomorrow' or 'To Morrow' because it's addressed to you," Whitney said. "Don't let me spoil it; you can suggest a title if you think of one, okay? Ready?"

"Ready and willing."

"Alright." Whitney opened by playing through the notes first so Graham would know where the tune was headed. Then he added the lyrics on top:

"We pass on the sadness of passing,
Find shelter from the rain.
We wave away the sorrow
To soothe away the pain.
The misery is mounting,
The damage will come due,
But I borrow against the morrow
To love today with you."

"To love today with you," Graham repeated, nodding, thinking, mathing it out. "To love today alongside you. To love in general, and to do it today with you. To love with you, like doing the act of love with you, today."

Graham counted through each version again silently on his fingers. His nods were accented with frowns, as his reasoning only made him more confused, but the smile never fell from his face.

Whitney stood, satisfied, watching Graham's mind chew through the meaning. "Want a hint?" Whitney asked.

"Yeah," Graham said. "Or no, just tell me. Which one is it?"

Whitney shook his head, smirking so hard it hurt his cheeks. "All of the above, that's the fun part. It's everything you heard all at once." Whitney took his guitar back off and stepped up to Graham's side to pack her away again.

"That's awesome, thank you." Graham leaned over to give Whitney another kiss, a peck on the cheek. "You know, if you need another rhyme after sorrow and tomorrow and all that, we can go get Sbarro's pizza to finish it out strong."

"That's an idea," Whitney said. "But why don't you figure out how to write me a love joke in return for my love song? I have also been sleeping with you for months and haven't made it into a routine yet, have I?"

"Yeah, you're right, I've really been slacking on that."

Graham trailed off and looked out at the river. Whitney put his arm around Graham's shoulder and felt him lean into the embrace. Once the peace was comfortable enough, Whitney had one more thing to offer.

"When the world comes back, and we can go out again, I've been wondering ... would you want to go on tour together?"

Whitney could picture it: he and Graham on the road in a camper with Honey Bun for a few months. Or he and Graham kickin' it in airports, taking turns driving rental cars, and happily defiling hotels across this great nation. Graham could open shows for him and really get his name out there, and Whitney could get all the joys of a two-man band without having to share any creative control of his music. It could work.

"They say traveling together is the real test of a relationship," Graham said. "But this would be traveling and your job rolled up in one. You think we could work together without ruining us?"

"I do," Whitney said. "Because it wouldn't be a collaboration so much as an accompaniment."

"Right, because we'd be company for each other. I get your meaning this time."

"So, is that a yes?" Whitney asked.

Graham grinned. It was a look that promised he, too, was about to say something clever. "It's a duet."

About the Author

L.A. Fields is a two-time Lambda Award finalist and author of literary, historical, and LGBT fiction. Works include the young adult *Disorder Series*, a modern retelling of the Leopold and Loeb crime titled *Homo Superiors*, and the Sherlock Holmes pastiches *My Dear Watson* and *Mrs. Watson: Untold Stories*. Fields has an MFA, a day job, and a calico cat named Kobb.